ARCHITECTS

OF THE

TAJ MAHAL

a novel over centuries

Between the Lines Publishing
1769 Lexington Ave N, Ste 286
Roseville MN 55113
btwnthelines.com

First Published: September 2024

ISBN: Paperback 978-1-965059-06-7

ISBN: Ebook 978-1-965059-07-4

Library of Congress Control Number: 2024944236

ARCHITECTS

OF THE

TAJ MAHAL

a novel over centuries

Allan Havis

To Dawn Goldfrank Baker, Aleks Rosenberg, Jim Ingalls,
Steven Adler, — and Nora Cohen for generous editing insight
on previous novels

"Whatever state of being one remembers when he quits his body, that state he will attain without fail."

Bhagavad Gita Eighth Chapter, Sixth Verse

Chapter One

My fears are as real as langsat. When unripe, langsat can be wickedly sour, but when ripe and translucent, they are heavenly sweet and have a bitter, citric, grapefruit aftertaste. Dreams come to me in the form of smooth orbs, not unlike the tiny, transparent fruit. My creative thinking begins with sensations which emanate from my two hands. Yes, these hands have imagination. These elegant, long fingers are worth more than ten flawless diamonds. My origins began in Shiraz within Arya, like the langsat. My life, so far, has been more bitter than sweet.

As one of a dozen architects in Agra, working under Ustad Ahmad Lahori, the emperor's court architect, on the palatial tomb bounded by infinite points of light and the apotheosis of all designs, my expectation for long life dwindles each day. It is the year 1637 and the weather has been challenging. We have been working on the colossal construction for nearly seven years. I will be dead before the Taj Mahal is completed. I expect to die before old age. I expect to die before my children are fully grown. I will die leaving my beloved wife Saanvi a small fortune. My life began when I fell in love with Saanvi, the most beautiful soul in creation.

Saanvi has no sense of time. But time is all I measure. I wish to believe in divinity, but in truth I am a material man wedded to a material woman.

I like a comfortable bed. I crave each month my wife's body. I do not fear the gods and I know in my bones that the gods do not fear me. When I die, the worms will consume me. My architectural structures will stand for many more years. Each mortal soul senses eternity because each waking day is a small eternity. My wife promises not to marry another man.

Twenty thousand artisans are at our command. These are good laborers. They are well paid, and they know the emperor will take their lives at a moment's notice.

The mausoleum will be an ivory-white marble miracle on the right bank of the Yamuna. A quiet river in Agra, Uttar Pradesh, India. The project was commissioned in 1631 by our fifth Mughal emperor, Shah Jahan.

Shah Jahan can be a figure of horrific menace. I met Shah Jahan once in his palace as a member of Ustad Ahmad Lahori's design delegation. It was a short session. Our delegation was searched for weapons and for poison. We came in peace. We left bearing precious gifts — small precious jewels and carved amber statues. We were warned that if we were to sell these presents we would be tortured to death. We were told that the massive palace would honor his wife, Mumtaz Mahal. We suspected that the structure would also house the tomb of Shah Jahan. The tomb will be the centerpiece of a 17-gaj estate, which will include a mosque and a guest house, and will be nestled within formal gardens bounded on three sides by a white crenellated wall.

My wife is not permitted, on pain of death, to tell family or friends that I am one of the leading Taj Mahal architects. Our children do not know about the Taj Mahal. The emperor's men will not hesitate to murder even them. The architects in this project know we are constructing a mausoleum which indiscriminately annihilates the lives of others.

The architecture of my dreams hovers like heavy clouds in summer. These visions are inspired masterpieces in my blood stream. My living soul is architecture. My legacy is my edifices of love. The architecture of our stature and our permanence is for an evolving society where cruelty and selfishness have been eradicated. My paternal grandfather taught me this humane philosophy when I was a boy. He said to me that a beautiful building can calm people's anger. We can be a violent people. My father's father was born in 1573 and he was a highly respected architect.

The years 1498 and 1526 brought to the foreground India's profound identity two events of historic significance: the earlier date marked Vasco da Gama's landing in Calicut after an ocean adventure circumventing Africa's southern tip; the latter date proved the creation of Mughal rule in Delhi. These markings have been acknowledged as milestones. In their calendar passing, India found her place in world history.

There have been seven magnificent buildings completed in my career. Two structures in association with Ustad Ahmad Lahori. Five structures that I alone claim to be my designs. Three are Hindu temples. These temples are my finest works, employing symmetrical forms and esoteric mathematical principles. I was in a meditative state with each design and what I remember feels like a dream. I studied Sanskrit texts for each building. Each temple adheres to the elements and beliefs of the Hindu cosmos. There is good and evil governing our life and our death. The powerful elements of dharma, artha, kama, moksha, and karma can be found in the flooring, the walls, the roof, the shape of doors and portals, and the invisible tension one can feel when our senses shut down. These profound elements represent ethics, prosperity, pleasure, spirituality, destiny. It is my assumption that my spirit will live in these three temples. I cannot prove this assumption. My wife will know my spirit if she eventually visits the Taj Mahal.

It is also my assumption that a temple's architect is equal to Hindu priests, pandits or pujaris. Again, I cannot prove this assumption.

I have dreams about the future. In these dreams I am a woman living on the other side of the world. I have a womb in these nocturnal visions.

These dreams embroider notions of dharma, artha, kama, moksha, and karma. These dreams always take the form of delicate, smooth orbs. My name is Mir Abdul Karim.

In our Las Vegas office, our staff finished setting up holiday decorations orbiting the fifteen-foot Christmas tree that towers over the leather lounge furniture. We were celebrating earlier than the previous Christmas, and of course the Resorts International commission fueled our expansive mood three years ago, only to be surpassed by the New York real estate developer Donald J. Trump's infusion of cash. We laughed at Trump, but we took his money happily. We knew all along that it was massive bank loans and not Trump's largess. Yes, there were of course ridiculous tales of junk bonds floating a mega-yacht of warm shit. Each Christmas, our design group anticipated and braced for Donald Trump's holiday visit. In ten days, it would be 1990 and we were hoping for a new decade of economic improvement. Throughout the last eighteen months, the U.S. economy had weakened due to the restrictive monetary policy by the Federal Reserve. George Bush isn't the sales star that Ronald Reagan was. With successful sales, it is never the product, but it is the sales agent. George Bush has a stick up his Republican ass.

We liked working properties on the East Coast. In my view, I am one of my firm's superstars, and its only female architect. My design choices are aggressive and balls-to-the-wall bold. My buildings are risky. I scare engineers. Fuck engineers.

The Las Vegas architecture firm of Steelman Partners on West Desert Inn Road was buoyantly practical, proud, and self-accepting about their undisguised affinity for casino and resort structures. I was hired soon after receiving national praise for my unconventional community center building in Seattle. The façade was homage to Marcel Breuer's design for the Whitney Museum on Manhattan's Madison Avenue. The building was aggressive and unapologetically brutal.

Led by ebullient Paul Steelman, a 1977 graduate of Clemson University and the son of an architect, Steelman began his career working for Joel Bergman designing many of the Nevada Mirage Resorts projects. Steelman broke new ground engaged in the public sector on the Atlantic City Master Plan. He intuited that entertainment architecture was going to be his lifelong practice and signature venue. Paul Steelman collaborated with gaming mogul Steve Wynn as his leading architect for nearly a decade, centering on The Golden Nugget in Atlantic City and Las Vegas, as well as the Mirage.

Through Steve Wynn's association and perhaps his quiet sadism, our firm entered into a series of complex meetings with Trump. Trump, the media whore with the crass Queens accent, already owned two casino hotels in Atlantic City. Resorts International, led by James Crosby, was in dire financial trouble with the Taj Mahal project. Trump and his wife Ivana dominated the tabloids for the last few years, and they teamed together on several prestigious sites, including the Trump Tower on Manhattan's Fifth Avenue, the Grand Hyatt Hotel renovation, and suddenly the completion of the Taj Mahal Casino.

Our firm knew that Crosby and Resorts International *twice* resolved licensing problems for the Atlantic City casino. In 1978 the Resorts persuaded the New Jersey Division of Gaming Enforcement that rumors regarding mob figures were untrue. A formal state inquiry revealed that several hundred thousand dollars paid by Resorts International to two lawyers had traveled through a Resorts employee to the Prime Minister of the Bahamas. The New Jersey Casino Control Commission voted to renew the casino license, accepting Crosby's explanation that Resorts International knew nothing about what had happened to the cash.

In my gut, I knew that James Crosby's death in 1986 would spell serious trouble for Steelman Partners. Without Crosby at the helm, Resorts International headquarters became rudderless. Crosby was a rationalist, a lucky man, and had integrity at least three days of every work week. He built an amazing gambling empire, although Crosby avoided casino tables because, he once said, he found gambling more boring than bingo and the house *always* holds the odds. He opened the nation's first public casino outside Nevada in 1978, the 750-room Resorts Casino Hotel in Atlantic City.

The Taj Mahal construction began in 1983, three years before I joined Steelman's firm. Resorts International, owner of Atlantic City Resorts Casino Hotel, transformed into a vulnerable takeover target. Moreover, the Taj Mahal had suffered numerous building and licensing headaches, and Crosby's heirs, lacking expertise in large commissions, doubted their ability to complete this mammoth hotel. Contributing to the design team was a very young architect, Francis Xavier Dumont from Atlantic City, who had little or no experience with projects of this scale.

Trump, owning two existing Atlantic City casinos, outbid his competitors to control the company for a little under one hundred million in 1987. Trump was then appointed chairman of Resorts International and he boasted that the Taj Mahal would be completed in the year. New Jersey prevented anyone from owning more than three casinos, so Trump schemed to shut down the original Resorts casino and designate it as a hotel annex to the Taj Mahal. The state officials approved that artifice almost immediately.

As the total budget ballooned to nearly a billion dollars, Resorts sought to raise a half billion to complete the Taj Mahal but struggled to find the financing. Television personality Merv Griffin made a surprise bid for Resorts International sparking Trump's ire and a notorious takeover skirmish. Aggressive lawsuits were filed however Griffin and Trump reached a quirky, stalemate settlement in 1988. Griffin bought the Resorts, and Trump won the Taj Mahal from the company for a quarter billion dollars.

Regrettably, I am withholding something private and criminal about this Resorts International narrative. Last year at this time, Trump had monopolized the holiday party and cornered me in a hidden wing of our reception hall. Trump kept calling me Rosy Baby, but my name is Roseanne L'Anse. My business card with a feint, stylish geodesic image tells the world that my name is Roseanne L'Anse. Trump liked asking for my card each Christmas. He liked leaning into my face and overwhelming my hearing in a booming voice an inch from my ear. "Rosy Baby. That's your name." He asked me about why I gravitated to a career in architecture and which architects were not getting proper notice nationally and internationally. I mentioned Sam Scorer, a British architect from Lincolnshire who championed hyperbolic paraboloid roof structures using concrete. However, Trump wasn't listening carefully. His hands were like a whirling octopus, and I suspected that someone that afternoon spiked my martini.

The Trump Organization recruited me to renovate a New York City office space on the 17th floor of The Trump Building on 40 Wall Street in October 2018. I was hired overnight to do a makeover of four thousand square feet and revise plumbing specifications. Partitions were needed and a change of ceiling height was added at the last minute. Improvements in area lighting and ventilation were part of the modest negotiation. The building, located in Manhattan's financial district, is a 72-story landmark property built in 1930. Trump acquired the property in 1995 after an extended vacancy. The work was finished ahead of schedule, and I was told that everything was acceptable. These small design assignments have become my stock and trade in recent years. My invoice to the Trump

Organization totaled $200,000 of which, I am still trying to collect an outstanding balance of $47,000.

My name is Rex Heuermann, and I am fifty-four years old. Five years later I find myself in solitary, in Yaphan, inside a dank Suffolk County Jail as investigators finished their search of my Massapequa Park home on Long Island for evidence and prepare for my upcoming trial. Several young women have been murdered in the vicinity. They were all escorts on Craigslist classified. Massapequa Park is roughly forty miles east of Manhattan. I am married with two offspring — a special-needs son, Christopher Sheridan, 33, and a 26-year-old daughter Victoria. I fear that my wife, Asa Ellerup, will never speak to me again.

I am an innocent man. God knows that. I speak to God now.

As I live and breathe, the news outlets are feasting on a trial outside of court. It is cold comfort imagining, in all probability, that I will never leave prison and yet a former president who grew up in Queens, miles from my home, will evade felony conviction.

Chapter Two

Roseanne L'Anse parked her 320i BMW sedan in the company's secure parking lot. She preferred the shaded area near the tall ponderosa pines. The yellow stripes defining the car stalls were fading from the harsh sunlight. Roseanne checked her makeup in her rear-view mirror and corrected a microscopic smudge of lipstick below her mouth. She smiled reflexively and climbed out of her car. She saw a small bruise on her ankle. There was no pain in or around her foot. Roseanne was curious how the bruise came to be. She tended not to bruise easily.

When turning her head, she spotted a homeless man on the ground holding a metal bucket. He was bald, bearded, and emaciated. His countenance projected a higher intelligence which devolved over hard times and miserable luck. He was a figure out of a Hieronymus Bosch triptych. He was calling out to Roseanne L'Anse. The words were incoherent, flying out of hell's tunnel. Las Vegas loved no one today.

Her profession gave her stability. She reminded herself that stability was a good thing. The day, early January 1989, was scheduled for a considerable battle with her Steelman colleague Derek Bolton. Bolton graduated Yale School of Architecture but had a flagpole up his ass broadcasting a lower pedigree. He was discrediting Roseanne L'Anse' work on Resorts International's previous hotel. Bolton was close to Trump. Roseanne knew she was ten times the architect than Bolton. His architectural contributions were safe, predictable, and derivative. Bolton was the color beige. Bolton feared her bolder aesthetic taste. Moreover, he was uncertain about his sexuality.

At her desk Roseanne found a note. It was unsigned. She tossed it away. A cup of hot coffee with a lid was near her phone. Her computer was already turned on. Her phone rang. She picked it up on the third ring.

"Hello."

"Roseanne?"

"Yeah."

"Bolton."

"What now?"

"Did you read the engineering reports?"

"Not yet."

"It's not a pretty picture."

"I don't give a flying fuck." she said flatly.

"You'll cause the firm to pay a heavy fine."

"Everything's to code, Bolton."

"You wish."

She was about to hang up. He apologized.

"Let me help you on this one."

"No thanks."

"The boss likes me. I can provide you cover."

"I don't need cover."

"Your recessed horizontal lines are getting tedious, Roseanne. That can't be your dominant motif. You're not Louis Kahn."

"What are we doing? A college studio critique without a panel?"

"Let's talk over lunch." he said.

"No. I don't eat lunch." she enunciated without tempo and hung up.

She swiveled to her drafting table and picked up the minor details from yesterday's work on the Steelman interior designs for Atlantic City's casino hotel. When Roseanne was in architectural school, she loved the freedom of speculative design concepts. These imaginary projects were profoundly enriching to the gratification within an architect's life. However, these very projects had little reality to the career and pursuits under the canopy of American architecture.

Nevada was known to be a friendlier state to builders, engineers, and architects all the while avoiding serious citations from FEMA in Washington. Her design firm was well versed in Nevada casino history, cognizant to the fact during the Depression era, her state legalized gambling to mitigate the economic pain. In 1931, Nevada paved the way for a host of gambling activities with the adoption of Assembly Bill 98. The state bill generated sizable revenue to Nevada. In liberal circles, licensed gambling and lottery tickets were interpreted as a tax on the less affluent and even the poor. Roseanne embraced every casino commission with open arms.

She left work at three o'clock to have her twice monthly therapy session with Dr. Lippman. She had no intention of returning to the office.

Roseanne entered Dr. Lippman's office on the third floor of a brick building a few miles from her office. She pressed the wall buzzer inside the waiting lounge. There was another patient waiting in the lounge. The patient looked remarkably like the actor David Duchovny. Dr. Lippman shared his office with another therapist. She smiled at the man and then picked up a copy of Time magazine on the coffee table.

When Roseanne stepped inside Dr. Lippman's private space, the psychiatrist surprised her by complimenting her business suit.

"It's a little chilly in here." she murmured.

"I can adjust the thermostat."

"Please. Thank you."

Roseanne sat down, choosing the upholstered armchair facing the office window.

"How was your day?" he asked.

"Fine."

"Good."

"I had a disturbing dream this week."

"Did you write down the particulars when you awoke?"

"Yes. I keep a notepad by my nightstand."

"What was your dream about?"

"India."

"Really?"

"Yeah."

"Do you like Indian food?"

"Not very much."

"Were you ever in India?"

"Yes. A dozen years ago with my husband on a business trip. His trip to be accurate."

"Why did the dream disturb you?"

"Herb and I were in Agra. Near New Delhi. Visiting the Taj Mahal."

"And?"

"It was nighttime. There's a long walk tourists have before getting to the main gate. The path is littered with vendors, touts, and creepy hawkers. The route is not well lit and the air in summer is rancid. One can smell urine. Herb is with me."

Roseanne stopped her account and touched the skin below her lip.

"Have you had this dream before?"

"No."

"Is there more to the dream?"

"Yes. Herb and I suddenly separate. He's with a woman wearing a dark red sari. Her hair is jet black and very long. Straps cover her ankles, but she is barefoot."

"Is she attractive?"

"I don't know. I couldn't see her face. Her perfume was pungent. She was singing to him. He seemed to know the melody and hummed along. I was threatened by all of this."

"Do you often go on business trips with Herb?"

"Maybe once a year if that. Most of his clients are in Nevada."

She reached for a tissue by the coffee table and blotted the invisible smudge below her lips.

"In this dream I continue walking along the reflecting pool guided by moonlight. I hear voices but there are no tourists to be seen. I must be the only person there and I think I'm imagining the voices. The voices are threatening. I'm bothered that Herb left me. As I approach the exterior wall of the mausoleum, I see a woman draped in white linen. It isn't a sari or any kind of garment. She has purple or blue skin. It's hard to tell the color in the dim light. Dry skin. She speaks English. She recognizes me. She knows my name. She tells me her name — Mumtaz Mahal. She was one of the wives of Shah Jahan — the emperor who built the Taj Mahal for Mumtaz Mahal. She was his favorite."

Roseanne crossed her legs and tried to read Dr. Lippman's mind. She had trouble unveiling his thoughts about her mental health and the significance of this ridiculous dream of India.

"Roseanne, this is a fascinating dream."

"Why does it bother me so?"

"A ghost is talking to you. A famous historic ghost at that. That would bother me too."

"And Herb?" she asked rhetorically.

"And Herb is not present."

"I guess it's my subconscious mind pranking me. I am working on Atlantic City's Taj Mahal hotel."

"Yes, your sleeping self, your deeper profile making logical connections to illogical things. I'm not a semiotician, but exotic and banal domes factor into the scenario."

"She touches my wrist in this dream."

"Interesting."

"Mumtaz Mahal asked me to trade places with her. I called out to Herb. And then I woke."

"Well, you're not in Agra. The emperor's wife is still entombed. And your husband appears to be faithful. You say she touches your wrist, in the present tense. But she asks you to trade places in the past tense."

"What does that mean?" she asked.

"I have no idea, Roseanne."

Chapter Three

On the day of Ivana Trump's memorial service, held at St. Vincent Ferrer Church in New York, the site for her burial was "consecrated so that she could have a traditional Catholic burial," according to the New York Times. The media gave this event respectable coverage and enough due diligence about Ivana's history as a New York City citizen and celebrity. The modest plaque identifying her grave posts only her name, her date of birth and death which was Bastille Day, July 14, 2022. According to the Bedminster executive staff, Ivana's plot cannot be seen from the main clubhouse, but is minutes away "at the back side of the first tee."

Five years ago, clerks had given township approval for two burial grounds at Bedminster. Kicking things off, the vest pocket land near the first link was designated as family grounds – Ivana Trump's interment. Donald Trump intended a 284-plot parcel to be developed at some future date for the public at large to buy perpetual Bedminster membership. Multiple plans from the Trump Organization had curious and bizarre offerings as grand as a thousand public graves and as select as an ultra-private plot which a Trump representative claimed would host "only Donald Trump and the very good Trumps." Architectural drawings were submitted featuring intricate stone obelisks twenty feet tall, a twined mausoleum and chapel allowing weddings, commitment ceremonies, religious confirmations, bar mitzvahs, and bat mitzvahs.

To Trump's critics, internet trolls, political cartoonists, clairvoyants, and late-night television comedians, it remained a mystery as to the benefits of a mortuary tax concession on a section of the golf course would help the former president because he had already escaped property assessments by lobbying New Jersey to determine the large parcel a farm. In Trump's official application, he had argued that hedges and trees had transformed into abundant mulch.

In 2017, it was reported in the Washington Post that Trump had announced plans to build a ten-plot cemetery that overlooked the first hole of the golf course for family members. "It's never something you like to think about, but it makes ineluctable sense," Trump conveyed excitedly to reporters. "This is such beautiful land, and Bedminster is one of the richest and most elite places in the country."

One entertainer at the Comedy Store quipped, "Do ghosts golf with a higher handicap or do they just enjoy cheating on the green?"

"New Jersey law exempts land used for cemetery purposes from income, sales and use taxes. The Ivana Trump burial site at Trump National Golf Club in Bedminster likely delivers a huge tax break," wrote Phoebe Wall Howard, for Detroit Free Press and USA Today.

A year ago in 2022, Rex Heuermann followed the Ivana Trump news story with keen interest and perhaps morbid fascination. He was skeptical that a former ski instructor in excellent health would have fallen to her death in her own home. The chief medical examiner from New York City proclaimed that she had died from blunt force injuries to her torso. However, hearing that Trump's first wife was headed for Bedminster convinced Rex Heuermann that there was surfacing a Trump family curse similar to the multigenerational Kennedy family curse. Rex Heuermann predicted that there would be another Trump fatality or attempted assassination before the next presidential inauguration, 2025. Moreover, Rex Heuermann believed that Trump's third wife, Melania, was destined to survive her husband and release a biting, best-selling memoir.

The architect read about Trump and Melania's well publicized trip to see the Taj Mahal in February 2020, eleven months before Trump would have to leave office and in the middle of his historic impeachment proceedings. Trump was the third president after Bill Clinton and Dwight Eisenhower to make an official tour of the Taj Mahal. The grounds around the Taj Mahal were cleared so that the president's inspection would be quiet, private, and completely secure. Melania Trump, age forty-nine, motivated her husband to make the visit. The press speculated that the couple was extending their fifteenth anniversary celebration weeks later as their nuptial date, January 22nd, had little fanfare in Washington. There were a few media whispers that Melania had heard the spectral voice and admonitions of Mumtaz Mahal along the Indian fountain gardens.

Rex Heuermann arrived ten minutes before his morning haircut appointment at Sports Clips on Hempstead Turnpike in Levittown. He had an MVP card for loyal clients, and he always requested the red-haired stylist nicknamed Barbarella. She kept her long flowing hair in the manner of Jane Fonda playing the title character of Roger Vadim's campy, science fiction, 1968 film. Barbarella, based on a French satiric series that centered on a space traveler and representative of the United Earth government, had little to do with advancing the feminist movement at the end of the 1960s. The Sports Clips' Barbarella loved the political realm of Trumpism.

Barbarella greeted Heuermann at the counter. She led him to the front barber chair in plain view of the store window. He smiled broadly and Barbarella touched his shoulder affectionately.

"On your way to work?" she asked.

"Yeah. I needed a cut a month ago but had no time."

"I thought you were keeping away from me, sugar."

"No way."

"How's your wife?"

"Grumpy this week. Sweeter last week." He replied. "It's the July heat."

"Take her upstate for a vacation."

"Yeah."

"I don't mean the Catskills. The Adirondacks. Lake Placid. Lake George."

"Maybe."

"MVP special? You have time, sugar?"

"Why not? I got the card."

The special included a hot steamed towel, vigorous shampoo, plus a neck and shoulder massage.

"Should I trim the eyebrows too? I see your garden's getting bushy."

"Don't touch the eyebrows, Barbarella."

She threw the apron over his massive chest and stomach. Then she wrapped tissue securely around Heuermann's neck. He eyed another guy in the neighboring chair who was as bald as a cue ball.

"What do you think of Ivana Trump's death?" he asked her.

"She's kind of young to have a bad fall."

"Yeah. I know."

"But" she continued, "she stayed faithful to Trump in his first election. Got to hand her some credit for that.

"True." said Heuermann.

"Like there were opportunities for Ivana to extort assets from her ex."

"True."

"They parented Ivanka, Donald Jr., and Eric."

"True."

"He apparently managed her funeral too."

"What do you think of her burial at Bedminster?" he asked.

"Well, Trump loves golf. He loves Bedminster. He can see her grave weekly when he's in Jersey."

"I don't know. Seems tacky to say the least."

"I think you're losing hair, Sampson." she quipped.

"Well, I've been on a Propecia generic for nine months and it hasn't done shit for me."

"Yeah, if it doesn't grow hair the generic — finasteride — will give you breasts soon enough."

"I had a bad dream about exactly that problem."

"Were you wearing a bra in your dream?" asked Barbarella with sudden solemnity.

Heuermann lifted one leg out and crossed himself under the haircutter's apron. His eyes darted around the salon. He looked angry as if a little tornado entered his head. Barbarella and Heuermann fell silent. The haircut was quick. Then came the MVP treatment. She asked him about his hobbies and vices. She knew he liked to gamble but Heuermann spoke about his woodshed in Massapequa Park on First Avenue.

"I build furniture at home, and I still build it in the same exact workshop," he said. "I have one tool that's pretty much used in almost every job, and it's actually a cabinet maker's hammer. It is persuasive enough when I need to persuade something."

"Not someone?" she joked.

"Something," Heuermann said, "and it always yields excellent results."

He looked at the wall mirror and the handheld mirror. He smiled with a little more boyishness this time and paid in cash. His tip was two five-dollar bills.

"Next time, don't wait four months to see me, sugar." She sang like a love bird.

Chapter Four

Mir Abdul Karim met with supervising designer Ustad Ahmad Lahori in the finery of the master's architectural headquarters atop a steep wooded hill, high above the city of Agra. It was raining lightly, and daylight was slipping away. Ustad Ahmad Lahori was smoking from a large water pipe. The air inside was pungent and heavy, despite two large open windows letting in a forceful, summer breeze. Ustad Ahmad Lahori coughed into his smooth fluid hands.

"I heard that you sent for me today," said Mir Abdul Karim with calm dignity, "and I did not waste time to make this appointment."

"Thank you, Mir Abdul Karim. It is always good to be a day early." replied Ustad Ahmad Lahori, while rubbing his heavy eyelids with an elongated forefinger and thumb. Mir Abdul Karim was shown by a palace guardsman to a seat alongside an elongated mahogany worktable. There was a partially completed model of a complex, ornate military structure.

"This is an approximation of the Red Fort for Delhi." said Ustad Ahmad Lahori with a sweeping wave of his right hand. "There are overtones from the Taj Mahal, but not terribly loud."

"It is heavy with thought." replied Mir Abdul Karim, his voice deepening with professional intimacy.

"Military formalism is indeed heavy. Do you not like the design?"

"I like it more than my face can show."

"Do you smoke?"

"I stopped some months ago. My health."

"My friend Mir Abdul, I wanted to meet with you weeks ago. Unfortunately, I was not feeling well. I want to speak today with the strictest confidence. You earned my trust. I beg you to say the same."

"I do, Ustad Ahmad. I say this without hesitation."

"Good. Good."

Ustad Ahmad Lahori inhaled a gust of smoke and his chest expanded. He closed his eyes briefly. A servant of the master architect appeared suddenly in the wings and quietly closed the studio's double doors.

"Mir Abdul, the Taj Mahal is intended to surpass all temples, mosques, and palaces in the entire world. You know this in your heart. You had a significant hand in our brilliance."

"Thank you, Ustad Ahmad. You are too kind."

"Ali Akbar Isfahani, was the master architect of the Shah Mosque, in Isfahan, Persia during the Safavid dynasty."

"Yes, I know."

"Initial work on Shah began in 1611. The magnificent edifice was completed in twenty-eight years. Ali Akbar Isfahani was the most distinguished student of Badi' al-Zaman Yazdi, the grand architect serving Persia's Shah Abbas."

"Of course."

"The Shah relocated the capital of his Persian empire from city of Qazvin to the central district of Isfahan."

"I had seen early drawings of the Shah Mosque as well as visiting the site nearing the mosque's completion, Ustad Ahmad. The Taj Mahal has no similarity with the Shah Mosque."

"No striking similarity, that is true. Ali Akbar Isfahani has his name inscribed at the Mosque entrance."

"I did not know this." replied Mir Abdul Karim.

Ustad Ahmad Lahori broke from the conversation to have a sip of alcohol.

"I have had good fortune and privilege." declared Ustad Ahmad Lahori with an air of strained ascetism. "I have too much wealth. I was wise with my wealth. My wealth and fame grew like twin brothers."

"Yes."

"You are not so wealthy, Mir Abdul."

"I am not poor."

"You have a wife and two children."

"Yes."

"You must provide for them."

"I do. Yes."

"You have a daughter is not like other children and who learns slowly."

"That is true. She is dependent on her mother. I provide for our daughter with much more earnings."

"I can help you, my friend."

Mir Abdul Karim removed his spectacles reflexively. It was a gesture when he was baffled and caught by surprise. Mir Abdul Karim looked vulnerable. He exhaled cautiously as if there was little air left in the study.

"I would not feel comfortable, Ustad Ahmad. Charity would destroy my self-respect."

"I do not offer charity."

"I cannot accept a loan."

"I do not offer a loan."

"What are you offering, Ustad Ahmad?"

"A business arrangement. I am one hundred times richer than you, but I am a coward."

"You are no coward."

"Mir Abdul, have you heard the rumors?"

"What rumors?"

"The emperor is adamant that my design can never be repeated again."

"I heard a few things."

"The emperor has hinted to a few of the elders that the master architect of the Taj Mahal must die as the construction is near completion."

"That cannot be possible, Ustad Ahmad."

"Several elders swear they heard the emperor would show mercy and spare the execution, by allowing the master architect to live but lose both hands to a sword."

"That is absurd."

"I would rather die than lose my two hands, Mir Abdul."

"As would I, as would I."

"I must live seven more years to finish the Red Fort."

"And in my bones, I know that you will."

"Would you consider my sincerest proposal?"

"Proposal?"

"Yes, my friend. I owe you more than money for your contributions to our Agra construction."

"Thank you." said Mir Abdul Karim.

"You have woven a modest thread of genius into our monument."

"I gave my best effort."

"I will supply your wife and children a five hundred thousand silver rupee annuity."

Mir Abdul Karim's jaw dropped like a broken hinge. His eyes squinted shut. How would he manage another minute inside the design study of Ustad Ahmad Lahori?

"Mir Abdul, you can claim the mantle as the master architect. I believe that you know destiny chooses heroes and history chooses villains. It could be your destiny to become a hero this year. You can claim the fame bestowed upon our project. I can tell the emperor that you are the master architect. The visionary. The tower of our team's talent. Do not berate yourself. Sometimes the student surpasses the teacher. You shape pure space and sky. No clutter. Your pencil drew lines from divinity."

Mir Abdul Karim rose carefully, finding his balance laying his hand atop the mahogany table.

"I can convince the emperor that you were the primary designer. I care not about the relativity of credits and titles. I am not a résumé. I am flesh. I will be faulted for withholding this news, but I will not be punished."

"You are asking me to be the murdered architect?

"Only if you believe the rumors."

"I will believe the rumors if the rumors truly force you to hide."

"I can prepare a contract."

"A contract?"

"For us to sign."

"My signature?"

"Sign with two witnesses, yes." reasoned Ustad Ahmad Lahori.

"The emperor will not believe that I was the principal architect hiding in secret."

"We can produce early drawings in your handwriting. I have a physician who will attest to my seizures and my inability to concentrate. Believe me, I have given this much thought."

"If the emperor senses this is a falsehood, he will torture you, the physician, and me."

"That is a risk, yes, Mir Abdul. But I intuit that the emperor will be pleased that our design team is fully transparent to him."

"I have seen one miserable victim of the emperor's torture. It is a fate worse than death. What if the emperor pressures one of the younger architects to confirm this subterfuge?"

"I have already spoken to our designers, and they are willing to embrace this arrangement."

"I need some days to think this through, Ustad Ahmad."

"Alright. Take two days and two nights, Mir Abdul. But we must not delay."

Chapter Five

That October day when Rex Heuermann met Donald Trump Jr. was dominated by inclement weather, horrendous street congestion, and impossible subway delays. It was at The Trump Building on 40 Wall Street in 2018 where the modest renovation was in early progress. The 71-story landmark property built in 1930 required minor work on the 17th floor. Steve Lafiosca, the vice president of property management for the Trump organization, was ostensibly the overseer of the building. Rex Heuermann's reputation for circumventing code restrictions and competitive pricing, won the bid to renovate the office space, add height to the interior ceilings, insert partition walls, and accommodate significant plumbing upgrades. The job was estimated between two hundred thousand and two hundred twenty-five thousand dollars. It was obnoxiously low ball. Lafiosca made the initial contact reeling in Rex Heuermann, but others in the Trump organization interceded along the way.

Rex Heuermann's trousers were soaking wet from the heavy rain. He looked like a towering mess of a man. His hair was saturated from the precipitation, and he forgot to bring along his comb. His folding umbrella was shredded by the afternoon gusts. There was a comic squishing noise from his water-soaked black loafers. Rex Heuermann was in the middle of a conversation with one of his subcontractors when Donald Trump Jr. surprised him. Trump was not alone. By his side was the Trump Organization's chief financial officer Allen Weisselberg and young blonde woman who appeared to be a new Trump organizational hire.

Weisselberg stepped over to Rex. He introduced himself and gave Rex his business card. Rex Heuermann was flustered by the surprise visit. Weisselberg thought that Rex knew about this visit days ago.

"I didn't know about this appointment." said Rex.

"Seems like you've fallen behind schedule." Weisselberg frowned noticeably.

"Actually, everything's on time."

"Mr. Trump doesn't think that's the case."

Rex threw a look at Trump who was whispering with the blonde by his side.

"Can I speak with Mr. Trump?"

"No." said Weisselberg in an adenoidal voice.

"But he's looking directly at me."

"He's looking at the drop ceiling you're installing. Mr. Trump doesn't see you."

"Oh, come on. Your boss is eyeing me as we speak."

Donald Trump Jr. shuffled overlooking more like a wax figure than human. The young blonde woman remained stationary like a statue.

"Hey Mountain Man," said Donald Trump Jr. with a sardonic smile, "we deduct one thousand dollars each day you are late."

"Mr. Trump, it's an honor to meet you. I voted for your father and, actually, my crew is right on schedule. I can show you the contract."

"Fuck the contract. You sad eyed bozos are late."

"I know you like to joke with everyone." said Rex.

"This is no joke and we'll be here next week with a bullwhip."

"A bullwhip?" echoed Rex.

"That's what he said." confirmed Allen Weisselberg while checking his iPhone.

"Mr. Trump, I can email you the contractual schedule."

"Email Mr. Weisselberg." said Donald Trump Jr. as he walked back to the blonde.

Chapter Six

In the bedchamber of Mir Abdul Karim, a cockatoo was chirping intermittently with percussive, rhythmic clicking. The bird was content, secure in a delicately wired bird dome which the architect had built for the family pet. His wife Saanvi was washing her feet with warm water and oils over a porcelain bowl. The area around their oval bed was illuminated by several odd, shaped candles admitting a jasmine scent. Mir Abdul Karim sat on the bed; his back supported by fat pillows of goose feathers. His sleeping gown was partially open, revealing tuffs of chest hair. He watched his wife lean over to reach the bowl.

"My feet hurt." said Saanvi.

"I know."

"On hot nights, they hurt more."

"Let me massage your feet."

"You are too tired, Mir."

Mir pretended to laugh. Saanvi splashed the water at her husband.

"We need to talk about something, Saanvi."

She put her finger to his lips. He kissed her finger. Her arm reached for his neck. Their mouths touched. They removed each other's garments slowly. Saanvi held his gaze for several moments. His skin was warm to her touch. They proceeded to please each other indirectly. This led to a full act of lovemaking. The candlelight created shadows of mystery.

Saanvi did not suppress her moans. Her husband forgot to massage her feet, but he felt very potent. He vocalized his orgasm in an unearthly voice.

"We need to talk, Saanvi."

"I don't want to talk, Mir."

"Ustad Ahmad Lahori asked about a special favor."

"He wants you to travel to Mumbai?"

"No, my darling."

"Where does he want to send you?"

"Nowhere."

"He always makes you travel."

"Not this time."

"Let us talk about Ustad Ahmad Lahori tomorrow."

"It is better now, Saanvi."

"You gave me a moment's pleasure and now you want to erase the pleasure?"

She kissed Mir's neck sending an arrow of heat into his heart.

"Ustad Ahmad will give us five hundred thousand silver rupees as a protective measure and a gesture of gratitude. I have a written document signed by him."

"Five hundred thousand silver rupees?" she repeated with a lilting laugh.

"It is no joke."

"But it is, you absurd man."

"I am absurd, but this is all true."

"What ugly crime will you be committing for five hundred thousand rupees?"

"No crime. Ustad Ahmad plans to inform the emperor that I was the holy mausoleum's master architect."

"Why would he do such a stupid thing?"

"You know why, Saanvi."

"I do not know why, Mir."

"I told you about the rumors."

"What rumors? That emperor Shah Jahan would slaughter 20,000 artisans once the Taj Mahal is completed?"

"Ustad Ahmad knows Shah Jahan extremely well. Shah Jahan will not punish that magnitude of crew. Shah Jahan excessiveness is focused on the holy mausoleum's creative genius."

"And that is," she paused to be painfully deliberate, "Your good colleague and rich overlord, Ustad Ahmad."

"Ustad Ahmad wants to build the Red Fort in Delhi next. I saw his preliminary drawings for the new architecture. He has unbridled ambition."

"So dear husband, you volunteered to be decapitated by the emperor?"

Mir blinked his eyes rapidly to blot away tears. He grazed his hand lover Saanvi's face. She gave him a stone-cold look. An expression of torment swept over his silhouette. He had guessed that Saanvi would not allow any understanding to his devilish bargain with Ustad Ahmad.

"My love, there is a fair chance that the emperor will do none of these cruelties. If that is the case, we will still receive the rupees."

"You became Ustad Ahmad's plaything. An alley cat. He may be enormously wealthy, but we have our needs met. We are not living on the streets."

"We have to provide for our daughter. Years from now, Saanvi."

"But you gamble with your life, with our love, with all of your children's future."

"Ustad Ahmad had already set this plan in motion before he asked my permission."

"How can that be, Mir? How can Ustad Ahmad prove something that is so untrue?"

"He paid many people to acknowledge the fiction."

"Is the entire city full of liars and whores?"

"No, not the entire city.

"Ustad Ahmad chose you to play martyr whether or not you wanted the role?"

Her husband stopped crying and tugged at his long black hair which braided down his neck.

"Saanvi, we can leave in the middle of the night and escape. Will that make you happy?"

"With a sack of food on my back?"

"No, Saanvi. There are elements in the mausoleum design which shows my creativity. It is not farfetched that Ustad Ahmad wishes to crown me as the leading architect."

"You work under him. He is the genius, and you are the apprentice."

"I am not an apprentice."

"You think I am crazy?" she shouted.

Saanvi stood and walked to the caged bird.

"We can discuss this tomorrow. Nothing is simple." he said, feeling irrationally hopeful and at the same time absurdly moronic.

"Why not kill Ustad Ahmad tomorrow and make it look like a fall from the stairway?"

"He is never alone."

This rejoinder gave her some encouragement. She allowed herself a simple smile.

"He talked to you alone, Mir."

"Yes, he did. That was very unusually of him, Saanvi."

"He'll talk to you again alone soon, my husband."

"I cannot kill another man, Saanvi."

"You can pay someone to kill Ustad Ahmad."

"No."

"You can ask to see the emperor and confess this plot."

"I have not enough stature to be giving an audience."

"You can write a sealed letter and pay the royal courier."

Mir saw an image of his crippled father on his knees. Mir's groin began to hurt from the lovemaking. The evening began with sex but ended with contempt. Saanvi's left breast became visible under the bed's blanket. Mir's inner eye conjured up the completed grandeur of the Taj Mahal. Mir gleaned the piercing melancholy of eternity.

Chapter Seven

Rex Heuermann was scrolling through the classifieds in Craigslist in early February 2018. He was shopping for used carpenter tools to replace a few items in his garage workshop. He liked calibrating reasonable prices and deals. He was quite sharp about sniffing out fraudulent merchants and merchandise before picking up a phone. Occasionally, he sold things from his workshop. Rex Heuermann also enjoyed skipping to the personals where women posted for friendship, massages, and escort services. He enjoyed the erotic photos and the advertising copy for escorts. He found many of the tag lines both titillating and ridiculous. After a few drinks, he would even reply back to a posting in the personals as though it were a video game with a virtual character in a black negligee.

He knew a few convivial Long Island building contractors who indulged their leisure time, their wayward eros, and their hard-earned cash on Craigslist's escorts. These construction guys were married. They had families. They were Italians, Jews, Irish, Polish, Russian, and Puerto Rican. They liked the Mets. They liked the Yankees. They drove Cadillacs, Volvos, and BMWs. Many went to church once a month. They coached kids' soccer teams and were Kiwanis leaders. They all took Viagra, even the younger men. He knew one fat bastard from Great Neck who used a penis pump and boasted about the personal engineering miracle during a five-card poker game.

"Prime the pump. Pump the prime." was the joke around the card table.

Rex would open the countless female advertisements and check out the photos of partially clad young women. He perceived the ads as entertainment, laughing at them and sensing the cheap eroticism within American capitalism. He enjoyed listening to jazz while scrolling, sometimes nursing a cold imported beer. His imagination embellished the full profiles of these females, particularly if some were leading double lives.

Rex was cognizant of the unsolved 2010 Gilgo Beach slayings which were close to Massapequa Park. By car it was fifteen miles between Gilgo and home. A crow could fly five miles directly. Newspapers had identified that the victims were young women advertising on Craigslist. He had heard rumors that Craigslist would soon curtain the practice of posting classified advertisements for personal relationships, body rubs, and disguised escort services.

Gilgo State Park stretched on a barrier beach along Long Island's south shore, enjoying the beautiful Atlantic Ocean and Great South Bay frontage. The park was undeveloped. Access to the land was limited to 4-wheel drive and required a paid permit. The state park was a "carry in and carry out" recreation site. Spectacular views and tranquility made this a popular destination. Anglers could surf fish in the ocean. Fishing was popular during the striped bass October migration. Anglers could also catch blue fish and a variety of salt-water species. Gilgo had protective rights regarding the piping plover and sea beach amaranth. Stewards guarded the natural resources. Swimming was always strictly forbidden at Gilgo. Bathers could die in the ocean.

Gilgo, by car, was roughly forty-five miles from midtown Manhattan.

On December 13, 2011, police revealed that the remains of Shannan Gilbert had been discovered in a marsh less than a mile from where she had vanished. A week earlier, her clothing and personal things had been located nearby. Authorities have underscored the fact that Shannan Gilbert's death was unrelated to the Long Island serial killer investigation. Gilbert was last seen knocking on a beach resident's door, pleading for assistance. Gilbert made an emergency 911 call that night, saying that she feared for her life. Her disappearance had sparked the search during which the first set of female victims was found. Shannan Gilbert's mother promoted strong speculation that her daughter, age twenty-three, had been slaughtered by the serial killer.

Since late 2010, eleven bodies have been found along Long Island's southern beach.

Sometime after midnight on May 1, 2010, Shannan Gilbert earning money as a sex worker, travelled in the vicinity where the remains of the previous Gilgo victims lay hidden. Unbeknownst to her at the time, the disquieting events in the dead of night would tie her to four young women whose corpses were covered by burlap. The case sparked one of the largest murder investigations in Long Island history. Two days later, Sherre Gilbert, in upstate New York, learned that her sister had not returned home.

The Gilbert family filed a missing persons notice and then the family drove three hours from their home to Oak Beach, Long Island, to look for Shannan. Eight days had already passed. They learned that Shannan and her ride had left New York City after midnight and headed to a gated community in Oak Beach.

"My sister met the client through Craigslist and went to his house around 2:00 a.m.," Sherre explained to reporters. "Her driver dropped her off and she was there for quite a while and then for some reason, she started to panic."

Sherre Gilbert added to her media interviews that something violent happened in that house to scare Shannan because of a 911 call her sister made inside the client's home. For a time, there was significant suspicion regarding Dr. Peter Hackett and Joseph Brewer, both residents of Oak Beach. Joseph Brewer was living alone and an unemployed financial adviser, recently separated from his wife. He had contacted Shannan via Craigslist for hired sex and her cell phone had Brewer's number the night she vanished. Two days later, her mother received a strange phone call from a Dr. Peter Hackett. The doctor informed Shannan's mother in Ellenville that he managed a house for troubled adolescents and young woman. He added that her daughter had approached his gated Oak Beach home that evening. He went on to say that he provided her medication to lessen her panic. Shannan's mother, Mari Gilbert, filed a wrongful death lawsuit against the physician. Police stated that Michael Pak, Shannan's outcall driver, and Joseph Brewer had passed polygraphs, and they were not suspects. Journalists had noted that Dr. Hackett refused to take a polygraph.

Shortly after Shannan Gilbert's body was discovered, Dr. Peter Hackett placed his Oak Beach home on the market in 2012 and relocated to Florida.

Rex had followed this crime story with interest. Newspaper and television reports saturated Long Island. He may have seen Shannan Gilbert's photos on Craigslist, recalling perhaps that she was using a fake first name attached to her phone number.

When Rex was in architectural school, he remembered one of his zealous literature professors, Ludwig Fink, praising an obscure Austrian novel by Robert Musil, *The Man Without Qualities*, first published in English around 1953. The title in German, *Der Mann ohne Eigenschaften*, was stuck in Rex's consciousness. Rex's professor came from Vienna, had a thick accent, and overdressed in dark, worsted wool business suits. Professor

Fink walked with a slight limp. Professor Fink canonized the novel as the pinnacle of European modern literature.

Rex's modern novel literature class spent two weeks on the book. The class had learned that Musil's sexual activities around the turn of the century, according to Musil's professed public statements and writings, were primarily with a prostitute. The professor speculated that Robert Musil was fixated with either the sex for hire profession or the milieu of prostitution and the private realms of men who sought out paid sex. This was, in so many words, empirical self-study for the novelist first, and collateral hedonism second.

Musil completed a university degree to become an engineer but pivoted to doctoral studies in psychology and philosophy. He had yearned for an immediate window into human behavior and, more importantly, the myriad detours which perverted moral rectitude. He had married a Jewish woman and they fled Berlin for Switzerland during the rise of Nazism. Musil was demoralized by the magnitude of Hitler's hypnosis of an entire nation. After his death, Musil's work was nearly lost to oblivion.

Two key and contrasting figures emerge in Part One of the Musil novel: a thirty-two-year-old mathematician named Ulrich and, Moosbrugger, a wandering, psychotic carpenter who became a criminal defendant charged with raping and murdering a prostitute. The book's narrator wasted no time informing the reader that all Europe suffered nightmares of Moosbrugger. Rex Heuermann's professor had spent one class session on the importance of this detail. His tightly strung professor kept repeating, "Imagine, an entire continent obsessed by a lurid murder and haunted by their collective dreams about Moosbrugger."

Rex Heuermann's professor punctuated the idea many times over that Moosbrugger represented the dark, subconscious energies in play under the civilized veneer of modern society. The classroom was given the definition of the German word, *zeitgeist* — the defining spirit or mood of a period of history and culture made manifest by the ideas and beliefs of the time.

Rex Heuermann saw Ulrich, representing elite society, and Moosbrugger, representing society's monsters, as two sides of a tossed coin that kept twirling. Whenever he mentioned Musil's book to friends during college or later during his building career, no one knew anything about the esoteric story or the obscure Austrian author. In one office visit with his college professor, Rex Heuermann expressed generous sympathy about Moosbrugger's plight and Ulrich's efforts to defend a hated incarcerated monster. His professor validated the act of empathy and sentience calling the emotions within his student as a mature rendering. Rex Heuermann joked to himself that Ludwig Fink could be a successful, debonair serial killer.

Chapter Eight

Roseanne L'Anse met her husband Herb for dinner at a small Italian bistro near his office in downtown Las Vegas. The arrangement was made on the spur. It was Herb's idea. He was famished and they drove there separately immediately after work. Herb Tennison was a tall, lanky gentleman hoping to bring back turtlenecks under a business jacket. He was a tax accountant. He arrived twenty minutes before seven o'clock and requested a quiet table in the restaurant's inner courtyard under the ceiling. The immense glass skylight was prominent. A potted Ficus was near his seat.

"I think it's my wife's birthday," he confided to the waiter.

"Better not guess," the waiter replied.

Herb ordered two glasses of Chianti and looked casually at the menu. Across the way sat two young women in revealing, low cut dresses. His eyes were drawn to their table, to their necklines, and to their stocking legs. The redhead was exceedingly charismatic.

"You must have avoided all the red lights on Paradise Road." said Roseanne as she pulled the chair from the table.

"I just don't stop when I see yellow." he said kissing Roseanne.

"How was your day?" she asked, sniffing the wine glass discreetly.

"Fabulous. Yours?"

"Fabulous."

"I told the waiter it's your birthday."

"It's not."

"I know."

"Why bullshit the waiter, Herb?"

"He'll bring out tiramisu with a candle. Maybe even sing for us."

"I'm trying to lose weight."

"Roseanne. You have no weight problem. You're gorgeous."

"What's the secret?" she pressed him.

"Secret?"

"I can read your mind. You're withholding."

Herb took her hand and held her warmly.

"Yes, well, I have good news and you'll like it."

Roseanne smiled quizzically. Again, she unconsciously touched the invisible lipstick smudge with her forefinger.

"Roger Edison, one of my golf friends, is a leader of his church's outreach organization. He called me this morning with news of an expectant mother who is thinking of adoption when she comes to term. A single woman in her early twenties. College graduate. White. Chloé with the accent mark over the 'e'."

"You never spoke about Roger Edison before." she replied.

"I thought I had, but anyway . . . Roger heard me talking about family ideas."

"Where is this conversation going?"

"Try the Chianti, sweetie."

"Herb, you've done too much groundwork without consulting me."

"I'm just relaying the news from Roger."

"I don't know Roger and I don't like Roger."

"This has nothing to do with Roger. She's drug-free and loves yoga."

Silence fell over the bistro table. Herb squinted his eyes as if a great weight bore down.

"Herb, you want a family more than I do."

"How can you measure that emotion, Roseanne?"

"In my profession, we measure everything as accurately as humanely possible."

"This is just the negative residue after two years of fertility clinics."

The waiter returned to take the dinner order. Roseanne ordered for the two of them.

"Herb, sometimes I believe in destiny. Fate isn't telling us to have children."

"At least would you be willing to meet with the woman?"

"Why would I want to meet her, for Christ's sake?"

"You might have a change of thinking." said Herb.

"Did you meet her?"

"Yes."

"And you liked her."

"Yes."

"Did you say that we were a *definite yes*?"

"No."

"Did your friend Roger Edson convey to her that we were a *definite yes*?"

"He didn't convey that to her either. She's having a baby girl."

"Who gives a fuck?"

"You wanted a daughter."

"I never said that."

"Do you like the Chianti?"

"It's not their best."

"I know how you feel about architecture. You don't have to give up your practice, Roseanne. I'm willing to stay home three days a week and always be around weekends."

"So, you'll be Mr. Mom?"

"You bet," he slurred as he was downing his glass, "and happier for it."

"You won't have the patience for the boredom, Herb."

"I have improved my patience reading Charles Dickens."

Roseanne laughed at Herb. It wasn't the line but his delivery.

"How much does this expectant mother want?"

"Just expenses with prenatal care and an eight-day trip to Hawaii or France."

"Oh, she can't decide between Oahu and Paris?"

Herb laughed this time. The waiter returned.

"Our apologies. The chef said we ran out of mussels."

"I'll have shrimp then." she shot back softly.

Herb studied his wife attentively as the waiter vanished.

"Roseanne, I really want to be a father and to parent a baby with you. This is extremely meaningful for me. I don't have much of an extended family. You have nieces and a loving sister."

"You know, I worry that you've planned this happy, idealistic Hallmark channel movie right down to the window drapery but won't be there after a month of diapering. You'll invent excuses and position me into a default parent. So, Herb. My answer is no. Tell Roger Edson to go screw himself. *I want* the eight-day trip to Hawaii."

"Your wish is my command. We'll go to Maui before the end of the month."

An artic wind blew in from Roseanne's direction.

"Honey, could you just think about Chloé for a week?"

"No."

"Just think about it for twenty-four hours?"

"No."

"Think about it over tiramisu?"

Chapter Nine

Shah Jahan's facial mole floated above his left eyebrow. The emperor tried over the years different herbal remedies to reduce the size of the mole, lighten the color, and control the manner in which the mole became enlarged like a boil whenever Shah Jahan's anger overwhelmed his composure. In the morning, he had his royal soldiers escort Mir Abdul Karim to the palace, Shah Jahan applied palm oil that was soaked overnight in cat urine to his full forehead. The ointment had an aggressive odor that could make weak men vomit uncontrollably. The emperor despised this one imperfection of his outward appearance.

There was a light rain that was cooling the gardens around the emperor's palace. Four powerfully built soldiers led the architect to the emperor's throne. The soldiers had surprised Mir Abdul Karim and his wife while the couple were asleep in bed. Mir was handcuffed with rope tied behind his back and he had a black hood over his head. The hood kept the architect's head dry from the mist, but the head garment made breathing arduous, particularly due to Mir's asthma. Mir was deeply frightened by the intrusion and the arrest. Moreover, the hood's fabric seemed to trigger an allergic reaction.

Upon entering the raised platforms which led to the palace throne, there were subtle string sounds coming from the musician holding a Tanjauri Veena. All well designed Veena instruments have a meditative sound, which may carry both the performer and listener on a spiritual journey. The royal soldiers bowed to the emperor and waited for a hand signal. The emperor slowly raised his right hand. The emperor's rings caught the light from one of the palace torches.

Mir was forced to sit on a wooden chair with high arm rests. The soldiers changed the rope ties so that Mir's wrists were tethered to the arm rests. The wood was smooth and did not feel abrasive to Mir's skin, despite the tight bonds.

The higher-ranking royal soldier whispered a few words into Mir's ear and Mir nodded in the affirmative. The soldier then announced to the emperor that before the palace this morning was Mir Abdul Karim, the master architect of the Taj Mahal project. The four royal soldiers then bowed to the emperor.

"Good morning, Mir Abdul Karim." spoke Shah Jahan. "Speak to me."

"I praise your name to the heavens," replied Mir.

"Thank you."

The emperor stood from his high throne, and he adjusted his floor length robe with both hands.

"Do you know why I had you summoned here, Mir Abdul Karim?"

"No, your highness."

"Ustad Ahmad Lahori provided my royal Brahmins evidence about the true identity of the palace's master architect."

"Your highness, that person is not me. I am younger than Ustad Ahmad Lahori and I am younger than Ismail Afandi."

"Why mention Ismail Afandi?" asked the emperor.

"Because Ismail Afandi made his reputation as a palace dome designer in Turkey and he shares credit with Ustad Ahmad Lahori with the genius design, my holy emperor."

"You say this to fool me, Mir Abdul Karim?"

"I swear on my children's lives, I am telling only the truth."

"I was upset and confused when the royal Brahmins brought me this news."

The emperor gestured to two men standing behind the soldiers. The two men had barbering instruments and began to shear Mir Abdul Karim's hair and beard. They were gentle but swift. Mir Abul Karim's eye grew large and fearful. The locks fell all around his feet. All the while the Tanjauri Veena supported a delicate musical tapestry. The nearby torches created a bizarre shadow of Mir Abdul Karim's head and torso on the tile floor.

"I have learned in life," explained the emperor, "that a man becomes honest when he loses his hair and his vanity."

Mir Abdul Karim was now completely bald and his open face naked. The emperor gestured again to the two barbers, and they opened Mir Abdul Karim's laced shirt. His chest was exposed. They began to shave his breast hair showing professional care. This was not physical torture, but decisively mental and spiritual. Mir Abdul Karim began to cry framed by a chiseled stoic face. His dark eyes were piercing. His pain was evident in his jutted jaw line and the odd turn of his oval mouth. One of the barbers applied a lotion to Mir Abdul Karim's hairless chest. Mir Abdul Karim recoiled slightly, perhaps sensing a stinging wave. The other barber sprinkled talcum powder liberally over the architect's head, neck, and much lighter along his cheeks and chin. The two barbers then lifted a long mirror in front of the architect. Mir caught sight of his new appearance and he shuddered at the indignity.

"Why did you hide your role as master architect, Mir Abdul Karim?" declared the emperor in a rhetorical jab?

"Dear emperor, while I did learn that you had influenced a major change in building materials from red sandstone to white marble, that knowledge does not designate me as Taj Mahal's master architect."

"Again, I ask you, why did you hide your role?"

"My expertise is interior design, and not outward manifestations. Yes, I brought elements of beauty, shadow, and sound into the structure, and no one is my peer in this regard. I acknowledge this truth. The delicate acoustics inside the main dome allow the single note of a flute to reverberate five times. The inner mausoleum is arranged around an octagonal marble chamber which I swear to you and to the Gods serve as my chief contribution."

"Did you think I would murder you for this contribution?"

"No, dear emperor."

"Did you think I would cut off your hands or your arms for this contribution?"

"No, dear emperor."

"You can be more truthful, Mir Abdul Karim."

The emperor approached the architect. The emperor extended his index finger and ran it along Mir Abdul Karim's chest. He believed that Mir Abdul Karim returned a furtive glance.

"Look at me, court architect Mir Abdul Karim."

Mir Abdul Karim raised his eyes and matched the emperor's stare for a fleeting moment. With this exchange, the emperor clapped his hands once. The royal soldiers at the end of the hall escorted a woman who had her hands tied behind her back. It was the architect's wife Saanvi Aashi Karim. There was no hood cloaking her head.

"I beg you, my holy emperor, grant me mercy. Qazim Khan, the reigning goldsmith of the entire continent, who designed and supervised the placing of gold at the apex of the Taj Mahal's crown, has far more status than me. Mukrimat Khan and I were recruited from Shiraz to supervise and administer the construction. Mukrimat Khan can corroborate what I am saying to you."

"Mukrimat Khan told me that you are the master architect."

"That is untrue, my holy emperor."

"Let us then ask you lovely wife what is false and what is true." said the emperor in a quizzical cadence.

Mir Abdul Karim glanced at his wife as she was escorted closer to the throne. The architect fell into a massive panic. He feared that the emperor would order a horrid action to Saanvi. He knew that she had nothing to add to the inquisition.

"You are the architect's wife?" asked the emperor.

"I am Mir's wife, that is correct, my holy emperor."

"Has your husband told you about the palatial mausoleum?"

"Yes, my holy emperor."

"Do you know the status of his profile?"

"He is one of many fine architects under the honorable Ustad Ahmad Lahori, the court architect."

"What else do you know about the mausoleum?"

"Not much else, my holy emperor."

"Do you know which royal personage is assigned to the mausoleum?"

"I do."

"Who?"

She held her tongue for a full minute in dire terror and cleared her throat with a gentle cough.

"Your favorite wife, the holy Mumtaz Mahal."

"You realize this information is totally forbidden."

"Yes, my holy emperor."

"What else do you know, Saanvi Aashi Karim?"

"Mohammed Hanif, Multan, and Quandhar were summoned from Delhi to supervise all masonry work. I know that construction was intended to invoke the grandeur of Persian architecture. I know that my husband was tasked to enhance the interior chambers and engineer acoustics beyond the abilities of any other living engineer. My husband serves you brilliantly, my holy emperor."

The emperor smiled broadly as if Saanvi Aashi Karim's comments were gems of palace entertainment. He was surprised by her sophistication. The emperor was expecting her to fall apart in utter dread.

"Do you love your husband?"

"I do, my holy emperor."

"Do you love him as you see him in this condition today?"

"I do."

"And I believe you. Is there anything else you have to say?"

"There is, my holy emperor."

"Say it."

"Ustad Ahmad Lahori is the genius designer, the master architect, and he wanted to share credit with my husband knowing how hard Mir works for the emperor. Ustad Ahmad Lahori must receive all the honor for Taj Mahal once the mausoleum comes to completion. Today I wish to bless Ustad Ahmad Lahori for his dedication and for his spiritual love to the palace family."

Chapter Ten

Late December 2018, at Manhattan's 40 Wall Street, The Trump Building, Rex Heuermann went to inspect the completed office floor renovation. The new raised tile ceilings were enhanced with soundproof insulation which were also introduced insulation into the partition walls. Soundproof double plated glass was installed quickly and to code. The delays with the remodeling were blamed ostensibly on the plumbing improvements and incorrect supply deliveries from New Jersey. The job surpassed the initial estimates by another thirty-three thousand dollars due to the rising supply and shipping costs of CPVC pipes and fittings. Perhaps a ten-thousand-dollar bribe might have moved the calendar with one supplier. Bribes were always worth the effort.

At the job site, he saw the elderly, bearded electrician from Ukraine, Andriy Kovalenko, on a ladder by the streetside window. Andriy Kovalenko had a glass eye.

"Why are you still here, Andriy?"

"I'm checking a short in one light fixture."

"Is it the lamp?"

"Of course, it's the lamp. My work is always perfect."

"When are you retiring?"

"Next year, or the year after next."

"Is your son taking over the business?" asked Rex.

"Yeah. He's ready. I'm ready. We're ready."

"Good to keep the business going."

"What about your boy?" asked the electrician as he replaced the lighting equipment with both hands.

"No, he's not inclined to get into construction."

"Why not?"

"Because he lacks aptitude. He's clumsy. He's afraid of people."

"Are you sure he's your son?"

Rex laughed coarsely.

"He's half me, half his mother."

"Mr. Heuermann, what's the difference between a drum, a wife, and a whore?"

"What?"

"You can beat a drum, you can beat your wife, but you can't beat a blowjob."

Rex paced the empty loft floor plan with mindless energy. He saw an invisible line to follow meticulously. He counted his steps and entered data into his cell phone. He rapped his knuckles against the sheet rock walls, listening to hollow sounds and sounds of wood studs. He checked the molding with his pen knife. He flipped on and off all the light switches on the walls. The architect flushed the two toilets and opened the bathroom sink faucets to time drain flow. Inspection was an art, according to Rex's professional bible of conduct.

"How much do I owe you, Andriy?"

"Four thousand."

"I have a check on me today."

"You are an honorable man, Mr. Heuermann."

"Yes, I pay my goddamn bills."

"Your last check bounced, my good friend." said the electrician with a playful wink.

Rex noticed two people entering the office floor as the front door was not closed. The lead individual was a short woman in a deep purple dress. Her hands were animated. Her companion was a much older man walking with a cane. They walked slowly, deliberately taking each step with distinction. They whispered to each other. Rex remembered seeing the man before. The man had visited Rex's office two weeks ago.

"Excuse me, Andriy. I think this couple is here to see my finished work."

"What's not to like?" said Andriy.

Rex walked toward the couple.

"Is it Mr. Templeton?" spoke Rex with some tentativeness.

"Yes." said the woman in a Hungarian accent.

"I must have given you this address."

"Yes." she confirmed with forced politeness.

"This job is close in scope to your project." said Rex.

"Yes." said both the woman and Mr. Templeton. His voice was hoarse and in a low octave.

"Notice the interior walls that bend gently and avoid harsh angles."

The couple nodded their heads.

"That's my electrician, Andriy."

The electrician waved his right hand as if shooting a TV commercial.

"You do a lot of work for the Trump Organization?" asked the woman.

"No."

"Why not?" she pressed.

"To be candid with you, the Trump Organization is notorious for paying late or shorting their contractors."

"Then why work for them?" asked Mr. Templeton as he lifted his cane.

Rex smiled shamelessly, thinking the answer was self-evident.

"For your resumé?" she guessed correctly.

"I didn't get your name." said Rex.

"Erzsébet Takács."

"Have you more questions, Erzsébet Takács?"

"Yes. I do. How did you get to be so tall?"

"My father was tall."

"And was he as broad as you?"

"No, he was not this broad."

"Mr. Templeton likes your work."

Rex looked directly at Mr. Templeton.

"Thank you." said Rex.

"I was told," said Mr. Templeton in a halting voice, "that you are very adroit with building code violations and city inspectors."

"That is my specialty, Mr. Templeton."

"But you must be adept handling bribes and gifts." said the Erzsébet Takács.

"I avoid bribes and illegal actions absolutely."

As Rex made that sincerely definitive pronouncement, it was as if he were polishing the halo above his skull.

"I believe you." she offered without irony.

"One of my first design projects in my early twenties was a bid to reorder the usefulness of an abandoned supermarket in Suffolk County. I proposed to the county board a mixed-use structure that accommodated a small daycare center for toddlers and preschoolers interfacing a senior center with some assisted living residencies. The plans were brilliant, but I failed to pay off a government official."

The electrician came down from his extension ladder and joined the conversation.

"Mr. Heuermann is Long Island's unsung genius."

This made Erzsébet Takács smile oddly and perhaps it was her first smile of the day.

"The work appears good enough, Mr. Heuermann." spoke Mr. Templeton, in the manner of sealing the deal. "For the pricing scale."

Rex Heuermann pretended to chuckle and appear convivial. His eyebrows frowned. Most business occasions, he was able to be convincing. Today was more ambiguous. He exchanged quick looks with his prospective clients. Suddenly, there was a detectable industrial odor in the loft office.

"We will finalize things tomorrow in your office." instructed Erzsébet Takács as she produced her asthma inhaler from her purse.

"Of course. Thank you, Mrs. Takács." said the architect.

At this moment as though choreographed by a Broadway dance team, Eric Trump entered the loft office from the rear service elevator. Behind him was a secret service agent in a pin striped suit and a young redhaired woman staffer from the Trump Organization. Eric Trump was talking on the phone, *sotto voce*. Also in Eric Trump's left hand was Rubik's Cube. Mr. Templeton and Erzsébet Takács took notice of the secret service gentleman. He walked with the grace of a ballet artist.

Rex Heuermann recognized Eric Trump. The electrician was guessing this visitor was a member of the Trump family.

Eric Trump glanced at the architect. The architect returned the gaze. Eric Trump put away his phone and stepped in the direction of Rex Heuermann. Rex was braced for a confrontation.

"I want to apologize for my brother." spoke Eric Trump.

"Why?" asked the architect.

"Because he lacks finesse with all of our subcontractors."

"I'm not a subcontractor."

"Who are you?"

"I'm the architect."

"You don't look like an architect."

"Who do I look like?"

"I don't know. A football coach for Notre Dame?" said Eric Trump, with self-amusement.

"You like Notre Dame?" asked Rex.

"Not into college ball, my friend."

Mr. Templeton shuffled closer to Eric Trump.

"The job is done as of this afternoon. The electrician is just changing a lamp or two."

"I like the restructuring, Mr. Heuermann." Eric Trump declared. "You didn't try to reinvent Rubik's Cube."

"No, that wasn't my agenda." replied Rex holding back phlegm caught in his throat.

"You have a preoccupation with clean and crisp geometric forms, like Le Corbusier.

"Le Corbusier?"

"You show a bit of immersion in industrial rationalism."

Under his breath, the electrician repeated the phrase, "immersion in industrial rationalism."

Mr. Templeton adjusted his hearing aid and leaned into the conversation.

"You display broad building techniques and inexpensive materials, and tip towards a machine aesthetic."

Mr. Templeton was deeply moved by Eric Trump's analysis. Rex Heuermann was afraid to accept the compliments and tried to change the subject.

"How do you solve Rubik's Cube?"

"Create white cross," shot back Eric Trump. "Hold the cube with the white face up. Solve white corners."

He turned to the secret service agent and continued.

"Solve middle layer. Create a yellow cross. Swap yellow edges in top layer."

Eric Trump than turned to the female staffer.

"Position yellow corners. Solve final layer corners."

Erzsébet Takács sauntered over and had no inhibitions addressing the Trump team.

"I was always offended watching Stephen Colbert mimic you with his inverted upper lip on his TV show." she proffered with sincerity. "You really are a talented, brave young man, and your father has to be proud of you."

Erzsébet Takács signaled to Mr. Templeton, and both shuffled off to the elevator.

"I apologize for her remarks." said Rex Heuermann, contritely. "They are prospective clients from Riverside Drive, new to this country, who wanted to see my current design work."

The electrician, tool bag in tow, left the space like the Cheshire cat. Eric Trump said nothing and handed the architect his Rubik's Cube.

Chapter Eleven

Roseanne L'Anse was flying swiftly through her modified interior designs for the corrected plans handed to her by colleague architect, 34-year-old Francis Xavier Dumont, who was outside the more senior Steelman Associates stable. Fortunately, she was rid of Derek Bolton's incessant interference with Atlantic City. Steelman had fired Bolton for a series of inept and inaccurate drawings, for delinquent due dates, and a noticeable attitude. Perhaps he was drinking during his working hours? There were rumors afloat. In fact, Bolton had accused Roseanne of cooking up the gossip. Nonetheless, she volunteered her knowledge of Bolton's sloppiness during one formal and very private inquiry two weeks ago. Bolton was told to leave on a rainy Friday afternoon and was given a large box to collect his things.

Steelman became indifferent to Dumont's ambitions.

Unlike Bolton, Roseanne was savvy about her professional conduct in meetings, about her model making and drawings, about her ability to prepare precise budgets, and her tireless diplomacy. She was the only woman in the firm. She either kept up with or surpassed the boys. Most impressively, Roseanne knew how to suppress her growing disgust over the key visual elements of the Trump project. The 51-story Taj Mahal Casino had more onion domes and minarets than any subcontinental recreational park, and enough mirrors and chandeliers to make Versailles look threadbare. With the updated, upper budget designs, and in strict dialogue with powerful HRH Construction, Dumont had redefined the palatial entry drive into the hotel with a pair of stupendous white gates, each with three two-ton elephants of cast stone in front, and a colossal fountain large enough to fill Hoover Dam.

The casino would be America's temple. This casino in Atlantic City.

In her recent team conferences with Dumont, he tried to remain in New Jersey but eventually relocated to Las Vegas. Roseanne quietly endorsed the firm's honest theme that the casino hotel was less homage to India's indomitable Taj Mahal, and more the ridiculous American fantasy of a night at the maharajah's palace.

"The maharajahs' palaces were known for great festivities, endless sex, fabulous decoration, fabulous food, and that's what I hope the Taj Mahal will be known for," Mr. Dumont said to Roseanne time and again. "The historic palaces were for an elite minority, but our Taj Mahal in Atlantic City is for everyone who wants to come."

In Roseanne's mind, she heard Dumont say that there would be naked bodies in the bedrooms and naked souls at the slot machines.

Dumont's role kept growing in magnitude, which mirrored the inflated car and truck capacity where at the most recent count, the hotel expanded to fifty-three hundred parking spaces, along with a twenty-two-space tour-bus terminal, a dozen restaurants, an arena seating over five thousand, a convention center and a casino the size of four football fields. Arriving gamblers and the occasional maharajah will walk up to one of the seventeen computerized check-in counters.

Dumont's central conceits were directed in the opulent private suites on the fifty-first floor, each of which is named after a renowned historical personality. The pièce de resistance, which crowns kitsch beyond all description, is the Alexander the Great suite, a forty-two hundred-square foot lunacy of gold-flecked purple carpets, marble and bronze statuary with a crater bath bookended by gilded Ionic columns and garish recessed ceiling lighting.

Competing for second place in vulgar excessiveness is the Michelangelo suite, capped by loud colored ceiling frescoes, the spacious Cleopatra suite's clichéd Egyptian theme, and the Napoleon suite's cobalt blue lighted in neon.

The Taj Mahal Hotel's interiors were created by Yates-Silverman Inc., with Jeffrey Higginbottom as principal designer. Thomas P. Pippett functioned responsibly as the owner's representative, coordinating construction until Trump took over for Resorts International. The overriding architectural concepts rested with Dumont in consultation with Steelman Associates. Dumont had confessed to Roseanne over drinks that his devotion to the Taj project would secure his career for life.

"Our casino hotel is not unlike building a cathedral." He said over and over to Roseanne.

"Have you ever seen Chartres Cathedral, Francis?" she asked demurely.

"Outside of Paris?"

"Yes."

"I'm guessing you have." he said politely.

Dumont was as earnest a young professional as anyone could imagine, and he never phoned in his commitments to this behemoth. As the Atlantic City project evolved, there were aspects of Taj Mahal Hotel and Casino, such as the dramatic elevations from the boardwalk, that were pleasant to the human eye. From that benevolent angle, the monotonous white tower vanished like a new moon, and the attractive colored onion domes and minarets of fiberglass, which Dumont claimed was inspired by John Nash's Brighton Pavilion, surfaced as an architectural reveal. However, the painfully obnoxious size of the tower dominates the skyline, becoming a blasphemous conflation of modernism and classical. To wit, revolting, oversized, silver windows, and endless, white aluminum in the form of artificial pilasters. Instead of any bejeweled, sculptured tiara that might suggest the Indian palace theme at the scale of a mega-hotel, there was a flat, prosaic ceiling with the obligatory branding seen a quarter mile away — the oversized, tinsel Trump sign.

The interior, while more fun and inventive than any other Atlantic City casino, failed as a visual statement of stature. Spaces defined by gold mirrors, Carrera marble, crystal chandeliers, and plum carpeting pleased no one in particular.

As so many architectural critics would eventually notice in print, The Taj Mahal — feathered up like a homely bride in Chantilly lace — was a ditzy tramp tricked by cheap plastic surgery. The Taj's decadence personified the expanding desolation in New Jersey's most misunderstood city. Transcending the crystal canopy framing a sea of slots and card tables, there was only unchecked elephantiasis.

In 1990, as a follow up act to Ivana Trump's hotel management appointment, Donald Trump put his brother Robert in charge of the Trump Taj Mahal casino. Despite the nepotism and the elusive Trump magic, the hotel suffered relentless problems with its grand opening, especially drowning in its slot machine errors, which took months to address and battalion of lawyers.

According to Jack O'Donnell, a former Trump Organization staffer, "Donald Trump screamed at his brother Robert, putting the blame for the slot machine debacle entirely on him."

Roseanne conversed once or twice with Robert Trump. He was always respectful and debonair in their exchanges. He had phoned on this afternoon just as she was preparing to leave early to meet the expectant mother, Chloé, that Herb had identified for their dubious adoption plan.

"Roseanne, Robert Trump calling."

"Hello, Mr. Trump." she said.

"Please, call me Robert."

"Hello, Robert."

"I'll be in Las Vegas next week and thought we should meet."

"Of course."

"Francis X. Dumont thought I should touch base with you regarding the historic themed suites. What does the X stand for?"

"Is there a problem brewing?"

"No. Not at all. I like the preliminaries, Roseanne."

"That's good to know."

"Can you check your calendar about best times?"

"Really, I'm very flexible next week, Robert."

"I'm guessing you had some interplay with Ivana."

"Very little, actually."

"I was told something different." said Robert Trump, half defensively.

"Who told you that, if I may ask?"

"To be candid, my brother."

"Thank you for letting me know."

"Let's pencil in next Wednesday for lunch or perhaps late afternoon?"

"Great. Fabulous."

"I'll email you to confirm, Roseanne. Thank you. And I like your telephone voice."

Robert Trump hung up as neatly as a freshly minted paper clip. Roseanne jotted down the time and date on her calendar and grabbed her jacket.

Roseanne went to her car and drove to TGI Fridays on W. Tropicana Avenue to meet Chloé. Chloé was hiding under an overlarge cowboy hat and drinking a cocktail from a red straw. Her tight halter top was tomato red. She looked like a forgotten lovechild of Las Vegas. Who needed to be pure in Nevada? The cowboy hat compensated.

"Roseanne?" asked Chloé and sounding smart.

"Yes." Roseanne spun around.

"I'm Chloé."

"Yes, you look like your photo."

"Thank you. Can I call you Roseanne?"

"Yes."

"Roger Edison is a really good guy."

"That's nice."

"Religious guys are the best. I guess Roger knows your husband."

"Yes. From church."

"Roger is *all there* for all the girls." said Chloé.

"That's nice to hear."

"You look upset. Are you upset?"

"No, not at all. Can I ask you one question?" asked Roseanne.

"Sure."

Roseanne took a pause and tapped her forefinger along the table.

"Are you afraid to be a mother, Chloé?"

"Should I be?"

"Do you want to be a mother?"

"Maybe."

"I have nothing more to ask you. Chloé."

"You asked two questions. You said you would only ask one."

Roseanne laughed shortly and stood up. The check was in her hand.

Chapter Twelve

Saanvi Aashi Karim hung wet laundry in the open patio of her home as the late summer sun was rising. This was the second morning after her visit to the emperor's palace. She was still terrified. There was a rumor that the emperor's guards would release Mir Abdul Karim soon as free man or bury him by week's end. She knew these rumors were not reliable and made certain that her children were spared these worries. Irrespective of the rumors, Saanvi Aashi Karim kept praying for her husband's safety and his prompt return home.

Several stray felines ran through the patio. She saw one calico cat catch a grey rodent with a very long tail. Saanvi Aashi Karim took the image as a benign omen since rats and mice were abhorrent in her home. Her children were still asleep. She heard noises coming beyond the walls of her patio. Then there was a harsh pounding at the wood door.

"We have your husband." snarled one of the guardsmen.

From a side window, Saanvi peered out to check if this were true. She opened the door.

"Why is he in chains?" she asked.

"It is for his safety." came the explanation as the shorter guardsman unlocked the cuffs behind Mir Abdul Karim's back. The black hood covered his head. Mir Abdul Karim's hands and wrists were severely bruised.

"Mir, my darling." she said softly.

The hood was removed. Mir Abdul Karim's tan face was free of bruises, but his eyes appeared bloodshot.

"Do I have to sign papers?"

"No." the guardsman told her.

"No writ of any sort?" she pressed the concern.

The shorter guardsman unfastened the ankle shackles. Mir Abdul Karim was now a free man. Mir Abdul Karim dropped to his knees due to dire emotional fatigue. His wife draped her body over his body. Her arms embraced his torso. She felt his fear. He quivered like a young bird fallen from a tree's nest. He gasped for air. She kissed his naked skull and tears ran down her cheek.

"I missed you each hour of each waking day, Mir."

"I missed you, Saanvi, my love."

"Is this ordeal over or will they come back for you?"

"The ordeal is over."

He tried to lift himself from the kneeling position, but breathing was difficult.

"Let me help you, Mir."

She held his right arm as he steadied himself and rose carefully. His knees cracked slightly from arthritis. She took notice that the palace guards also shaved Mir's eyebrows. He looked like a holy monk begging alms.

"Your hair and beard will grow back."

"Yes."

"What do we tell the children?"

"We tell them the truth. They are old enough."

"Do you return to work?"

"Yes. Of course."

"You will follow orders from Ustad Ahmad Lahori?"

"He might pretend to be following my orders, Saanvi."

"So, this farce will continue?"

"Ustad Ahmad Lahori has been meticulous in demonstrating this fiction."

"What is the emperor planning then?"

"He is cunning. He will dig deeper. I sense the emperor will be testing Ustad Ahmad Lahori a year from now. He will trick Ustad Ahmad Lahori. The emperor is a trickster. Perhaps the biggest issue is ambiguity of design. And, of course, the fog of truth. I have given inspiration to the Taj Mahal and the source of this stems from my paternal grandfather's brilliance. I am proud of my contributions. I have inherited his practical genius. But I swear to you, Ustad Ahmad Lahori is a glorious architect who dominates marble creation. We have to credit him for architectural greatness even if he is a coward. I have proven to the emperor that I am not a coward. In the meantime, money will be given directly to you from Ustad Ahmad Lahori. You must accept this money, but you cannot tell your sister or our neighbors about this. You must practice at things invisible, Saanvi. Or our family will suffer for our deceptions. Our children will be cursed if you are not working towards the invisible. Good lies can be poetry."

"We lie because of Ustad Ahmad Lahori, and we must also praise Ustad Ahmad Lahori?"

"I told you, my love. I have proven to the emperor that I am not a coward. I have demonstrated my loyalty as the emperor's servant. He and I share values that endure beyond a lifespan. The emperor loved his wife as I love you, Saanvi. The emperor's guards would have killed me by now if the palace judged me wrongly."

"He will be buried with distinction inside the grand Taj Mahal."

"Yes, Saanvi."

"And if his guardsmen come back to murder you, you will be tossed into a commoner's pit."

"I am not afraid of death now."

"You say that, but you don't mean that, my husband."

"Any burial can be sacred."

"Your burial will be unlike the emperor's internment."

"All burials mean life eternal."

"Only the emperor will be eternal."

Mir was able to walk with more joy.

"You must be hungry, my husband."

"I am."

"And you need your sleep."

"I live to sleep, Saanvi."

"Your eyes are bloodshot."

"Bloodshot, yes."

"You lost weight. You look like a bag of bones."

"I am a bag of bones, my love."

"Are you telling me everything?"

"Yes. Nothing held back."

She intertwined her fingers with his.

"The clouds are moving furiously."

"Yes."

"That means fate will twist suddenly."

"Don't be superstitious, Saanvi."

"What if Ustad Ahmad Lahori buys your murder?"

"Pays an assassin, you mean?"

"Yes."

"Then he can lie without fear, but the Gods will punish him for eternity." said Mir.

"I dreamt that Ustad Ahmad Lahori ordered your death by paying one thousand rupees."

"When did you dream this?"

"Every night that you were in the Palace prison."

Mir hugged Saanvi. Emotions swelled up. They cried in unison and their tears wet their skin. She swept away her bangs to see him as their noses touched together. Her hair brushed his face. Birds on the patio were singing. Fear left Mir and Saanvi. Their tears were sweet nectar.

"What else did you dream?"

"I dreamt about barking dogs."

"Our dogs?"

"Yes, Mir. Our dogs were fighting the dogs from Hell's gate."

"Say no more."

She fell silent.

Dogs played a strategic role in Mir's life. He wanted to describe to Saanvi about how a circle of dogs protected him when he was a boy. He wanted to tell her about his recurring dream about dogs. The nocturnal canines were his, were from Mir's imagination, but they appeared much larger than reality. The tails of the dream dogs fanned powerful winds that formed a mighty tornado higher than the Himalayas. The twisting winds moved the crescent moon. The dogs howled and howled which forewarned the enemies of Mir Abdul Karim. He interpreted the dream as a sign from the Gods that he could trust animal spirits in the event of another palace arrest. How coincidental that Saanvi was dreaming about the same animal.

Chapter Thirteen

The week that began with Labor Day, 2018, was seasonably mild and sunny in the New York tristate area. Rex Heuermann felt highly encouraged about the departing days of summer and welcomed comfortable bidding jobs and keeping busy around the clock. He addressed a panel of three women from the non-profit foundation, The Children's Garden of Manhattan, that early Wednesday in September. He was making a power point presentation with his laptop, and he was wearing his lucky paisley silk tie.

"My firm was founded in 1994, and I recently finished my work on the new Target at 600 Broadway in Soho. It was a big job. It was a successful assignment. We collaborated with Target's design team to integrate the store's aesthetics into the upscale neighborhood. RH Consultants and Associates worked on the escalators and elevators in the existing landmark building built in 1884, re-structured multiple floors and provided new ADA-compliant entrances for the retail space. ADA is short for the Americans with Disabilities Act Standards for Accessible Design."

"As we have collaborated with the big-box retailer on aesthetics, restructuring floors and walls, we also renovated the lobby of the property, which isn't managed by Target. RH Consultants has been involved in roughly 300 projects across New York City, where all our projects were concentrated. Lately, our projects celebrated design solutions for small spaces and individual apartments. We conducted the full build-out of a 12,000-square-foot Foot Locker in The Bronx near Yankee Stadium. We also obtained the Certificate of Occupancy for the three-floor space at 30 East 170th Street."

"Another exciting project was the renovation of a 2,800-square-foot hair salon, Bellami, at 410 West 14th Street in the Meatpacking District. We restructured the salon's upper floors and redesigned the historic marquee. Bellami is a top-tier hair salon."

"Moving on, we provided architectural and design services for the building owner of Savoir Beds, a very upscale bed brand. The company sells handcrafted luxury beds. RH took on a full renovation within an existing Upper East Side building for the showroom, which made its city debut within the last 10 years. The build-out includes herringbone wood flooring throughout, recessed lighting details and built-in illuminated display niches to showcase the client's pieces. The existing mezzanine above the first-floor level was cut back to expand the ceiling at the entryway."

"We also provided architecture and interior design for a doctor's office at 60 Gramercy, a renovation that included raising the interior floor to make it ADA-compliant. Additionally, we did a gut renovation of a two-bedroom apartment at Central Park West. Other notable projects include work on the Savoir Beds store in the Upper East Side and a full build-out of a 52,000-square-foot Burlington Coat Factory in Brooklyn."

"RH Consultants has been based out of Manhattan since its founding. Our projects have included work for Catholic Charities and the John F. Kennedy Airport, and we specialize in expediting services, serving as an intermediary between projects and the Department of Buildings."

Rex stopped talking and smiled mechanically. He thought he was charming enough and he deliberately paced himself to be appealing to the three-women panel. Fast talking would have projected a dishonest architect.

"I hope that wasn't too long and perhaps you have questions?"

"Have you any photos of your work with non-profit orgs?" asked the oldest panelist with very neatly trimmed grey hair.

"Actually, I have very little experience in the non-profit sector. I was a consultant to a few foundations but did not actually building for them."

"How do you outbid your competitors." asked another panelist wearing oddly shaped spectacles which tied behind her neck.

"Well, when I do successfully outbid another firm, it's probably first on my sustained excellence, and is always forcefully reinforced by my low overhead and my select elite staff who work on a salary *plus* profit-sharing basis. I know reasonable pricing and cost-saving measures as well as my best competitors, but no New York architect knows how to navigate building codes like me. No one! Of course, I'm proud of this fact. These cost efficiencies are passed directly to my clients. Plus, I never price gouge even if the job timeline is a near emergency."

"And how is your 'on-time' record, Mr. Heuermann?"

"Second to none."

"Others say the same."

"I am an honest architect."

"May we contact your references?"

"By all means."

"Do you have questions for us, Mr. Heuermann?" asked the elder woman panelist.

"Yes, in fact I do. Three questions please."

"Please."

"Do I have to work with a committee or is there a point person in your organization?"

"There will be a point person."

"That's good."

"Second question. If you become angry with my subcontractors, would you please consider speaking to me first?"

"We can do that. Yes."

"Can you give me your organization's promise not to change the goals, the budget, and the specifics of the project once we bring in the crew?"

"That is a strange question." murmured the panelist wearing the twisted tortoise shell glasses.

"Why is that a strange question?" replied the architect.

"We are a charitable foundation. Our goals are always shifting. You do understand that charitable foundations are vastly distinct from for profit corporations?"

"Yes. Naturally. This goes without saying."

"We can promise you to always keep you informed." said the quiet, mousy panelist.

"That's cold comfort." Rex raised his voice.

"Thank you for coming today, Mr. Heuermann. We will get word back to you by next week."

"Sure. Although I did bring a contract today thinking we could exchange signatures."

"That's a sanguine mind at work."

"I had sensed that your leadership wanted a quick start. Yes, I am an optimist."

"The Children's Garden Foundation likes optimists."

"Do you want me to leave you a copy of the contract?"

He opened his attaché and pulled out the papers.

"Please leave the papers on the table, Mr. Heuermann."

Rex Heuermann gently lowered the contract pages over the wood table.

"The architect must be a prophet... a prophet in the true sense of the term, and if he can't see at least ten years ahead don't call him an architect."

"How stately to think that." said another panelist just entering the room.

"Frank Lloyd Wright made that statement. I only am quoting him."

"It's nice to quote the century's greats." said the fourth panelist.

"Mr. Heuermann, you are so very tall." said the elder panelist.

"Yes, I am very tall."

"Were you tall in high school?"

"Yes, I was."

"When did you discover Frank Lloyd Wright?"

"My last year in high school. But certainly, my first year at college."

"Do you like the Guggenheim Museum?"

"Of course. Everyone loves the Guggenheim."

"Whenever I visit the Guggenheim, I suffer vertigo." said the elder panelist while taking a few pills with her glass of water.

"Well, maybe you should skip the next visit?" said the architect.

"I was being sarcastic, Mr. Heuermann."

"So was I. And no one gets my sarcasm."

One of the panelists laughed behind her powder blue handkerchief.

Chapter Fourteen

Roseanne L'Anse's husband Herb was in the kitchen preparing dinner. He liked to cook salmon quick style, relying on shallow poaching. Rather than submerging the fish into a poaching liquid, Herb placed the salmon with the skin still present on a bed of shallots, parsley, and dill, with California Chardonnay. He would use his favorite saucepan, bring to a simmer, cover, and cook. The fillets absorb the flavors of the aromatics. Herb preferred the wild-caught Pacific salmon varieties Coho, Sockeye, and King. He drank the Chardonnay while preparing asparagus, brown rice, and salad. Herb wore an apron that had the printed words, "Please Kiss the Chef!"

She joined him when he was setting the table.

"Dinner looks sumptuous."

"Thanks, darling."

"I met Chloé."

"Today?"

"Yes."

"Oh, good."

He kissed her.

"Over lunch."

"Where?"

"TGI Fridays."

"Why didn't you tell me this morning you would be meeting?"

"I wanted to see how it would go first."

Herb frowned without thinking.

"Smells good. I'm hungry." she said, while helping him remove his apron.

"I didn't have lunch, Roseanne."

"How was work?"

"Shitty." replied Herb.

"What happened?"

"We're getting audited?"

"Nevada or IRS?"

"Both."

"Sorry, darling."

"Skip the subject. Tell me about Chloé."

He poured her a glass of white wine. She sipped slowly. He brought the food to the table with amazing agility.

"Well?"

"Chloé didn't impress me."

"How was she dressed?"

"Does it matter, Herb?"

"She had a deep plunge halter top and a cowboy hat."

"Cowboy hat?"

"Yes. As in rodeo."

"What did you perceive?"

"I asked her a few questions. I wasn't trying to be judgmental. I tried to be charming."

"I'm sure you charmed her, darling."

"Because you went through our church."

"Why are you judging her after a short lunch?"

"I'm just saying that she didn't impress me."

"Adoption doesn't mean we adopt Chloé. It's her baby who is up for adoption. We will never see Chloé once the baby is born."

"I know, Herb. I really do know that."

"The legal paperwork will prevent her from seeking visitation rights."

"I realize that."

"Even if by chance we run into her at Home Depot, there is no obligation to establish contact."

"I've never been to Home Depot, Herb."

Remarkably, their attention was directed at the salmon.

"What did you ask her?"

"I asked her if she was *afraid* to be a mother."

"Why ask her that?"

"I think that was a fair question."

"That's a question for her therapist."

"Does she have a therapist?"

"What else did you ask her?"

"I asked her if she *wanted* to be a mother."

"And what did she say?"

"She didn't have a good answer."

"And?"

"I stopped asking questions."

"And?"

"And I picked up the lunch check."

They sat down to eat. Herb appeared half perplexed and half upset.

"Roseanne, this wasn't a good way to meet her."

"I paid for her lunch."

"Roger Edison vouches for her."

"I don't care. I'm not wild about Roger Edison."

"There really isn't a more ideal situation for adoption from a white mother in our community."

"I realize that, Herb. Honest to God, I do."

"Could we try to meet her together and give her more grace?"

"More grace?"

"You know what I mean."

"Let's not pursue this project, darling. I don't want to raise someone's child. Please understand that."

"The baby would be our child, Roseanne."

"And Roger Edison would be the uncle or the godfather?"

"Roger Edison would be neither."

"You're fifty-three years old, Herb."

"So?"

"You're too old to become a father."

"Nonsense."

"I'm too old to become a mother."

"You're forty-two. That's not old, Roseanne."

"I'm a working architect. I was profiled by Architectural Digest. I love my profession."

They lapsed into a chilly silence. Herb cleaned his plate.

"We can hire a nanny."

"No."

Roseanne left the table and looked for her hidden pack of cigarettes in the garage.

Chapter Fifteen

Saanvi Aashi Karim went to the market on a blustering morning as autumn was surrendering to winter. She was bundled carefully with extra clothing, gloves, and fighting off a persistent cough. The grey sky broke with sudden precipitation mixing rain with hail. This was a day when she needed more fortification and strength. She needed a loved one.

There was a line at the food merchant tent. Customers were impatient. She saw familiar faces but felt unwilling to engage in small talk. A thief entered the tent and stole some food in a large sack. The small crowd hardly reacted to the commotion.

An older woman, talking to herself, stood behind Saanvi. Her piercing voice was grating and getting louder. Saanvi ignored the chatter but felt the older woman's walking stick brush against Saanvi's leg. After a few more jabs of the stick, Saanvi turned to face the woman.

"Stand away. Please. Your stick keeps hitting me."

"Shut up." said the older woman.

Saanvi studied the woman's face. There were deep lines carved into her jowls and hair above her lip. One eye was sagging. Her skin was seriously pockmarked.

"I asked you politely."

"Shut up."

The older woman's stick scraped along the wood floor and over Saanvi's foot. Saanvi's cried aloud.

"Your husband will die this week. He has no hair."

The older woman tapped her stick. Mucous oozed from her nostrils.

Saanvi decided to flee the merchant tent. She was unsettled by the older woman's aggressive energies, and she felt vulnerable to a stranger's curse. How did the woman know that Mir had no hair? The older woman followed her out of the tent and down the alley.

"What do want?" cried Saanvi.

"I want you to look at me." came the rejoinder.

"I am looking at you. You are disgusting."

"I told you the truth. Your husband will die."

"Go away!"

"He has no hair. He is as bald as a baby's bottom."

"Go!"

"Give me money. Then I will go."

Saanvi threw a handful of coins at the older woman. The older woman laughed.

"There's your money. Go."

The older woman strained as she lowered her twisted torso, bending at the knees and at the waist. Her hair became longer and snakelike. The older woman transformed into a monster. Saanvi detected a pungent odor circling the monstrous woman. Saanvi wanted to vomit. The older woman picked up the scattered coins. With the help of her walking stick, the older woman lifted her body to a standing position. Her head and neck were cantilevering like a diving board. Her hair slipped into knots. Her saree under her coat was shredded at her legs.

"This is not enough money." whispered the older woman. "I know you have children."

"I have no children."

"You are lying. I can heal your husband."

"My husband is not sick."

"I can heal him." she repeated and turned away. The hair below her neck suddenly grew longer and darker. "You know what I am able to do."

"You can heal him?" Saanvi doubted it.

The older woman walked away from Saanvi. The unforgettable odor vanished. Saanvi allowed herself to take a full breath. Saanvi was still nauseous.

She proceeded to return home. She would shop another day and let this day wash away. She had to see Mir. Saanvi had to see his health. He was not going to die.

Mir was home. He was wearing a robe and a towel. His eyes were red with exhaustion.

"Saanvi." he muttered delicately.

"Yes."

"I am hungry."

"Good. You ate nothing yesterday."

"That was due to my fever."

"Is your fever gone, Mir?"

She touched his forehead. It was cooler than the last few days. Mir said nothing.

"Where are the children?"

"With the tutor. The tutor is working late today." he answered.

"When will you return to work?

"Tomorrow."

"You can wear a hat."

"Yes, I can wear a hat."

"It's been two weeks since you went to building site."

"Yes. Nothing has changed there."

"What will you say to Ustad Ahmad Lahori?"

"Nothing to say. He knows what happened. He is the master architect in control, even if he proved otherwise to the emperor."

"Would he ever kill you?"

"No."

"Are you so sure?"

"Only the emperor will be my executioner."

"I met a frightening old woman at the market. She assaulted me."

"Did she rob you?"

"No."

"What did she do?"

"She knew things about you. She said you would die soon. She offered to heal you."

"There are a million old women like her." he said, filling up his smoking pipe.

"She was different, Mir. She knew you lost all your hair."

"And she can restore my hair?"

"Maybe."

"With the boiled toxins from a cobra?"

"I know that I will run into her again."

"Find out how much she will charge for her medicines. I have miserable ingrown toenails."

"Stop joking, Mir."

"Do I look pathetic without eyebrows and hair? Abject unsightly lump of a man."

"In my eyes you are always beautiful."

"I sense in my bones that the next atrocity will be the loss of my hands. I can feel the sword's blade."

"We can move our family in the middle of the night. We can change our names, Mir."

"You think the emperor has not stationed men to watch every step I take?"

"It is a gamble to stay here. It is a better gamble to look for refuge."

"At least the children do not know the circumstances, Saanvi."

"Yes, my love."

Saanvi happened to glance outside their largest window. The older woman was standing thirty paces from their home.

Chapter Sixteen

It was the fourth Thursday in April 2019, "Take Your Child to Work Day." The precise date was April 25th. The architect's daughter Victoria was in the office helping him with a PowerPoint presentation. Victoria was a genius preparing PowerPoints. She had an amazing eye arranging graphics with captions, simplifying flow charts, balancing ideas with key words, and choosing colors which popped off the screen. She had more talent than her father.

Today she wore a colorful print blouse with ruffled collar and puff sleeves. Victoria's hair was tied back in a short, neat ponytail and she had on her favorite gold ring earrings. The architect's daughter was a recent fine arts graduate of New York Institute of Technology and her skill set included 3D/2D Animation, Modeling, Sculpting, Autodesk Maya/Mudbox, ZBrush, ToonBoom Harmony, Photoshop, Illustrator, and editing in After Effects/Premier. Prior to working for RH Consultants, Victoria had a sales position at Macy's which she converted to part time.

Victoria was both a genuine support to her father in a host of office chores and she provided an emotional benefit to him during late hours of stress. He enjoyed her company and her natural sweetness which generated throughout the day. Her sense of humor made the architect laugh. As the morning hours tapered off, she phoned the local deli to deliver sandwiches to RH Consultants while her father was completing drawings for a proposed retail store renovation.

Victoria put away her work and flipped through a few YouTube segments on her desktop. There was a cute video of two little girls in colorful party dresses visiting their mother's Park Avenue law firm. The little girls had their hair pulled up in sophisticated styling. Rex Heuermann leaned over Victoria's shoulder to see the video clip from NY1 cable news.

"How darling." said Rex.

"Look at those little dresses."

"Both pink."

"I remember when I came to your office at that age."

Victoria's father nodded and placed his hand on her shoulder gently. He admired Victoria's spontaneous kindness, wit, and optimism. For three years she also had volunteered as an animal caregiver and kennel helper for Bideawee in Wantagh, Long Island.

"I ordered deli, Dad."

"Thanks."

"I can work late if you need me."

"No, you can cut out about five o'clock. I'm good."

"Okay."

"Do you have a date?"

"No."

"Are you sure?"

"I'll tell you if I had a date."

"You don't tell me everything, sweetie." said Rex in a teasing tone.

"I prefer dates on the weekend."

"Really?"

"Home late, wake up late."

"And you rely on the zodiac." he asked.

"No, I don't."

"You ask every guy what his goddamn sign is."

"Only for fun, Dad."

"But you had your chart drawn a few times."

"Because Trish is good reading charts."

"She's quite a character."

"Trish can read minds. No shit, Dad. She can do your chart. Your birthday's six months away. Perfect time for astrology."

"Sure." he said with an avalanche of sarcasm.

"It's a great birthday gift. What to give a guy who has everything?"

"Stick with Hermès silk neckties."

"That's a Father's Day present."

"Did you order me a roast beef on rye?"

"Yeah, with a dill pickle and root beer. Extra Dijon mustard."

"And you?"

"Tuna. Diet Coke. I looked at the calendar in September. Your birthday is Friday the 13th."

"Yeah, and I was born on Friday the 13th."

"I didn't know that, Dad."

"That's why I lead such a charmed life."

Victoria laughed as the phone rang. She answered the call in a professional voice as the architect returned to his desk. Hanging up, Victoria laughed to herself.

"Today is also International Chocolate Day, National Hug Your Boss Day, National Peanut Day, National Defy Superstition Day, National Kids Take Over the Kitchen Day, and I could go on."

"National Defy Superstition Day?" muttered her father.

"You bet. Friday the 13th!"

"Are you superstitious, Victoria?"

"Not really. But I do hold on to lucky objects."

"Like what?"

"One of my high school friends once gave me a bowling pin. I have lucky days whenever I polish it with *Tried-and-True Danish Oil*."

"Never knew that."

"What about you?"

"What about me?"

"Do you have a lucky object?"

"I have a few tape measures, but my *Stanley Fatmax* twenty-five-foot tape measure has been lucky enough."

"Anything else?"

"I like my Glock 19."

"Can a gun really bring you luck, Dad?"

"Yeah, honest to God." said her father.

"Please tell me that you never used the Glock."

"I never used the Glock."

"Should I believe you, Dad?"

"I hope so, darling."

"Why do you own guns?"

"Everyone has to have a hobby."

"Guns are not a hobby."

"In America they are."

"Do you keep secrets from me?"

"No. Why should I?"

Victoria suddenly changed the subject sensing that her father's face was getting flush.

"What's your most proud design in your entire career?"

"I don't know exactly. I loved my imaginary custom homes which I created in architectural school. Minimalism with precision wood detail and innovated recessed windows and doors. Very Scandinavian. In terms of my commissioned work, probably it would be the full build-out of the 12,000-square-foot Foot Locker a few blocks from Yankee Stadium."

"What's the most impressive renovation you've seen in New York?"

"Eero Saarinen's lovingly restored 1962 TWA Flight Center at JFK Airport. Sort of a theme park hotel projecting midcentury modernism. You can spot Le Corbusier's Ronchamp absorbing Las Vegas buzz. The building's liquid curves are like bars of feminine soap, foisting buttresses like a fat bird on bony legs."

"And the most beautiful building in the entire world?"

Rex Heuermann closed his eyes and ran the question through his mind.

"Maybe the Hagia Sophia in Turkey? No, that's not right. It's India's Taj Mahal."

"Have you been there?"

"No. Haven't been to India or Turkey. The Nobel laureate Rabindranath Tagore described the magnificence of The Taj Mahal as a teardrop on the cheek of the universe."

"What a cool thing to say."

"Yes."

"A teardrop of beauty or of sadness?"

"Probably both. Tagore opposed imperialism and promoted Indian nationalists. He barely avoided assassination in 1916 by Indian expatriates during Tagore's stay in a San Francisco's Palace Hotel."

"You read so many weird political things."

"You know that I'm a history buff and I love stories of political menace. The Tagore assassination plot failed when his screwed-up killers got into an argument."

"What sort of argument?"

"If memory serves, there were two opposing factions. The Khalsa Diwan Society based in Stockton, California, and the Hindustan Ghadar party with headquarters in San Francisco. Ghadar was hellbent on inspiring a revolt against British rule of India. Independence came in 1947. And Rudyard Kipling called the Taj Mahal, 'the embodiment of all things pure'."

"Kipling was a jerk, Dad."

"Was he?"

"He was into imperialism and racial hierarchy. 'The White Man's Burden'."

"'The White Man's Burden'" repeated Rex with his Long Island accent. "Don't mock me, Dad."

"I'm not mocking you, pumpkin. An impure man can have thoughts of purity."

Chapter Seventeen

Chefs at the Trump Taj Mahal Casino presented their signature dishes to local TV media during the resort's pre-opening on March 17, 1990. Donald Trump had appeared at a New Jersey Casino Control Commission hearing twelve days later, to field a battery of skeptical, challenging questions on gaming and informal ties to organized crime. He was half brash, half diplomatic.

Roseanne L'Anse arrived at the Trump Taj Mahal Casino on the same day, in anticipation of the official hotel opening April 2nd. It was her office's protocol to inspect the project's final touches and represent her architectural firm at the ceremonies. She was greeted with professional hospitality at the front desk and was given one of the smaller suites as a special courtesy from the Trump Organization. There were fragrant, luscious flowers on her glass coffee table, a bottle of Moët champagne on ice, a bowl of fruit, and a signed copy of Donald Trump's *The Art of the Deal*. Next to the gifts was a printed flyer with the following words:

"One step beyond your wildest dreams, there is a billion-dollar dream come true. The utterly fantastic Trump Taj Mahal Casino Resort, where every day is a holiday, and every night is New Year's Eve. So, take a magic ride to the eighth wonder of the world — The Trump Taj Mahal Casino Resort in Atlantic City. You've got to be there to believe it."

Ornate chandeliers, Persian rugs, gold taps and sinks in the restrooms and gold elevators were ready to welcome the hordes of guests and spectators who arrived at the opening ceremony to see a command performance hosted by Michael Jackson. This was New Jersey's tallest building to date. The entire April day was planned to be a gargantuan spectacle. Management hopes were very high. The casino expected to make over two million dollars during their opening day.

Roseanne unpacked her luggage and decided to take a shower before walking the premises. The flight felt long. She was impressed with the high-end bathroom vanity elements, accessories, and lighting. The bathroom tilework, in particular, pleased her. The interior suite's beauty and understated luxury compensated for the monolithic kitsch of the hotel's exterior statements. The hotel should not be written off as a joke or a Disneyland concoction. Still, a part of her felt like a whore for selling out in the execution of this commission.

Touring the hotel casino's expansive bedizened spaces, she spoke with two workers untying the giant stone elephants outside the façade. She met Bob Klinger, of Mays Landing, planting tulips outside the main casino entrance. Full of cheer, electrician Jack Jamieson of Pittstone, Pennsylvania was finalizing adjustments on a chandelier in the casino lobby. Hidden from public view, were the immense costume shops where seamstresses and tailors were sewing costumes for the hired hotel actors. Scores of actors were hired for the opening week's publicity antics. She witnessed their rehearsals in one of the unlocked ballrooms. When not rehearsing the actors floated desultory and bored through the maze of hotel corridors.

Roseanne strolled by the hotel boutiques. Many of the shops were not opened yet. She entered *Accents*, part of the Taj Mahal Casino's *Spice Road* shopping corridors, observing a prominent line of designer Cartier sunglasses prices from $520 to $1,800. Luckily, Roseanne remembered to pack her affordable Ray-Ban wirerimmed sunglasses from Las Vegas.

In the open expanse of the casino's sea of slot machines, she ran into two executives from HRH Construction who were key players on the project, and they were effusive with pride.

"What a week it will be!" said the older HRH executive to Roseanne.

"Yes, that's for sure."

"Congratulations." uttered the other executive who appeared to be sporting a thick black toupee with hints of distinguished grey hair.

"Thanks, and congratulations to you guys at HRH."

Roseanne rounded out her hotel inspection stumbling into a professional photo shoot for a well-coiffed Donald Trump, in an expensive and well-tailored black suit and solid red tie, who was posing in front of the gaudy supersized genie lamp adjacent to the neon lights projecting the words: Trump Taj Mahal Casino Resort. The genie lamp struck her eye as brilliantly absurd satire that could have been a Jeff Coons Museum installation. She kept a safe distance from the photography team. She was relieved to not be seen by Donald Trump, thanks to the flashing cameras and general tumult.

Moreover, Roseanne had an epiphany how ludicrous, after several long and arduous years, this architectural commission turned out. The importance of the commission was the sheer size and volume of the edifice. The highly vaunted Trump publicity machine, always on steroids, was never perceived as a negative ingredient to Roseanne's firm and to her personal portfolio. America's spiritual vulgarity became incarnated to new heights. However, seeing a troupe of actors looking like escapees from an Arabian Nights movie pushed her tolerance past the red zone. These actors were simply mirroring the tacky Indian costumes for the concierge team, the bell hops, along with the reception and casino crew.

She returned to her suite feeling a sudden tug of fatigue from the transcontinental flight. Roseanne slipped off her shoes, massaged her toes, and saw there was a flashing light on the bed table's hotel phone. It was a long, rambling voice message from Herb. He apologized profusely that business problems suddenly surfaced, and he couldn't make the flight to Atlantic City in time for the opening. He added that they could chat tomorrow in the middle of the day or in the evening. The tone of his voice was caring and contrite, but Roseanne processed the news poorly. Cancelling this late truly ticked her off. April 2nd was a Monday, and she knew his weekend was originally wide open.

Roseanne opened the champagne and poured it liberally. The Taj Mahal was one of her largest jobs. She often was there for him on his professional celebrations. Herb's priorities were thoroughly upside down, she thought. She wondered if his decision not to make the flight was an unconscious quid pro quo in response to her shunning Chloé's baby adoption. Her relationship with Herb was deteriorating ever so slightly. Herb's news began to burn her inside.

There was a powerful jolt in Roseanne's gut knowing she would spend a night in the stupendous structure that had her sweat, DNA, and blood. Seeing the casino hotel animated by staff and media ghouls penetrated her aesthetic numbness. She was an essential architect to the elite team, but she began to feel like a trashy, architectural whore. The derogatory term was bandied about at her architecture school. She loved the term as a young woman, but she threw a boomerang hard. Atlantic City, home of America's televised beauty pageants, had devolved into a whore's gambling hell on the Jersey shore. The casino patrons were pensioning senior citizen Italians, Jews, and Puerto Ricans from Philadelphia, Newark, and New York with one-day roundtrip bus tickets. Roseanne wasn't a cheap whore, but this evening no modifier mattered. Having forfeited the best years of the last decade, this was Roseanne L'Anse's overture into the 1990s.

The next afternoon Roseanne met with two of her office colleagues who flew overnight.

They annoyed her and she was short with them. They told her that New Jersey's governor James Florio was with them when they checked in during the late morning. They asked her about the V.I.P. parties over the coming days. They wanted to be able to see the Michael Jackson show and go backstage to meet the singer. She admitted to her ignorance. They thought she knew more than she was willing to say. If she had three martinis and a pistol, Roseanne would have murdered them.

That evening Roseanne walked out of the Trump Taj Mahal Casino Resort and found her way to the boardwalk. The weather was pleasantly warm for early April. She saw many couples holding hands and walking along the boardwalk. Silhouetted by the boardwalk lamps there was a dramatically tall man with a thick neck walking alone, swinging his arms oddly. He was wearing sunglasses, and his sandy hair was windblown. They would soon be passing each other. They looked at each other. She saw that the man was not older than thirty and he seemed in an unhappy mood. He had binnacles strung around his neck. Was he wearing sunglasses because the boardwalk's night lights were too intense?

The tall broad guy was Rex Heuermann, recently hired as an intern architect at Greer Construction Corporation in Freeport, New York.

In seven months, Rex Heuermann and Elizabeth R. Ryan had planned to marry at Saint Peter's Church in New Brunswick, Middlesex County, New Jersey. Rex Heuermann loved Elizabeth Ryan. She loved him. They trusted each other and showered each other with small gifts every few weeks. She made him laugh day and night. They enjoyed their relationship and their physical affection. They were not shy talking about marriage to their friends. Elizabeth wanted to get pregnant. That was her secret. Her friends knew. She didn't want Rex to know.

Rex Heuermann was in Atlantic City planning to spend the weekend with some drinking buddies. They could be coarse like him. They knew that Rex Heuermann had a raunchy sense of fun. They liked to gamble. For some odd reasons, he mixed up the dates and came a weekend early. Rex

Heuermann decided to make the best of things. He bought an expensive steak dinner on the boardwalk just before sunset. He drank a few beers. He thought about sex and roulette tables. He didn't feel very lucky this particular night. Still, the evening sky was an aphrodisiac. He felt an urge pulsating from his groin.

Rex Heuermann saw Roseanne L'Anse coming from the boardwalk shadow. One of the streetlamps was broken. He liked her figure and the movement of her hips. She was an older woman but very attractive to him. There was something sexy about her walk. There was something classy about how she controlled her hands while strolling ahead. He felt a frisson of unconscious recognition as they passed on the boardwalk. He took one more look at her derrière.

Roseanne moved briskly and she was concerned about her safety. She looked back out of instinct. The towering stranger had disappeared. That struck her as peculiar. He should have still been within her sightlines. She knew what saw, a large lumbering guy with an off-putting vibe. She thought best to reverse her course and return to the Taj. At least her mind had drifted from the resort's grand opening.

Chapter Eighteen

Ustad Ahmad Lahori walked around the palatial grounds along the south bank of the Yamuna River. It was soon approaching sunset. He was deep in thought about current problems with a delayed shipment of marble and disciplinary matters with his top design team. Moreover, he was fending off recent rumors suggesting that the Mughal emperor Shah Jahan had decided to erect a replica structure like the Taj Mahal, in black monotones, across the Yamuna River. The clandestine reports were coming from reputable sources which intensified Ustad Ahmad Lahori's worries. The rumors had identified the emperor's sons were not in support of a competing palace projecting the powerful magnitude of the Taj Mahal. The gossip included the immediate dangers to the court architect and his most elite artisans tied to the construction. Adding to the intrigue, many strangers were visiting the Taj Mahal site as the project was nearing a finishing phase. Some were caught drawing the Taj Mahal on parchment. These suspicious visitors without credentials were murdered by the emperor's guards and their bodies were thrown into the Yamuna River.

Running through his mind was the slippery problem of Mir Abdul Karim. Ustad Ahmad Lahori believed that his efforts to persuade the emperor about the architectural hierarchy of the Taj Mahal were rock solid.

The emperor had heard in the last few years that Mir Abdul Karim was a rising master architect known for unique flashes of brilliance. It did not stretch credibility to exalt Mir Abdul Karim as the true Mughal court architect. The emperor accepted the explanation Ustad Ahmad Lahori presented in front of the emperor and the emperor's sons. The emperor had placed a cobra by Ustad Ahmad Lahori's feet during the palace session. The emperor had conveyed to Ustad Ahmad Lahori that the cobra would strike him if he uttered one false note. Ustad Ahmad Lahori dreaded all snakes, particularly at close range, but he managed to maintain his composure during this hour-long interrogation. The cobra was placed inside an uncovered wicker basket with two snake handlers nearby. Only during the last few minutes did the cobra threaten Ustad Ahmad Lahori's personal space.

The emperor's sons were harsher to the architect over the remaining questions and verbal challenges. They whispered to the emperor aggressive assumptions that the architect was manipulating perception and breaching the high trust bestowed. Ustad Ahmad Lahori could read the whispering lips and the body language. The sons gestured to the cobra. Had the cobra moved within striking distance of Ustad Ahmad Lahori, the Emperor would have judged the proceedings against the architect.

Ustad Ahmad Lahori had intuited that the emperor was profoundly invested in the architect's decades of loyalty, fidelity, and service. The emperor's initial anger about the discovery of Mir Abdul Karim's role as the primary agent behind the inspired concepts birthing the Taj Mahal. The revelations about the mausoleum's chief designer bore tragic weight.

The emperor convinced himself that Ustad Ahmad Lahori's fear of snakes would weed out the truth. The emperor would defer his decision about Mir Abdul Karim's execution for at least another year. This was a rational plan in light of the estimated completion date for the Taj Mahal. The emperor had informed his sons and the palace guards about the postponement. The emperor made it clear to his inner circle that Ustad Ahmad Lahori would not be executed prior to the celebration of the Taj Mahal's premiere.

It seemed more than coincidental when Ustad Ahmad Lahori saw the emperor and his palace guards by the Yamuna River banks as the sun left the horizon. Thinking about the Emperor was a sign of the emperor's immediacy and commanding power over all of his Mughal subjects. The architect acknowledged the emperor's presence by bowing slowly from a very far distance. One of the guards mounted a horse and trotted to Ustad Ahmad Lahori. The pounding of the horse's hooves carried in the gentle wind. The helmeted guardsman held a sword.

"Climb up." said the guardsman, extending his empty hand.

Ustad Ahmad Lahori hesitated.

"Mount up!"

Ustad Ahmad Lahori grabbed the guardsman's wrist and jumped onto the horse.

"Hold tight."

The horse trotted briskly to the riverbanks. Ustad Ahmad Lahori felt the urge to vomit. The air felt cold and stung the architect's face. The architect ordered himself to contain his sudden nausea. The guardsman stopped his horse as they approached the emperor. The full moon was visible in a cloudless sky.

"Ustad Ahmad Lahori."

"Yes, my emperor."

"Do you always walk the grounds?"

"Yes, my emperor."

"Alone?"

"Yes, my emperor."

"Dismount when you are addressing your emperor."

Ustad Ahmad Lahori slid off the horse awkwardly, stumbling on his feet.

"The soft evening light is beautiful, Ustad Ahmad Lahori."

Ustad Ahmad Lahori nodded his head in agreement, still resisting the need to vomit.

"You look ill, Ustad Ahmad Lahori."

"I am fine, my emperor."

"Do you believe in an afterlife?"

"Yes, my emperor."

"Where does the soul ascend to?"

"The soul is purified and comes back as an infant, my emperor."

"You truly believe that notion?"

"I do, my emperor."

"Does it matter where your carcass is buried?"

"On that point, I am unclear, my emperor."

"My view, for what it is worth, the soul must be in sanctified circumstances if there is a transition into immortality."

"Yes, my emperor. Sanctification is the imperative."

"Where will your body be placed, Ustad Ahmad Lahori?"

"I have not made preparations to date, my emperor."

"How can that be?"

"I am superstitious, my emperor."

"What do you mean to say, Ustad Ahmad Lahori?"

"If I make plans about my burial now, I think that I would invite an early death, my emperor."

"Coming from my court architect, you are too rational and too enlightened to think that."

"Most of the time I am very rational. I have my weaknesses, my emperor."

"You have a beautiful wife and children, Ustad Ahmad Lahori."

"Yes, my emperor. I love my wife and my three children."

"How old are your children?"

"They are all grown. They are adult."

"I asked how old they are."

"My son is nine and my daughter is seven, my emperor."

"Which is your favorite?"

"I have no favorites, my emperor."

"Fathers have favorites."

"I fancy my youngest daughter, my emperor."

"What is her name, Ustad Ahmad Lahori?"

"Prisha, my emperor."

"Does your wife know that you prefer Prisha?"

"No, my emperor."

"I think you should tell your wife that you prefer Prisha."

"I will, my emperor."

"Do your children know about the Taj Mahal?"

"No, my emperor."

"What do they think you are doing, Ustad Ahmad Lahori?"

"They think that I am renovating your personal palace."

The emperor began to laugh without self-consciousness. He loved the improvisational manner of this discourse.

"Your wife knows?"

"Yes, she knows, my emperor."

"About the Taj Mahal?"

Ustad Ahmad Lahori nodded and then bowed his head to show respect.

"This mausoleum is breathtakingly beautiful, Ustad Ahmad Lahori. I know in my heart that you are a major force in the design. The dome of my dreams. The spires of a perfect sky. The exacting geometry of sculpted beauty. The Taj Mahal will never age. The Taj Mahal is a form of design that existed before man. And it will outlast civilization. The Taj Mahal does not mark time. That is its truest secret. Birds cannot light upon the dome. The angle upsets all flying birds. Rain dances over the four smaller domes. Moonlight flirts with the four kiosks. The smoothness of the surfaces speak to the moonlight while the noontide sun bakes the soul which lifts the edifice effortlessly."

Ustad Ahmad Lahori nodded his head. He felt humbled by the rolling words. The emperor studied the architect as though Ustad Ahmad Lahori was art on the wall. There was silence interrupted by the sound of an owl.

"I know that you fear torture by my palace guards." explained the emperor. "I know that you fear a painful death. You imagine the worms consuming your buried carcass and maggots defiling your broken grave. You see the obliteration of your life. You leave your body and join the invisible wind. There is nothing after you expire. You see the departure of your manhood. No strength in your loins. The erasure of your creations. You question now whether immortality will be granted by the gods. If the gods are in a good mood. Can you negotiate for immortality? Will the gods listen to you? You are not worth more than an insect. I must tell you; I look at everything. And I will educate you, here and now, that you will know cold emptiness before you will know a very frigid death."

"Yes, my emperor."

"You accept what I am saying?"

"Yes, my emperor."

"I know that you pushed Mir Abdul Karim into the principal leadership against his will."

"Not so, my emperor."

"Exactly as I say."

"I cannot lie. Mir Abdul Karim is a man of genius. I am not his equal."

"Look away."

Silence. The guardsman held his sword above the horse.

"Yes, my emperor."

"Complete the Taj Mahal."

"Yes, my emperor."

Chapter Nineteen

In the early days of December,1990, Donald Trump had already defaulted on the mountainous debt from his infamous Taj Mahal casino. All the newspapers were feasting on the scandalous news and on Trump's expanding humiliation. Business journals were taking pot shots at his crumbling stature. Marla Maples was also a point of media focus during Trump's initial months of his tawdry affair with her. If his father, Fred Trump, merely wrote his son a check, the liquidity would be directed to resolve that debt. Fred Trump wasted no time by dispatching an attorney to the Trump Castle Hotel to slip cash overnight into the sick casino's coffers.

The Trump lawyer, Howard Snyder, walked right up to the casino cage. Snyder smiled like a TV game show host. He straightened his necktie and collar. He then opened his wallet. His hand held a certified check for $3.35 million, drawn on Fred Trump's bank account. He and the clerk exchanged a few niceties. The clerk presented stacks of chips. The lawyer strolled past several rows of slot machines, past a roulette table, past one of the open bars, and centered on a Blackjack table. There were people who didn't acknowledge the lawyer's presence. Snyder nodded his head to several women watching from a distance. The dealer then paid out the full amount in 670 gray $5,000 chips. It was that obvious and Snyder didn't care. The following day, the bank wired an additional $150,000 into Fred's account at the Castle. Returning to the casino, Howard Snyder, dressed in a subtle plaid jacket, collected the total amount in thirty more chips. He believed he executed the mission nearly perfectly as planned. Fred Trump got the phone call from Snyder and was complimented for a job well done.

The scheme allowed Fred Trump's son to apply the unofficial loan in whatever way was urgent. Reporters later discovered that the Castle met its bond payment the day Fred Trump's attorney bought the chips. A collateral benefit behind this maneuver allowed Trump —patrons who hold gaming chips are not paid interest. Everything was breaking for Donald Trump.

New Jersey's Casino Control Commission investigated the chip purchase intrigue the following year. The Commission decreed that it was an illegal loan, breaking the New Jersey's rules about casinos receiving money from approved and appropriate financial sources. A local newspaper quoted a casino lawyer saying, "Fred Trump is ineligible for licensing, and Trump Castle should be required to return the money, a move that would almost certainly force it into bankruptcy court."

Ironically, after enough time the casino kept the cash propelling the commission to fine the casino $65,000. The fine was far from overwhelming. Still, it didn't save Donald Trump. A year later, the Trump Castle fell into bankruptcy, and Donald Trump forfeited half the casino to his creditors.

It wasn't just his assets in Atlantic City. Trump's real estate portfolio was shaky and the portfolio's health profile was cloaked from view. The New York media had reported that Ivana Trump was suing to nullify the revised prenuptial agreement they signed on Christmas Eve of 1987, which was either a unique holiday gift to Ivana Trump or to Donald Trump. It was leaked quickly that the prenuptial gave her approximately $25 million in the event of marital dissolution.

One of Ivana Trump's tactical ideas for striking down the prenuptial was more than obvious: simply demonstrate that Marla Maples was rapidly emerging in the public eye as her husband's newest paramour. His latest whore. At the same time, Marla Maples was expressing her irritation of being sequestered and cloaked with each Trump romantic escapade. Donald Trump's mistress had engineered her stealth behavior for an extended period up until the summer of 1989, when Trump transitioned Marla Maples onto his $30 million yacht, the Trump Princess. Donald Trump bragged to the press that his luxe yacht was an "incredible toy" and "the ultimate toy."

In mid-February 1990, the New York Post front page exploded with the headline, "Best Sex I've Ever Had." The naked quotation allegedly came from Marla Maples. It was reported by close associates of Trump that he was ecstatic by the decadent publicity. Donald Trump wanted the world and also Ivana Trump to know his unending sexual prowess. Trump was still married to Ivana, but he would divorce her before the end of the year.

Marla, absolving herself about the many media leaks, would often whisper into Trump's ear with her soft southern drawl. "I just never know what to do in these situations. It's so hard for me." Trump would respond by nibbling on Marla Maples' fingers and hinting to her about leather bondage games. At least that was reported by Marla Maples' manicurist and yoga instructor.

Trump explained to Marla Maples that his real estate luck hit headwinds in Atlantic City. The casinos failed to approach their respective benchmark profits. He boasted to her that he had mastered the art of handling construction companies with mob connections. Atlantic City was beholden to some of the hidden stars of gangland. He loved how the casinos allowed him to be creative with cash flow problems. To his surprise, his father Fred Trump accepted many of the outrageous stunts, from brief case cash to kickback bonuses tying elected officials to Donald Trump.

Donald Trump wanted his father to visit Atlantic City and return every summer. He wanted his father's admiration. But that never happened. Donald Trump feared secretly that his father judged him about the casino failures. Fred Trump expressed his disapproval over the vulgar newspaper headlines and cover stories about his son Donald. He told his son that this was shaming the family name. Moreover, acting out for the media would not add profit to the Trump company. Profit was the bright North Star. Sex was Uranus; small, distant, and dark.

The only time Fred Trump visited his son at Atlantic City, Fred Trump spoke incessantly about dying and the aftermath of his death. This behavior annoyed Donald Trump. Fred Trump was consumed by his mortality, while Donald Trump was convinced of his invincibility. Donald Trump hugged his father outside the Taj Mahal Casino. Fred Trump pulled away awkwardly. They avoided eye contact. Fred Trump coughed into his open palms.

Chapter Twenty

Mir Abdul Karim awoke before dawn and washed his face, hands, and feet. The weather was brisk, dry, and windy. The trees were howling in the distance. He could not remember his dream and his anguish, but he was prepared to return to work. Eleven days had passed since he had seen his design crew and his supervisory master, Ustad Ahmad Lahori. Mir Abdul Karim anticipated the cold stares of his architectural colleagues. They would wonder why he was hairless. They would speculate if there was a powerful curse or some illness eating at his soul. Some of these men would suspect this was the wrath of the emperor and a lesson to all about any acts of defiance or deception. Mir Abdul Karim would not tell the truth to his crew or to his colleagues this week. He wanted to live another year. Money was losing more and more importance. Destiny was wicked. He lost interest in physical sex.

He hummed a melody which he had learned when he was a child. He dried his damp feet. A mosquito bit his neck. He slapped his skin. There was his blood inside the mosquito's mouth. A piece of his life was now an element within a flying insect. He felt diminished.

Ustad Ahmad Lahori walked over to Mir Abdul Karim. An arm fell along Mir Abdul Karim's shoulder. Ustad Ahmad Lahori was demonstrating affection. It looked like affection but felt like poison. Ustad Ahmad Lahori felt confident. Ustad Ahmad Lahori was in command.

"Mir Abdul Karim. We missed you."

"I was sick."

"Yes, well now you are better."

"Work returns health."

"Yes." smiled Ustad Ahmad Lahori. "Look at my clean, white hands. Look at my dexterity. I am immaculate."

"I want to see the new marble." requested Mir Abdul Karim.

"Why?"

"Moonlit changes the color of northern marble."

"Moonlit changes the color of everything. Moonlight changes a man's mood."

Mir Abdul Karim found himself perspiring pressed by some magical heat.

"Moonlit discolors marble."

Ustad Ahmad Lahori pursed his lips and attempted to broaden his smile.

"You are in a peculiar mood. We will keep the marble cold, and the color will be steadfast."

"Bone white marble is bone white." pronounced Mir Abdul Karim, seeing the pale color before his eyes.

"Marriage is an idea between a structure and the architect."

"I am only focused on the integrity of the marble arriving to our site."

"How is your wife, Mir Abdul Karim?"

"She is fine."

"Is she?"

"She is fine, I said."

"She worries about you all the time." said Ustad Ahmad Lahori.

"Some women sew clothing."

"Does your wife sow?"

"No, she does not sow."

"She is a beautiful, older woman, Mir Abdul Karim."

Mir Abdul Karim wanted to murder the court architect.

"Is it the cat who plays with the mouse?" continued the court architect. "Or is it the mouse who plays with the cat?

"A cat's tail is longer than the rodent's." replied Mir Abdul Karim.

Mir Abdul Karim bent with pain and then stretched, reaching for a pitcher of water. He was suddenly thirty. He poured water into a glass cup. He touched his face with wet fingers. He drank from the cup. He looked up and coughed. There was an open fire at the far side of the studio. There was a chimney made of stone. There was a sleeping dog on a half-rolled rug. Sunlight had noise, at least to discerning eyes.

"It seems we are missing men."

"We are missing men." echoed Mir Abdul Karim.

"You knew."

"We both knew. This sets us back. Weeks delay."

"The emperor took some men."

"The emperor killed some men."

"How do you know?"

"How do you pretend not to know?"

"I drink heavily at night."

"I do not believe you."

"Believe what you want, Mir Abdul Karim."

"I believe in an empty landscape. We have nothing."

"I hope you are wrong."

"I am right."

Ustad Ahmad Lahori changed the expression on his face. He became vulnerable and innocent.

"I once believed in the harmony of numbers, in the geometry of beauty." came Ustad Ahmad Lahori's most quiet voice.

"Yes, the geometry of beauty."

"The perfect wall has no boundary.

"You convinced everyone to lie, everyone to tell your lie."

"Mir Abdul Karim. Do not judge me. Do I dare judge you?"

"I cannot judge you."

A hawk flew into the studio. The sound was unmistakable. Their eyes followed the hawk.

"Years ago, we were honest with each other."

"Yes, Mir Abdul Karim."

Mir Abdul Karim coughed into his hands.

"When we die, there must be a moment to feel we will have no more life."

"Many die in their sleep."

"Do you think your death is coming?"

"I will die at midnight."

"Yes. You will die at midnight."

"Did you give rupees to my wife, Ustad Ahmad Lahori?"

"Did she not tell you that?"

"She did not." said Mir Abdul Karim.

"What did she tell you?"

"She told me your nature."

"She is astute."

"My wife is astute. She is smarter than me. I told her once to leave me.:

"Then she must truly love you." replied Ustad Ahmad Lahori.

Mir Abdul Karim remained silent. His hands reached his face and his head dropped. He began to cry. Ustad Ahmad Lahori looked away.

"I will leave you alone, my friend." said the haughty court architect.

Chapter Twenty-One

Rex Heuermann took a weekend business trip to Atlantic City during the last days of October 2006. That is what he told his wife. Halloween was Tuesday. He left his family on Long Island. He liked the casinos in Las Vegas and Atlantic City. Without traffic it was less than a three-hour drive along the Garden State Parkway. He booked the Taj Mahal Casino Resort, and it was his first stay at the fabled Trump hotel.

He brought a thousand dollars and his lucky corduroy sports jacket. A college friend from New York Institute of Technology taught him the art of counting cards while playing Blackjack. Mastering this skill takes serious concentration and, if done consistently, will increase the player's odds considerably against the house.

The counts for each card value work best when intuitive, essentially delineating the frequency a player had seen that card before the current hand started. The array of these values is a direct function of the number of decks in the Blackjack shoe, which is usually six in Atlantic City. Therefore, the number of times a player will have seen a card might range from zero to twenty-four. Outcomes will most often take on the following values: Zero — Draw, One — Player Won, One Point Five — Player Blackjack, 2 —

Double Down and Player Won, Negative One — Dealer Won / Dealer Blackjack, Negative two — Double Down and Dealer Won.

Rex Heuermann knew he couldn't drink alcohol while counting. His plan was to play Blackjack Friday night and win a few hundred dollars. Saturday night he would play the slots for an hour, have a few drinks, see a show, and maybe get lucky meeting someone exciting and reckless. Regarding Sunday departure from Atlantic City, he expected to drive home after breakfast and eleven o'clock check out time. He promised his wife that he would be home before Sunday dinnertime.

At the Blackjack table nearly two hours of intense card play, the architect was beating the house by at least eight hundred dollars. Maybe over a grand in chips. He kept an eye on his wristwatch with a sharp reminder to end Blackjack by ten o'clock sharp. Counting cards and personal luck put him in the winning column this Friday evening. He loved to beat the house.

A young woman was eyeing a few men at the card table. She observed that the oversized architect was about to call it a night and sidled over to him without any subtly. She had fitted into one of the tightest, low-cut dresses in New Jersey. Her shoes were tomato red matching her earrings and party gown.

"Did you win big, baby?" she asked Rex Heuermann.

"I did okay, sweetheart." he replied in a raspy voice.

"You look like a winner."

"That's right."

"Are you here all by your lonesome?" she said with sensitivity and sincerity, parting her teeth.

"Yeah. I guess it shows."

"It shows. Do you want privacy? I'm very extroverted."

Rex Heuermann studied her intensely. She was about twenty-five years old. Maybe Puerto Rican? Maybe Italian? Not Irish or Polish. She was not unattractive. Her breasts were large and dominated her petite frame. Long black hair draped her bare shoulders. She looked athletic and strong. Her mouth was sensual. Her nose was rather sharp and long, like a predator bird. Rex liked her eyes. They were tough and sexy. He thought she had hissed like a cat when a flurry of half smiles crossed her countenance. He imagined what her tail might feel like in his two large hands, and in his mouth.

"Buy me a drink?"

"Are you old enough to drink?"

"Oh fuck, are you a cop?"

"No, sweetie."

"If I ask that question and you are a cop, you have to tell the truth."

"Is that from a fairytale?"

"Yeah." she laughed and then asked, "What's your favorite fairytale?"

"Rumpelstiltskin." offered the architect.

She touched his wrist. Her skin felt warm. Her face became less severe. He thought he could have sex with her tonight. He reminded himself that manners always count, even inside a New Jersey casino. She picked him up at the Blackjack table. She could have selected another guy with a pile of winning chips. There was a sweet inflection in her eyes, despite the over applied mascara and false eye lashes. Clearly, he read her thoughts. She was available without a big price tag.

"Okay, I'll buy you a drink."

"Thanks, big guy."

"Are you hungry?"

"No. Not really. But you look like you want a T-bone porterhouse."

Rex Heuermann laughed in carefree amusement. They walked to the cocktail lounge and waited to be seated by the hostess.

"What's your name?" he asked.

"Hazel."

"That's a nice name."

"What's your name?"

"Rex."

"Doesn't that mean king?"

"I guess it does in some languages."

The hostess escorted them to a table under soft lighting. Hazel was assessing the architect's inner world while watching his large hands playing with the table napkin.

"What do you like to drink?"

"A screwdriver."

"Okay. How about an appetizer?"

"If I eat anything, I won't be able to remove my dress."

Rex Heuermann chuckled at the gibe.

"What do you drink?" she asked innocently.

"An IPA beer."

"Are you married?"

"Yeah."

"Do you love your wife?"

"Of course."

When the waitress sauntered over, he gave the order.

"What do you do?"

"I'm an architect. What do you do?"

"I work for a travel agency."

"Cool."

"Tell me something you haven't told anyone in a long while."

"Let me think."

"It has to be the truth, Rex."

"Of course. Only the truth matters." he guaranteed her.

The architect then told a bizarre teenage story.

"Okay. Back to high school. I nearly offed a member of my drama club during a backstage prank. It was 1980."

"1980?"

"1980. Yeah. Berner High School in Massapequa. Long Island. The club mounted a production of *Arsenic and Old Lace*."

"Don't know the show."

"I thought everyone knows *Arsenic and Old Lace*, Cary Grant was in the film."

"Who's Cary Grant?"

The architect wondered if she was playing dumb for the fun of it.

"It's a black comedy about whacky sisters who poison and bury a lot of old geezers in their basement. I was on crew. I worked behind the scenes as a stage tech for the school play, as was the classmate, who also helped paint the sets. During one rehearsal, I added a lot more weights to the base of the pulley system which lifted and lowered the stage curtains. When this girl pulled on a lever to drop the curtains while holding onto a rope connected to the system, her body went flying toward the auditorium ceiling. I helped her down and said I was so sorry. She thought she was going to die."

"Wow, Rex."

"Kind of a mean thing to do." he confessed.

"Yeah."

"What about you?"

"A secret to tell?"

"Yeah. Play fair."

"The priest at my church where I lived growing up was a lech. I was thirteen. He flashed himself. I told the police. I was able to identify a mole on his thigh. He was busted." she said flatly.

Chapter Twenty-Two

Roseanne had volunteered to speak to her high school, Las Vegas Academy of the Arts, on Career Day. The school had sought her out several years in row, but she finally relented when her calendar eased considerably in the fall of 1991. She was unburdened by the Taj Mahal Casino project and had smaller, more manageable jobs on her docket. She spent the previous weekend writing a clear summary of her work in architecture, her educational path, her challenges in a male dominated field, and her love of Nevada. She visited the school during the week of Halloween and the school had been decorated accordingly.

The assembly of juniors and seniors filled the auditorium to capacity. The principal introduced the three invited speakers that afternoon. All the honorees were women. Roseanne was the third guest to approach the podium.

The first speaker was a Nevada Assembly Legislator who was raised in Las Vegas. She began with an ebullient preamble about her learning disorder as a child and how her faith in Christ helped her evolve into a high achieving middle schooler. She was a high school class president and knew early in her life that she was destined for public service in government. She took a tangent about the beauty of teen celibacy and surprised the audience by saying that she was a distant relative to one of the victims of Stephen Morin, a serial killer lined to forty murders from 1969 to 1981. Three of deaths were young Las Vegas women.

The second speaker, who appeared very young, from the University of Nevada Las Vegas, was a celebrated medical researcher who was leading a new treatment for endometrial and ovarian cancer that had impressive clinic trials. The doctor emphasized her team's focus upon the action of immunotherapy, dramatically emphasizing the miraculous therapy to activate and energize T-cells for cancer treatment. Her final words prophesized the end of all cancers by the year 2049. Roseanne wondered to herself how the researcher telescoped to that particular year. Roseanne would not live that long.

The principal introduced Roseanne L'Anse.

"With additional pride, our last distinguished speaker is an alum of Las Vegas Academy of the Arts. I think I know the year of her graduation, but I will keep that a secret. She is a graduate of Yale School of Architecture. Her prolific work was featured in Architectural Digest, particularly attuned to her innovative approaches to small churches and chapels in America's vast southwest. In the private sector, Roseanne L'Anse has stretched her eclectic portfolio from public schools to hotel casinos. She is known for her blunt interaction between wood and concrete, between stone and metal, and the illusion of inverted weights. Please welcome Roseanne L'Anse."

Roseanne L'Anse stood up. She felt all the blood rush from her head and feared she was about to hit the floor. She took one step back, her hand steadying herself along the auditorium wall. She closed her eyes for a moment or two, stopping the room from spinning away. The principal could sense that Roseanne was looking faint and unsteady. He was about to extend a hand to help her. Roseanne smiled to herself and began to approach the podium slowly. She detected a strange odor overhead. The odor of something burning that shouldn't burn. Her fingers tapped the microphone. Her tapping foot on the ground. Everything was magnified. She smiled to the students awaiting to hear her voice.

"Thank you for this nice welcome. I remember this school so well. The colors have not changed. I was a crazy kid. I really was. School was hard. I was shy. I avoided people. I hid in the art classrooms. And now I'm an architect. I build things. Big, beautiful things. Some things are actually too beautiful. Some buildings take you by surprise."

Roseanne looked into the front rows of the auditorium. The students looked so young. She felt dizzy once more and took a second to refocus. Her eyes glanced down. She took a breath and smiled.

"If I were a man, my journey would have been different. It would have been easier and faster. But this is not a race. There isn't a finish line. I wonder if there is a young architect in the auditorium right now. Stand so I can see you please."

Roseanne squinted and strained to look around.

"I see you. I really do."

She smiled warmly and looked down.

"I see so much talent in front of me. So much energy."

The principal nodded his head and listened intently for the next few minutes. When Roseanne paused for several seconds, he stood and reached for her elbow. He sensed that she had finished her formal remarks. She pulled her arm closer to her side and then adjusted her podium microphone to continue her address.

"So don't take for granted any obvious professional choices. When we analyze our chosen discipline — mine being architecture — we witness many incredible incarnations. Architects have not only designed buildings and plazas, but also sublime objects and shrines in Ancient Greece, magical environments for theatrical Renaissance performances, elaborate gardens in Europe's seventeenth century, wonderous temples in Japan, China, and the subcontinent. All of these creations were dedicated towards the human experience and a lasting spiritual horizon. I ask myself each year why architecture matters and how architecture enhances the quality of life. Ethics should trump unlawful financial gain. See past the forms and shapes which buildings assume. If standing architecture projects power, it is my hope that it is not an oppressive power. Public edifices and public spaces grant us existential placement. Some situations are common, some are diverse, but every physical encounter should steer the way to our humane and mortal self-reflection. The baby's nursery is an architecture statement. The soldier's graveyard is an architectural statement. All is heritage. All is epiphany. Thank you."

The high school audience responded with respectful applause. The principal thanked the three speakers and concluded the program by saying that Las Vegas Academy of the Arts touches all aspects of society, and that the perceived gulf between the arts and the sciences is effectively non-existent in 1991.

The adjacent reception room had a dozen high school faculty mingling with the guest speakers. The buffet table looked sumptuous. Roseanne helped herself to black coffee and a bran muffin. A history teacher approached her cordially.

"I wish we could have seen projections of your buildings during your talk." he said.

"Yes, that might have been nice." replied Roseanne.

"Is it true that your 1987 Seattle community center design stands out as your most celebrated work?"

"Probably so. Acclaimed for the poured concrete liberties against natural wood."

"How do span your work from inspired faux adobe churches in Santa Fe to garish casinos in Atlantic City?"

"Garish?"

"I'm trying to be witty."

"Oh, I see."

"Very eclectic."

"Thank you." said Roseanne, turning her back to the teacher. She then was facing the Nevada assemblywoman. The two women were a foot apart. Roseanne felt shorter as they made eye contact.

"That was a wonderful speech." said the assemblywoman.

"Thank you. I greatly enjoyed your address." returned Roseanne.

"This is progressive high school."

"Yes, it would seem so."

"How's the coffee?" The assemblywoman suppressed a smirk curling over her lips.

"Not bad."

"Would love a martini. It's almost five o'clock."

"Yes, an extra dry martini." smiled Roseanne naturally.

"Do you have children?" asked the assemblywoman.

"No. Do you?"

"No."

"My heart goes out to you and your family. I have to ask you about Stephen Morin's crimes. "

"Yes?"

"How did you feel when he was arrested?"

"Relieved to a point. A serial killer was removed from society."

"Which distant family member was she?"

"She was my niece."

"Oh God, I'm so sorry."

"Not so distant." said the assemblywoman.

"How do you burn this from memory?"

"Time helps."

"Does it?"

"It was over ten years ago. He converted to Christianity once he started his prison sentence."

"Is Stephen Morin still alive?"

"No, executed. Lethal injection after midnight. March 13, 1985, Texas"

"So sorry for you. And your family. No person should suffer such hell."

"Thank you. My niece was just eighteen."

Chapter Twenty-Three

Saanvi woke early and sensed that her husband was not at home. This was becoming a pattern over the last few weeks. Mir left for his work at the Taj Mahal site without having breakfast. He reminded her that he kissed her lips before leaving the bed each day whether she was awake or not. Sometimes she imagined the taste of his lips, but this morning the sensation was without definition or flavor. She was thirsty for water.

Saanvi could not recall her dream, but something during the night frightened her. Her bed clothes were damp from perspiration.

After washing her face and hands, she tended to her two children. They were in the kitchen snacking on flat bread and sweet jam. Her nine-year-old daughter Ananya had jam on her cheeks and chin. Her seven-year-old son Kian ate with more fastidiousness. She poured her children freshly squeezed nectar. Saanvi's open hand ran through Ananya's long black hair. Seeing them at the table was routine, but this morning had a peculiar air.

"How about some yoghurt and fruit?" she asked them.

"Where is Bāpa?" asked Ananya.

"Working with the men."

"Which men?" asked Kian.

"The white marble men from Makrana."

"We don't see Bāpa anymore."

"That's not true, my love."

"He leaves before we wake; he comes home after we are in bed." said Kian.

"Only for a week or two. Be patient."

"Why does Bāpa look sick?" Ananya said, poking her mother's arm.

"He is not sick. He just lost his hair. That happens with age."

"Bāpa is too young to lose hair, Mātā."

"Some men suffer this loss early, but hair is not a signifier."

Saanvi's children stared at her with a variety of skepticism. Instinctively, Ananya and Kian knew their mother was covering the complete story about their father. Saanvi wondered to herself if Mir was deliberating leaving for work in the dark and returning home in the dark. A way to be less seen by street people. A way to tempt the gods to increase human folly. A way to prepare oneself for an early death.

Death would erase Mir's history. Death would prevent Mir from owning his life.

Death entered the room. Death walked the street. Death flew with the black crows. Death smoked a dry leaf. Death sung a song. Saanvi would not see Mir anymore. Her intuition told her that her husband would be murdered before the end of summer. Saanvi knew he wanted more years. To grow old with her. To see the river flow.

Saanvi glanced at herself in the mirror. She saw a mature face with perfect features. This was the woman Mir craved.

Saanvi waited for the children's tutor to arrive. Something to expect. The tutor was on time and his sandals were falling apart. Saanvi set up the table for the tutor and the children. She gave the children a kiss and waved her hand to the tutor. Saanvi carried a small leather bag and shoulder strap. She looked for her money. She grabbed a white shawl.

She hurried to the market. Saanvi's hands became cold. But it was summer. As she approached the crowded streets ahead, she spied a pack of aggressive monkeys chasing people and climbing on women's legs. Sometimes stray dogs attack a young monkey, and the monkeys seek revenge against the village dogs. A few men had monkey sticks and hit the animals. The monkeys were showing their teeth. A dozen monkeys were joining in a choreographed formation. More monkeys than people. There were nauseating monkey shrieks. This overture to a sweeping brawl began to frighten Saanvi. Some of these monkeys were known to be violently wild. Last year a monkey seriously injured a toddler.

Saanvi darted into a back alley. A small black monkey followed her and touched her leg. She kicked back with all her strength. The monkey managed to scratch her exposed ankle. Saanvi began to bleed as she ran. The monkey vocalized something which sounded guttural and hellish. A bystander threw a rock at the monkey which spared Saanvi further encounters with the beast.

Saanvi decided to forego the market and visit her mother, Divya, to calm her nerves. She also wanted to dress her wound. Her mother's home was a fifteen-minute walk away from the melee. Her mother was surprised to see her.

"Saanvi?" she said as she opened the door.

Her mother saw the distress in Saanvi's face.

"I need to sit down, Maa."

Saanvi hugged her mother tightly and entered her small home.

"You do not look well, Saanvi."

"There was fighting in the market."

"Fighting?"

"Monkeys attacking."

"Monkeys fighting each other?"

"No, attacking people."

"Someone or some animal must have hurt a baby monkey."

"I need to wash my ankle."

"Were you bit?"

"No, it was a scratch."

Saanvi's mother kneeled down to see the wound.

"Not good, my child." she spoke flatly.

Her mother went to find clean cloth and some alcohol. Momentarily Saanvi's mother returned and cleaned the wound. The bleeding had stopped before arriving at her mother's home. The scratch was not deep, but three fingers wide.

"Do you need money, Maa?"

"No. I have what I need.

"You look thin." said Saanvi.

"I am always thin."

Her mother's smile was like a frown, as she bandaged her daughter's ankle.

"Is this better?"

"Yes, Maa. Thank you."

"How is Mir?"

"He is back at work."

"Not sick?"

"Not sick. But no hair growth."

"I am sorry. Who is with the children?"

"The tutor."

"I can help watch them."

"I know. Yes."

"Are you hungry?"

Saanvi's mother went to her kitchen. Saanvi followed her. There was food on the table. On one plate was rice. On the other two plates were cooked vegetables in a dark sauce. There was flat bread fresh from baking wrapped in a clean white cloth. A brown pitcher of water was brought over while flies were hovering over the plates and the pitcher. Saanvi's mother whipped a washcloth into the air.

"I have premonitions, Maa."

"About what?"

"About Mir's murder." offered Saanvi.

"Who would hurt him?"

"The court architect. Or the emperor."

"Is this Mir's fear too?"

"Yes."

"Does Mir carry a weapon?"

"No."

"He should carry one."

"A sword will not protect him, Maa."

Saanvi's mother handed her daughter a charm, strung on a leather cord. There were various red colored gems with a highly textured surface.

"This will protect him, Saanvi. He should tie this around his neck or wrist."

They finished eating. Her mother made two cups of tea. Her mother tied her hair braids behind her neck and then rubbed her neck as if to provide relief to sore muscles. Saanvi stood and walked behind her. Saanvi's fingers massaged her mother's neck and shoulders.

"Thank you, darling."

"I need to go. The tutor will be leaving soon."

The women hugged. Saanvi kissed her mother on the mouth. The door closed behind Saanvi.

She walked back in the direction of the market. Saanvi intuited that the monkeys would be gone. They were gone. The market was not crowded at this hour. Vendors were packing their products in preparation for going home. The sky was darkening with heavy rain clouds. In the distance,

Saanvi heard galloping horses. She looked off into the distance and the dirt road was widening inexplicably. Merchants pushing carts peeled away. The two horsemen had masks over their faces. Saanvi panicked and quickened her pace to be out of harm's way.

The horsemen were focused on Saanvi. Their horses trampled over her body.

Chapter Twenty-Four

Hazel expected a reaction from Rex Heuermann about her scandalous church anecdote, but the architect said nothing. He gave her a vacant look and noticed that she was looking at his wedding ring.

"I'm married."

"I can see that."

"What do you think of married men?"

"They're fine, what do you want me to say?"

"You can be more honest with me, Hazel."

"Well, I like the joke about married men."

"What's the joke?"

They both took sips of their drinks.

"You know, medical studies show that married men live ten years longer than single men." Hazel played with her long black hair. "But is it worth it?"

The architect laughed into his beer.

"Got a boyfriend, Hazel?"

"Yeah, kind of."

"Where is he?"

"He goes to Alaska seasonally to work on oil rigs."

"Is he there now?"

"Yeah, about to come back in two weeks."

"Good for you." said the architect.

"Yeah."

"Does he see girls in Alaska?"

"No."

"How do you know?"

"I would know."

"There are a lot of girls there."

"He said they all look Eskimo."

"You mean, Inuit or Yupik."

"No, I mean fucking Eskimo." she said adamantly.

"I'm staying in the hotel."

"The Taj?"

"Yeah, the Taj."

"Are you inviting me to your room, Rex?"

"Not exactly."

What they didn't address at the cocktail lounge was the Eastbound Strangler. The paranoia about the strangler would soon consume Atlantic City and the neighboring communities. The unidentified serial killer would murder four young women. They would be identified by the police as prostitutes and discovered in drainage ditch November 20, three weeks from today. Their cadavers, behind the Golden Key Motel in Egg Harbor Township, just outside Atlantic City, would be placed face down, facing east, about sixty feet apart from one other. They would be found clothed except for their feet. The coroner would find strong reason to believe that all four women had been strangled to death.

"Would you like another screwdriver, Hazel?"

"No, thanks."

"I'm getting a little sleepy." he said swigging the last of his IPA.

"Yeah, you look like you're running on empty."

The architect signaled for the waitress.

"Check, please?" He rose to his feet. "I need the restroom. I'll be right back."

Rex Heuermann took out his wallet and put down a hundred-dollar bill.

"Are you really coming back?" she asked.

"Do I look like a liar?"

"Yeah." she grinned flirtatiously.

"Do I look batshit crazy?"

"No."

Rex Heuermann extended his forefinger and ran it just under Hazel's lips. He hurried to the restroom to relieve his bladder. Standing in front of the urinal he asked himself if Hazel would be at the table upon his return. He was in Blackjack card counting mode and gave odds at even money. He washed his hands thoroughly and looked into the mirror over the decorative sink. He seemed old and exhausted. He had put on weight on his face. There were bags under his eyes. His hair was a mess. He forgot to bring a comb. He ran his fingers through his hair and dabbed on a little water to keep a cowlick down.

He walked slowly back to the cocktail table. Hazel was gone. The waitress caught the architect's eye and pointed to one of two lounge exits. He looked in the ascribed direction and saw Hazel wave to him with cash in her hand. Rex Heuermann shot back with a very masculine smile, bursting with inner confidence.

She took his arm and they walked to the resort's bank of elevators.

"What floor?"

"Sixteen, sweetie."

"Oh, that's too high. I get nose bleeds."

He wasn't certain if she was playing a game with him. He felt that she was going to ditch him along the way.

"Suit yourself."

The elevator doors opened, and they both got in. There were four other resort guests in the elevator. Hazel began to hum a Stevie Nicks song.

"I like that." Rex said.

"Fleetwood Mac was a great band." said one of the resort guests with a husky voice.

On the eighth floor, two guests walked out of the elevator.

"You're even bigger inside an elevator, Rex."

On the tenth floor, a single guest exited the elevator. Hazel took a half step away from the architect. Nervously, he pressed the button for the sixteenth floor although the button was already lit.

They stepped out into the corridor. Behind them a bald man wearing a black suit and a black necktie also left the elevator while looking at his wristwatch. The architect found the key in his right pocket. He dropped the key and stooped to get it. He looked at Hazel's shapely legs and glanced quickly at the suited man walking away.

"Like the view, Rex?"

"The view is always pleasurable when one is surprised."

They were standing in front of his hotel room, 1624. He opened the door and kissed her on the mouth.

"Goodnight, Hazel. I'm much too tired."

"What?"

"Maybe I'll see you tomorrow."

Rex Heuermann entered his room and closed the door. She was stunned by his behavior.

Chapter Twenty-Five

Mir Abdul Karim was rolling up parchment drawings when two laborers entered his studio at the Taj Mahal grounds. They were agitated and awkward at his worktable. It was the end of a difficult construction day. The architect's interior monologue was directed at the spacing problems of the new kiosks which Ustad Ahmad Lahori demanded of the design team. These were new specifications which violated the perfect geometry of Mir Abdul Karim's principal concept. The chronology of the total design using geometric centering had become an intricate dialogue between Ustad Ahmad Lahori and Mir Abdul Karim. Ustad Ahmad Lahori had stumbled without much grace over his justifications to Mir Abdul Karim, in front of the other leading team members. This colored the day and ruined the fragile, deteriorating partnership between the two architects.

"What?" asked Mir Abdul Karim.

"We are so sorry, Mir Abdul Karim."

"Why are you sorry?"

"Sorry to be here and to be respectful to your family.

"What are you saying?"

"We were ordered to find you and tell you the news."

"What news?"

"Your cherished wife." said one laborer.

"Saanvi Aashi Karim." said the other laborer.

"What about my wife?

"Something happened."

"What happened?"

"There was a terrible accident. In the market. Horses had trampled her."

"Horses?"

"Cloaked men riding black horses."

"How bad is it?" demanded Mir Abdul Karim.

"She is gone, Mir Abdul Karim. She is dead. She died upon impact."

"Saanvi? How can you say such a thing!"

"We cry for you, Mir Abdul Karim. We cry for you."

"Which men on horses?"

"No one knows."

"No one in the market saw these men?"

"No." said the laborer. "They will say nothing. That is what we heard."

"Are they afraid of these men?"

Both laborers nodded in the affirmative.

"This cannot be true. Where is her body?"

"Guardsmen delivered her body, wrapped in a fine silk weave, to your home."

"With my children at home?"

"The guardsmen were instructed to be discreet. That is all we know, sir."

Mir Abdul Karim fell to his seat, his head dropped onto the table.

For a brief moment, Mir Abdul Karim vanished from the earth. The men left him alone. They bowed at the studio door and vanished. Then nightfall choked all living things.

The pounding of Mir Abdul Karim's heart was so powerful that he could not catch his breath. He poured a cup of water and drank. Water spilled from his mouth. He closed his eyes. A fly landed on his face. He tried desperately to slow his breathing and find his sense of bodily control. His body was about to implode.

Many minutes transpired while he was blind. He was able to breathe normally again.

Mir Abdul Karim was determined to return home, stunned to find himself able to walk alone. His eyes were wet and bloodshot. There were his children, still with the tutor. Saanvi's mother was there. She was taciturn, sitting behind a wall. Saanvi's body was in the house too.

Mir Abdul Karim could feel Saanvi's spirit. Saanvi was alive and present. She was warm. He could almost hear her sweet voice. Suddenly he was overtaken by grief and horror. All was an illusion. He wanted to die. His tears were bitter acid. Where was his beloved Saanvi? How can he join her? He had to join her. Why were the gods doing this to him?

Mir Abdul Karim's head dipped quickly, and he passed out. He dreamt that he died and went to a new century halfway around the globe. The obscene noise he heard inside his head was thoroughly modern.

Saanvi was dead. She was not prepared for this outcome. Returning home.

Saanvi's mother came over to Mir Abdul Karim. Her hand caressed his head. She said something inaudible. There were tears in her eyes. She kissed the back of his neck. Saanvi's mother walked away. She went to find the children. They were playing in the courtyard outside the kitchen with some musical toys. From inside the sounds from the children were so familiar and innocent to Mir and the mother of his departed wife.

Mir assumed that Saanvi was murdered. He withheld that feeling from Saanvi's mother. He was clouded about the instigator's identity. Who hired these cloaked men on horses? Was it Ustad Ahmad Lahori or the emperor?

Why murder her? In front of so many people. Why terrorize a defenseless family? Why were the people at the market unwilling to give testimony?

Mir was torn inside about his next action. He wanted to die and join Saanvi in the invisible world. He truly craved death. He wanted to get revenge and kill the two assassins. He cursed the gods. He wanted to blow up the Taj Mahal site with explosives. He wanted to abduct Ustad Ahmad Lahori and torture him until he revealed the truth.

Mir's head began to spin. He lost consciousness and entered a dreamlike state. His body sank into quicksand. There was a rush of a waterfall crashing brutally, separating his limbs like twigs. Mir had succumbed to oneirophrenia or an unfamiliar liminal realm in the forest of hell.

He suspected that he just died. But the world would continue without him.

His eyes focused on a hazy image of Saanvi. She was approaching him in wisps of smoke. Her arms were outstretched. He reached out to touch her hands. She enveloped his fingers. Their faces touched. And then their outstretched tongues.

The sting of final kiss.

He tried to say words, but his throat was dry. She opened her mouth, but there was no language. He tried to read her lips. She studied his. Nothing was discernible.

His ravaged mind asked Saanvi if he was no longer alive.

"Yes, Mir."

The image of Saanvi was fading but her beautiful head was nodding to Mir. His fingers ran through her silky hair.

"I love you, my darling Saanvi. We cannot be separated." came a disembodied voice from the open window. It was Mir's inflection but not quite his true voice.

"I love you, my darling Mir. We cannot be separated." came another distant voice.

Wind blew night away.

When Saanvi's figure disappeared, Mir heard her voice inside his head.

"Do not abandon our children, Mir. I beg you please."

"I love you, my darling Ma. We must be separated." came another
distant voice.

Win Steve might...

When Steve's hand disappeared, Ma's soft low voice made his
head...

Do not abandon our children, Ma. Does you pray..."

Chapter Twenty-Six

On an unseasonably warm, sunny Tuesday, February 16, 2021, Rex
Heuermann followed up to see Tony Ambrogio who invited the architect
to the Jersey shore for business and relaxation as his house guest. Ambrogio
refused the architect's preference to stay at the Holiday Inn. Their
appointment was changed four weeks in a row, due to Ambrogio's non-
disclosed medical issues. The architect suspected either plastic surgery that
was botched or another vanity concern.

Rex was unclear if the Ambrogio project would be based in New Jersey
or in New York. Although he wasn't licensed to practice architecture
outside of New York, Rex occasionally provided in-depth consultation and
unofficial design solving tasks. There was always a creative and legal
workaround if the money was good, the client was cooperative, and
headaches were minimal.

Ambrogio owned a large home in Spring Lake, New Jersey which was
seventy-five miles north of Atlantic City. The architect had dined once at
the upscale Spring Lake house at the end of the summer. Ambrogio was
happy with Rex Heuermann's affordable architectural work in his
Brooklyn and Queens apartment buildings, and the architect was satisfied
how quickly Ambrogio paid his last invoices.

Ambrogio had phoned him about some large apartment buildings in Atlantic City that was held in a group investment in which Ambrogio held the controlling interest. Top floors needed restructuring, better plumbing, electrical, and slightly higher roofs. Heuermann would be hired in a flexible, consulting capacity. Ambrogio swore to Rex Heuermann that there were no mob names tied to the buildings.

The architect wasn't so certain of that pledge.

Ambrogio asked Rex Heuermann when he would secure his New Jersey license to practice architecture. The architect said he needed a few days to study New Jersey building codes and sign up for the state exam. It wasn't a big deal. Ambrogio believed him.

Coincidentally, on the following February day, the Trump Plaza Hotel and Casino in Atlantic City was scheduled for demolition. The acclaimed casino opened in 1984 during a decade of decadence in the Gilded Age of Reaganism. The hotel hosted grotesquely grand events, boxing championships, and killer parties for the elite and richest of the rich from Hollywood mansions to the Metropolitan Opera to the best part of The Bronx —Yankee Stadium. The scandalous pandemonium over the years coupled by well publicized bankruptcies filings forced Trump to abandon Atlantic City by 2009, when Obama entered the White House. Trump's new obsession would be Obama's birth certificate.

When Trump Plaza finally went dark in 2014, the controversial hotel was the most broken casino in Atlantic City, taking in as much cash in eight months as the Borgata casino did in half a month.

Wednesday morning, February 17, in less than a magician's moment Trump Plaza imploded. The tower fell like a trick top hat into clouds of dust. Three thousand sticks of dynamite blasted the guts from the massive structure. Chunks of the hotel had tumbled to the streetscape. It was as if Atlantic City witnessed the wrath of an angry God or the amusement of an ironic God.

The Trump Plaza's grand finale began precisely at 9am. The building died blanketed by a voluminous mushroom of ash sweeping the beach and boardwalk. Cheers were heard from a large viewing party who had paid to take photos from their Fords and Toyotas. Marty Small, the popular city mayor who had blasted the abandoned hotel as a shitty hell hole, told local media: "I got chills. This is a historic moment. It was so goddamn exciting."

Tony Ambrogio and the architect sat in Ambrogio's Mercedes sedan. Ambrogio had two cups of coffee in his hands. He gave one cup to the architect. Their eyes were fixed on the disappearing Trump Plaza. Ambrogio told Rex Heuermann a special gem from the Ambrogio philosophy: flawed public leaders have intimations of their political dethroning when statues are vandalized, and their palaces burnt.

"Destiny laughed at Trump." Snapped Ambrogio sipping black coffee.

The joke of Trump's evolving stature? Would the Trump Plaza demolition be his last municipal statement and the beginning of his lasting public humiliation?

"Think about it, Rex."

The thought ran through Rex Heuermann's mind.

According to city planning officials, some of the hotel's debris could be used by environmentalists keen to create an artificial fishing reef off Atlantic City's coastline. Trump Plaza was the remaining Atlantic City to bear Trump's name. The Trump Taj Mahal had been renamed as the Hard Rock Hotel and Casino while the Trump Marina became the Golden Nugget Atlantic City.

"Screw Trump." laughed Ambrogio. "Screw his wife too."

"His wife was a whore in disguise."

"How do you know?" asked Ambrogio.

"I know because I was on the Trump payroll."

"You billed him?"

"Yeah, and that bastard stiffed me."

"How much?"

"He still owes me ten thousand dollars."

"You actually worked for him?"

"One job. Manhattan."

"Before his election?"

"No, after. 2018. The Trump Building. 40 Wall Street."

"You worked for the Trump Organization."

"It's one and the same thing. It's a mom-and-pop joint. Just no mom."

"So, you took orders from Eric Trump?"

Rex Heuermann suddenly looked perturbed, ashen, and aggressive. His breathing became heavy and animalistic. There was something about how Tony Ambrogio framed his patronizing question. There was the tone of his voice. There was that diamond glint in Ambrogio's eye. There was that oily Ambrogio smile.

"I didn't take orders from anyone, Sal. I'm a licensed architect, not a plumber."

Ambrogio locked stares with Rex Heuermann. For the first time in their short encounter, Ambrogio feared the architect.

"Let me walk that back, friend." said Ambrogio with deference. "I respect you. I admire your artistry and your integrity. You don't overcharge clients. You never arrive late for appointments. You're a fucking smart guy. I like you, Rex. I want you to like me."

Rex nodded with his mouth partly opened. His face looked menacing.

"You know, Trump's son-in-law Jared is such a fucking asshole. And his old man is an even bigger asshole. Kushner hires a prostitute to screw his brother-in-law, films it, and then sends the tape to his sister to scare her from testifying before a grand jury."

"That's how Jews do business I guess." said the architect, annoyed by the digression.

"Rex, last night, you didn't get the full tour. My wife made things awkward, perhaps. See, I have a talking parrot named Caesar in my upstairs office. Asleep. Caesar's the most intelligent parrot who ever lived. He's seven years old. And laugh if you must, but I learned a hell of a lot from this parrot. He repeats phrases that have philosophic importance. He avoids everything else out of my mouth. Isn't that incredible?"

"Like what?"

"Like, 'we're born alone, we die alone, but we are family.'"

"Your parrot said that?"

"Caesar said that."

"Yeah, it is weird."

"We all have these rare encounters with animals, Rex, sometimes in our lives."

"Tell me about the Atlantic City project, Tony."

"I'll get to that in a minute. Did you ever keep a pet?"

"Not really. No."

"No?"

"Members of my family have allergies."

"What about when you were a young guy?"

"Maybe. I don't remember."

"Close your eyes. Think about it." said Ambrogio like an upholstered therapist.

"I had a cat in college with a few roommates."

"See. I kind of suspected that."

"The cat had a pronounced look in his eyes."

"Really?"

"When I was alone with the cat, I saw an expression in his eyes like he knew he would die someday."

"Really?" gasped Ambrogio.

"That's right. The cat looked worried."

"Did you roommates see that look?"

"No, just me."

"That's fucking incredible."

"Yeah, I know." muttered the architect.

"And you're only remembering this now?"

"Yeah."

"Are you shitting me?"

"Yeah, I'm shitting you, Sal."

Ambrogio started his Mercedes and secured his seat belt.

"You think you're funny, Rex?"

"I was trying to make you have a good laugh."

"I forgot to laugh."

"Did you get work done on your eyes and nose?" asked the architect with a little sugar. "You look good, Sal."

Presidential historian Michael Beschloss posted a tweet hours after the hotel explosion: "Metaphor alert: next to the bankrupt Trump Plaza and Casino, just imploded this morning, remains the Atlantic City convention hall where LBJ accepted Democratic nomination in 1964 and touted the Great Society."

Chapter Twenty-Seven

Roseanne flew back to Las Vegas business class. She applied her frequent flyer miles for a free upgrade to spare her firm additional costs. There was no way she would return home by coach. She told her associates that her plans upon returning to Nevada included a few days of home vacation. Roseanne felt emotional drained by the Taj casino opening and the ordeal of multiple points of contact within the Trump management team. Steelman and Associates certainly made a lot of money from the initial commission and the modified extensive designs in extra innings all the way into the first weeks of 1990.

She was able to fall asleep during the flight immediately after a glass of chardonnay. Her seat companion was a slight, older woman who was self-contained and quiet. The woman's perfume was a tad too pronounced but Roseanne diverted her thoughts from the problem.

Herb indicated that he could adjust his work schedule to meet Roseanne at the airport but at the last minute he phoned her saying she would need to taxi home. This news irritated her. Since he missed the Taj opening, at the very least she thought he could drag his ass to the airport for her. The last six months were feeling very rocky in their marriage. Their romance could use a booster shot, perhaps a three-day vacation away from phones and fax machines. Clearly, a week away together would be ideal, but Herb would block that suggestion during tax season.

When the cab dropped her at her front door, Roseanne experienced a weird sensation in sudden flashes. Her hands seemed to tingle. The house felt foreign from the street view. She tipped the driver as he carried her luggage to the front steps. Roseanne fumbled for her keys. Perfume was lingering in her nostrils, which seemed bizarre. She opened the door and gave a sigh of relief to be home. It was just a little after four o'clock. Herb said that he would get home before six thirty. They would either go out for dinner or he would bring home Szechuan chicken with hot and sour soup. She should phone him soon.

Placing her luggage in the hall, she wandered the house. First, a tour of the kitchen and then the bedroom. The house looked very neat. Herb wasn't that neat.

She looked at the backyard through the living room windows. She slid the patio door open and stepped outside. The peculiar perfume was still present. There was a hummingbird by the potted plants. She heard a gardener several houses away with a power tool that became grating on her nerves. Returning inside, Roseanne went into the master bathroom and inspected things. She looked within the small waste bin by the toilet. There were many crumbled tissues, a torn business envelope, and an empty bottle of Pepto Bismol.

Roseanne went through the tissues as though she were part of a CSI unit. One of the tissues had a lipstick smear. It was a color unfamiliar to her. She threw the tissue back into the metal bin and left the bathroom.

In the kitchen, she opened a bottle of Pinot Grigio and helped herself to a full wine glass.

Her mental concentration surrounding her strategies ahead. How should she confront Herb? Should she confront Herb? What good will come of this confrontation? What will he say to her about her discovery? She recalled the Richard Pryor joke: "Who you gonna believe? Me or your lying eyes?"

She found a favorite CD to play. It was the Miles Davis album *Sorcerer* recorded in May 1967 with a stunning color photo of actress Cicely Tyson, who at the time was Davis's girlfriend. The first cut, *The Prince of Darkness*, had a skip. She advanced the CD and found comfort from the jazz compositions culminating with Miles Davis' *Limbo.* Davis eventually married Cicely Tyson.

Her thoughts raced wildly. Who was the bitch Herb had over while she was in Atlantic City? What was her age? How long was this affair? Was this an affair? Should she murder him with a dull kitchen knife or poison him with slow action Drano?

She heard Herb's car. She jumped off the sofa and walked to the front door. She opened the door. The glass of Pinot in her right hand.

"Hi darling." said Herb with warmth and a broad smile.

"Hi Herb." returned Roseanne.

He leaned casually for a routine kiss. She allowed the kiss but reflexively pulled away. Roseanne could see that Herb had cut himself in the morning shaving.

"Hungry?" He pointed to the takeout bag under his arm.

"Not very."

"I am. Missed you, Roseanne."

He proceeded calmly into the kitchen. She thought of a third way to kill him. In the bathtub and tossing the hairdryer once he got wet. That would acquit her.

"I saw the Taj opening on cable news."

"Good, Herb."

"I really think Las Vegas media should cover this success."

"Impossible. It would benefit Atlantic City."

"Still, hometown gal scores big."

"Herb, let's be honest with each other."

He kept unpacking the Szechuan containers, splitting his attention.

"Sure." he replied wearing a business grin.

"Did you keep company with anyone? You know, while I was away."

"Yeah, I golfed with Ralph."

"I mean a woman."

"A woman?"

"You know, something with a vagina."

"Yeah, I slept with the NBC TV weather reporter. Kimberly Lake. The tall blonde who likes pearls and does live reports in the rain."

"Herb, there was a woman here. So, stop bullshitting."

"Roseanne, what's gotten into you? Bad flight?"

"Do you have a girlfriend, or did you hire an escort?"

"Come on. Quit this game, honey."

"Look at me, Herb."

He turned slowly and his discomfort began to sweep his face.

"I don't want to play twenty questions."

"Did some idiot friend talk to you?" he asked.

"No."

"One of our idiot neighbors?"

"No."

"Did you go through my laptop?"

"No."

"You know my password."

"No."

"Then stop this prosecution."

"I went into the bathroom."

"And?"

"There's a tissue with lipstick."

"Maybe it's blood. I cut myself shaving."

"It's fucking pink lipstick."

"Maybe it's your fucking lipstick."

"I never use pink lipstick, you asshole."

"Did you really marry an asshole?"

"Yes."

"Could we just sit down and eat? I missed your opening. I fucked up. Okay. But fighting isn't going to fix this. I hate when we have these fights."

"Did you ever really love me, Herb?"

"I still love you, darling."

"I have to move out."

"Roseanne."

"Or you need to go."

"I'll go crazy without you."

"I doubt that."

"We can try marriage counseling."

"We tried counseling."

"Then forgive me, at least."

"I can't forgive you, Herb."

"Why not?"

"Because you broke your fucking vows."

Chapter Twenty-Eight

The day after the guards brought Saanvi's body to the family, Mir struggled with the immediate funeral arrangements. Although there was a burial yard outside of Agra, Mir spoke to Saanvi's mother about the best course of action.

He honored Saanvi's clothing and personal items by not touching anything, leaving her earthly presence immaculate.

The Zoroastrian exposure of the corpse to birds of prey was the normal protocol, but individuals of high distinction were burned on a pyre, and their ashes were buried under a stupa or a top — shrines to the departed and vital for family members to visit over the years. In more recent decades, cremation became the privilege of every villager.

Several nights each month it was common to see dead tree branches and kindling gathered for the burning of the dead. The belief that creation would allow one's soul to ascend skyward toward the landscape of the gods assuming the soul led a holy life. On the other hand, it was also understood that many souls, without great stain in their respective lives, would descend to the underworld with other souls. The ashes of the cadaver would travel to a body of water to be dispersed with deep respect.

Mir believed that Saanvi's ashes should be released into the river Yamuna. Firstly, he explained to his children how their mother had died. The children were shielded from seeing Saanvi's corpse. Then, Mir articulated the stages of a soul.

"Before birth, the soul lives invisible and free."

The children listened.

"At birth, the soul has a sky of memory which means too much to retain."

The children nodded, not certain what Mir was saying.

"The baby learns. The toddler learns. The child learns. Memory is architecture which grows and towers upward."

The children nodded again.

"Sickness can take the body. Aging can take the body. A physical accident can take the body. But the soul is invincible and eternal. You will be reunited with mother in the future."

The children nodded a third time. Saanvi's mother was in the room listening to Mir.

"We will go to the pyre and free the soul. We will take the ashes to the river."

Mir began to cry. In a few minutes, the family put on outside clothing for the short journey to the wood pyre. There were two neighbors present to cart Saanvi's body on a wooden wheelbarrow.

"I thought that my life would end first. But the gods have complex plans which we cannot fathom." he said, directed at his children and Saanvi's mother Divya. The neighbors offered a few words of kindness.

It was a forty-five-minute hike to the pyre. There were four laborers present to help the controlled fire. There were buckets of sand and buckets of water. There was an empty urn too.

Mir held his children close to his body. Saanvi looked away, not wanting to see the pyre lit.

"I love you forever, Saanvi." said Mir in a hushed whisper.

Chapter Twenty-Nine

Roseanne rescheduled her gynecologist appointment several times over the last two months running into late September 1991, partly due to work complications. But she was also giving into a discernible reflex of avoidance. For most of her adult life Roseanne had a dire fear of cancer. She had a combination Pap-HPV test last year and there were complications.

Thirteen months ago, she had undressed from the waist down. The gynecologist had her lie on her back on the exam table with Roseanne's knees bent. Her heels rested in supports stirrups. Her doctor inserted a speculum into her vagina and took samples of her cervical cells using a soft brush and a spatula. Roseanne's HPV test came back positive.

She was informed that she had a type of high-risk HPV that was linked to cervical cancer. Her gynecologist, Dr. Brigitte La Follette, told her over the phone that the test result doesn't mean that she had cervical cancer at that time. However, her doctor explained that this was a warning sign that cervical cancer could develop in Roseanne's future. She scheduled a follow-up test with Roseanne to see if the infection had cleared and to check for signs of cervical cancer.

There was a history of cancer in her family which impacted her maternal grandmother, and two aunts. Her mother was able to sidestep the genetic destiny.

Roseanne had many long conversations with Herb about their actuary tables, their mortality, their likelihood of surviving one another rather than perishing together. Would Herb be better off than Roseanne? Would Roseanne be better off than Herb? Which member of this marriage was more spiritual and capable of carrying on while maintaining an invisible and inaudible conversation with a deceased spouse?

Roseanne thought Herb had more emotional bounty for this complex task as the designated survivor.

"I will speak to you from the grave, Herb," she often said to him, "and I encourage you to find another good woman to take care of you. And if I cannot make my voice heard to you, please imagine that my voice, keep that voice inside your head for eternity."

Herb would cry whenever Roseanne spoke these words.

"I will instruct this woman to be a good caretaker, Herb."

"Shut up, Roseanne."

"How can I shut up, Herb. I love you with my entire body and soul."

Roseanne was early for her follow-up visit to the gynecologist. She signed in at the reception desk and got her garage parking ticket validated. There were many women in the waiting room. She wondered which ones were confronting a question about cancer cells and which ones were present for comfortable issues, like pregnancy or menopause conditions.

The nurse called her name and Roseanne followed the nurse to a private room.

She was told to undress and put on the paper fiber gown. Sunshine poured in behind the window's white curtains. She was given slippers. The room felt chilly, but she attributed the discomforting temperature to her anxiety. She read the framed photographs and posters in the examining room. The framed items were celebrating the achievements of the two gynecologists as leaders of Nevada's medical community in women's health. She saw an ant crawling on the counter, near the jar which contained cotton swabs.

Roseanne's doctor entered the examination room. The doctor's hair was tied up in a heavy bun. Dr. Brigitte La Follette appeared tired and distracted. She had a clipboard in her right hand.

"Hi, Roseanne."

"Hello, doctor."

"Everything looks acceptable. I'm sorry the nurse asked you to disrobe."

"So, this is good news?"

"Yes, I think this mostly good news."

Roseanne seemed puzzled.

"Let's keep checking this every year. Just to be safe."

"Sure."

"Everything fine at work?"

"Yes."

"Still lots of travel? Atlantic City?"

"All done with Atlantic City, Doctor."

"Are you following the Clarence Thomas confirmation hearings?"

"A little bit." said Roseanne.

"It's so outrageous."

"Yes."

"What a creep this guy is. I feel so badly for Anita Hill."

"Yes."

"Putting pubic hairs on Coke cans." said the doctor in a clinical voice.

"Yes."

"Biden's a terrible chairman of the Judiciary."

"I haven't followed the hearing." admitted Roseanne.

"I'm glued to the hearing. It's out front in America. Women are chattel, at least to the panel of male Senators."

Roseanne had not expected a political editorial from her African American gynecologist today.

"I feel terrible for Anita Hill. She could be you. She could be me."

"Yes." responded Roseanne.

"Women have no credibility in this country."

"Yes."

"Her career is ruined," added her gynecologist, "but his damn career is set for life on the Supreme Court."

Roseanne exchanged quiet looks with her doctor.

"So, I don't have cancer?"

"No. It's far better news than we thought weeks ago."

"But I have to be seen twice a year?"

"Yes, let's be cautious."

"Have you always been this political?"

"I'm not political. I'm speaking as a woman professional to another woman professional. You are an architect."

"Yes, I am an architect."

"You faced uphill battles, I'm sure."

"Yes, a few."

"There could be more female architects."

"Yes, many more, in fact."

"You must sense professional double standards."

"Occasionally." replied Roseanne softly.

"You're a successful architect."

"I've been fortunate so far."

Roseanne fell silent.

"Clarence Thomas is married to a white bossy woman. Did you know that?"

"No, I didn't. Does it matter?"

"It's another incongruity in the narrative."

"Whose narrative?" asked Roseanne.

"Clarence Thomas' narrative. As a far-right conservative who benefitted by affirmative action. Did you know that miscegenation laws were still on the books in 1967."

"No."

"And seventeen Southern states plus Oklahoma still enforced laws preventing marriage between whites and non-whites. The last state to repeal its laws was Alabama in 2000."

"That's truly terrible."

"I'll say. Did you ever live in a southern state?"

"No."

"I started my practice in Georgia. Well, that was a total disaster."

The doctor opened the examining room door slightly to signal the nurse to join them.

Chapter Thirty

Shah Jahan was the fifth Mughal emperor, reigning from 1628 until 1658. He started life as Mirza Shahab-ud-Din Baig Muhammad Khan Khurram, the third son of Jahangir. He battled frequently with his youngest brother Shahryar Mirza and eventually prevailed as dominant for the throne. He claimed that it was his divine destiny and in his countless dreams his plotting was reaffirmed. Furthermore, key individuals within the court were surprised that Shahryar Mirza was defeated so quickly. Shan Jahan crowned himself emperor inside the enormous Agra Fort among a large attending crowd. According to historians, attendees were stripped of any weapons and ropes prior to entering the Agra Fort. Besides his sibling Shahryar, Shah Jahan slaughtered a long list of rivals who lusted for the throne.

As a child, he had benefitted from a robust, academic enrichment befitting his privilege as a Mughal prince, which circumscribed cultural arts and sciences, sports, and martial combat. His tutors were chosen for their brilliance, their versatility, and their absolute fidelity to the court. According to his archivist Qazvini, prince Khurram was barely versed in basic Turki conversation and had little patience towards a serious study of the language.

Khurram had expressed a passionate affinity to Hindi literature since his childhood, and his Hindi letters were alluded to in his father's biography, Tuzuk-e-Jahangiri. In 1605, as his father's health had deteriorated rapidly, prince Khurram reaching puberty, kept a vigil by the emperor's bed. In light of the menacing times preceding Akbar's death, the boy faced assassination threats from his father's many enemies. To ensure his safety and the needed rule of law, the prince was forced to withdraw to his own bedroom by his grandfather's protective household staff. There were guards posted outside his room each night.

Under Shah Jahan's ironclad, authoritarian rule, the Mughals reached the pinocle of their architectural greatness, cultural influence, and political supremacy. As the third son of Jahangir, Shah Jahan led ferocious military attacks against the Rajput of Mewar and the Lodis of the Deccan. Regarding high profile, foreign campaigns, Shah Jahan aimed his sights against the Portuguese, the Deccan Sultanates, and the Safavids. As emperor, Shah Jahan had no qualms suppressing the deadly force countless local rebellions, and he was tested relentlessly against the tragic Deccan famine in the first years of his reign.

In September 1657, Shah Jahan fell seriously ill, and he designated his eldest son Dara Shikoh as his heir. This personal action triggered a deadly competition among his three sons, from which Shah Jahan's third son Aurangzeb triumphed becoming the sixth emperor. Without remorse or hesitation, Aurangzeb killed his brothers, including Crown Prince Dara Shikoh.

After Shah Jahan surprised the court, recovering from his illness the following year, Aurangzeb jailed his father in Agra Fort from July 1658 until his death in January 1666. Aurangzeb's bloodthirsty behavior shocked the land. Nonetheless, Shah Jahan was laid to rest next to his preeminent wife Mumtaz Mahal in the Taj Mahal. His historic reign was known for removing the humane policies implemented by Akbar. During Shah Jahan's rule, Islamic revivalist waves like the Naqshbandi swept in to redirect Mughal customs and values.

Francois Bernier, a French doctor from the Duchy of Anjou who visited India from 1659 to 1668, wrote that the relationship of Shah Jahan with his daughter, Jahanara Begum, transgressed respectability as it was widely reported that they had entered a sexual relationship. Niccolao Manucci, a Venetian writer, physician, and a contemporary of Bernier, disputed the incestuous rumors. Manucci's work was appraised as reliable and comprehensive with regard to the salient events and specifics under Mughal rule.

Historian K. S. Lal had speculated that the allegations were fueled by the Mullahs and courtiers' biased partisanship. Complicating the perception was Aurangzeb sentencing Jahanara in the Agra Fort which inspired the inflaming, salacious gossip. During the war of court succession, the nobles and courtiers had been caught between two dangerous, polarizing factions. Eventually, Aurangzeb claimed the royal throne. He worked arduously to convince his supporters of his virtue and his destiny to rule the land. The Mullahs grew to embrace Aurangzeb. Without a doubt, Aurengzeb was determined to eliminate Shah Jahan and Jahanara in one fell swoop.

The Shah Jahan Album, also known as *The Emperor's Album*, features fifty illustrated and calligraphy folios, forty-one of which belong to the Metropolitan Museum in New York City, and nine of which reside in the collection of the Freer Gallery of Art on the National Mall in Washington, DC.

As seen in this album, the single-page painting attains prominence in Mughal art from the mid-sixteenth century onward. This spectacular album, which contains intimate nature studies, portraits of the royal family and various dignitaries, and fine examples of illuminated folios of calligraphy by renowned calligraphers, offers a glimpse into the courtly life and diverse interests of its patrons.

The album was initiated by the Mughal emperor Jahangir and passed onto his son Shah Jahan who added several paintings, illuminations, and calligraphy folios. It eventually came into the possession of Shah Jahan's son Aurangzeb.

From the exquisite Folio within the Shah Jahan Album: *The Emperor Shah Jahan with his Son Dara Shikoh*:

This impeccably painted portrait, encased by intricate borders, depicts the future emperor Shah Jahan appraising rare gems with his favorite offspring. Balancing a tray of emeralds and jewels, the father studies a ruby in one hand, while the inquisitive boy holds a peacock fan and a turban ornament. The elegance of royal living is celebrated in the textured specificity of the jewels, the luxurious furniture, the court fabrics, and, most dramatically, the large platform in all of its simplicity showcasing aesthetic patterns and vegetation. The diminutive painting was a work employing ink, opaque watercolor, and gold on paper. The spectacular margins consist of gold and opaque watercolor on dyed paper. The painting's height appears to be under sixteen inches and the width just under eleven inches.

Nanha was the artist. The calligrapher was Mir 'Ali Haravi.

The date — approximately 1620.

Chapter Thirty-One

Roseanne L'Anse left work early to treat herself to a Thai massage at a new location in Las Vegas. Her friends from the tennis club recommended this spa. It seemed that everyone at the club was having lower back problems.

Roseanne booked an appointment the day before over the phone. She was asked if she had any current allergies, if she had any medical conditions, and if she was experienced in traditional Thai massage. She conveyed that she was in excellent health and that she had little knowledge of Thai therapy. Roseanne was then asked her age which made her uncomfortable. She asked the spa why her age mattered. The spa was insistent on knowing this detail. Roseanne relented and stated that she was over forty-five.

At the spa's entrance, Roseanne noticed extremely tall indoor plants and she suddenly had a sensation of being amid carnivorous tropical pitcher plants. The artificial lighting inside the spa suddenly produced vertigo. She shielded her eyes with one hand and stepped closer to the front desk. She addressed a Thai woman in her mid-twenties.

"I have a five o'clock appointment."

"Your name please?"

"Roseanne L'Anse."

"Can you please spell it?"

"L. *apostrophe*. A. N. S. E."

"Thank you. Have a seat."

Roseanne sat down. Her vertigo lessened. She closed her eyes. In a few moments, she fell asleep. Time drifted in her vague dream. She floated down a humid riverbank and the river's sounds were overwhelming. There were large birds cawing in unison. There was the undulating drone of insane, desperate insects fighting death. There was a full moon looking too large for the night sky.

Roseanne opened her eyes and stared at her massage therapist. The therapist was a petite young person of indeterminate gender with long black hair. Roseanne was sprawling over a thick cloth mat on the floor. Roseanne had no memory of how she went from the lobby to the massage room. Lavender incense sticks were burning nearby. The therapist lifted Roseanne's two legs high into the air. Roseanne had another blackout. She heard sounds but could not see.

"Are you okay?" asked the massage therapist.

"What?"

"Are you okay?"

"I fell asleep."

"You were talking in your sleep."

"Was I?"

"You have to save someone's life."

"Did I say that?"

"You did."

"You picked up my legs."

"Yes."

"Am I pregnant?"

The massage therapist pretended not to hear Roseanne.

"Am I?"

The massage therapist flattened Roseanne's posture. Roseanne's face was pushed into the mat. The massage therapist walked along Roseanne's back and ass. This was mildly painful. Roseanne groaned. The massage therapist seemed to weigh more with each step. The incense sticks were making Roseanne nauseous. Roseanne simply passed out again. The only color in the room was black.

"Where am I?" asked Roseanne.

The massage therapist answered her while continuing the strenuous massage.

"Where is my blouse?"

"Hanging on the hook."

"Are you the same therapist from the start?"

"Yes, I am the same therapist."

"Are you a woman?"

"No. I am a man." said the massage therapist.

"You are a small man." replied Roseanne.

"Yes, I am a very small man."

"I think I must leave now."

"We have more time."

Roseanne crawled up into a crouched position, most of her weight on her knees. Again, the pungent incense smoke filled Roseanne's nostrils and the back of her throat.

"Why did I ever come here!"

Hearing this offended the massage therapist. Roseanne tried to open the door, but it was locked.

"Open the door please."

"Yes." said the massage therapist, unlocking the door and turning on the hall light as a courtesy to Roseanne.

Roseanne sat in her car for a long time. She was afraid that she would black out again while driving. She saw herself in the car's rear-view mirror. She saw that she had men's eyes and a high forehead. She was not a woman, and her skin was swarthy. She had an Adam's apple. She could not recognize how much she resembled Mir Abdul Karim because she had never met Mir Abdul Karim.

She started the car and drove home. Her hands were men's hands on the steering wheel.

"Who am I?" she asked herself.

Her voice deepened and sounded masculine. What will Herb say when he sees her this way? Will he walk out on her? Should she blame Herb for leaving?

"Goddamn it, Herb." she cursed.

It was a long drive home in difficult traffic. She wanted to say aloud, "I am a man from India."

Really, what will Herb say? She stopped the car. She unbuttoned her blouse. She put her hands on her breasts. Her breasts were still very big. Sensing this gave her some relief. She buttoned her blouse and got out of the car. Herb was expected late tonight.

Roseanne opened a bottle of Pinot Noir and poured herself a tall glass. She looked for a pack of cigarettes in the laundry closet, having found no cigarettes in the garage. Behind the Tide detergent box was a half empty pack of Newport menthols. This discovery immediately eased her nerves. She lit up on the small deck outside her kitchen. Her outdoor jacket was unbuttoned, and her scarf blew in the wind. It took her three attempts to light her cigarette. The blended taste of wine and tobacco moved over her tongue languidly. She swallowed slowly. Smoke came from her nose. The image of the stranger in her rear-view mirror was still haunting her.

Her fingers touched her face carefully. Tracing the contour of her nose and mouth, Roseanne reminded herself that her features were feminine. She imagined to be sightless for a moment in order to recognize herself.

"I'm losing my mind." Roseanne announced to no one present.

In her imagination, the facial composition of Mir Abdul Karim was losing definition like a sandcastle eroding by the incoming tide. Still, as Mir Abdul Karim's image was fading away, she sensed the powers of Mir Abdul Karim's architectural genius. She felt the inner pangs of being possessed by another soul. And yet, the feeling was something akin to self-discovery.

Roseanne took another drag from her cigarette. Smoke rolled off her tongue and lip. The wisps of smoke assumed the quick artist sketch of a cherub. The image, which comforted her, lasted a second and then disappeared. Lifting her wine glass, she drank with gratitude and noticed her red lipstick along the rim of the glass. She was a woman after all.

Chapter Thirty-Two

Saanvi's mother, Divya, had moved her belongings to Mir's home the day after her daughter had her funeral ceremony. Mir paid two men to carry her clothing, her kitchenware, her bedding, her tapestries, her favorite chairs and a mosaic table, her potted plants, and her decorative ceramics.

Divya was still numb from shock. She was in disbelief that Saanvi left this world so young. She knew that the task at hand was caring for Saanvi's two children. Mir told Divya that he had to return to work and the children's tutor was insufficient in providing supervision every day. Divya did not associate in any way the possible ties between Saanvi's death at the market and Mir's architectural capacities under the emperor's grandest projects within Agra. Mir suppressed his suspicions about the agency of a marketplace murder.

Mir talked in his sleep. The walls were thin. Divya heard phrases and utterances. She wanted to question the grandchildren's father. At the same time, Divya was empathic to Mir's visible devastation. He had yet to mourn properly. He lost significant weight. Capillaries around his nose were ruptured. Without hair and with blackened bloodshot eyes, he appeared sickly and wan. Over breakfast tea and sweet bread, Divya sat very close to Mir.

"You say things in your sleep."

"Do I?"

"I hear you, Mir."

"Can you not sleep?"

"I sleep. I wake. I try to go back to sleep."

"What do I say?"

"You say Saanvi's name over and over again."

"Yes."

"You say things about the black horses."

"What about the horses, Divya?"

"The men are masked."

"Is that what I say in my sleep?"

"You say that Ustad is a bad man."

"Ustad?"

"Yes, Mir."

"Don't listen to my babble."

"Who is Ustad?"

"There are so many men named Ustad in Agra."

"But who is the bad Ustad?"

Mir put down his cup of tea.

"You are hiding the truth to Saanvi's mother."

"I do not hide anything, Divya."

"How long do you wish for me to live under this roof?"

"Until the children are older."

"If I am to live with you, I must know the truth, Mir."

"I'm hiding nothing from you."

"Who is the bad Ustad?"

"We are a team of architects, Divya. He is on the team. He leads the team."

"And how is he bad?"

"He fears the emperor as we all do."

"Why do you link the bad Ustad to the men riding horses?"

"As a threat."

"A threat to you?"

"Yes."

"That makes no sense. His horsemen stole what you need to live."

"Divya, you are twisting meaning from my night dream words."

"Would the horsemen kill your children next, Mir?"

"I don't know. If I act stupid, my children might die."

"Why didn't the horsemen kill you first?"

"If they were to kill me first, there is no further logic to increase the pressure."

"The gods are watching you, Mir."

"How do you know?"

"Old women know such things."

"What do the children tell you?"

"They tell me they see Saanvi early in the morning."

"Do they talk to her?"

"Yes, Mir."

"Does she talk back?"

"Yes."

"Do you hear her too?"

"Yes."

"I will kill the men who took Saanvi from us."

"How?"

"With a sword."

"Where is your sword?"

"I keep it where I work."

Divya knitted her thick eyebrows. She ran her forefinger across her lip. Her heart was aching for her daughter.

"If you fail, these men will kill you, Mir."

"They cannot. I am already dead."

"You must not ever say that in front of your son and daughter."

She walked away from Mir. He continued to drink his tea. He lit a pipe to smoke. His daughter Kavya walked into the room. She was barefoot and wrapped in silk.

"Baapi, where is my toy monkey?"

"I do not know, Kavya."

"Did someone take it?"

"I do not think so."

"Help me look for my monkey."

"I am tired, daughter."

"Please, Baapi."

"I will find you a new monkey toy."

"It will be different. I know."

"I will look for the monkey tomorrow. Maybe the monkey is playing a hiding game with you?"

"A game?"

"A game, yes, Kavya."

"I hear Maa."

"Yes."

"She talks and it is like a whisper. I wish I could see Maa."

"You hear Maa, but you do not see her?"

Kayva leaned closer to Mir, held his arm firmly. She nodded her head sadly.

"Can you sleep?"

"I am afraid to sleep."

"We need to sleep, Kayva. Tonight, you will go to sleep early. Where is your tutor?

"My tutor is not here, Baapi."

"Is she late?"

"Yes, she is very late."

"Then Nani will watch you and your brother."

"Do not go."

"I have to go to my work."

"Does Maa talk to you?"

"Yes, she does."

"Do you see her?"

"Yes, Kayva."

Mir and his daughter heard crying in the next room. Mir rose and shuffled quietly to see. His son Vihaan was sitting in a chair with his head in his hands. Mir wrapped his arms around the boy as he kissed Vihaan's head.

Chapter Thirty-Three

Rex Heuermann had purchased a Nevada timeshare owned and managed by the Hilton Corporation. In 1994, the company's initial foray into the blossoming timeshare market began with the Las Vegas premiere of The Flamingo, a fifteen-acre establishment minutes away from the Las Vegas Strip's whirling energy. The Long Island architect was thrilled at the idea of owning an asset far from his home. His wife, Asa, was not aware of the acquisition until many months later and her reaction was caustic and suspicious.

"Why didn't you consult me?" she pressed him.

"I wanted to surprise you."

"I've no desire to go to Las Vegas, Rex."

"Las Vegas is changing. It's family friendly now."

"Bullshit."

"La Vegas has Broadway shows. Great shopping. Fantastic singers."

"Wayne Newton?"

"Come on. The Grateful Dead just played three nights in Vegas. And Sting opened for them."

"How much did you pay for the Goddamn timeshare?"

"Very little. It was a steal. I negotiated them down thirty percent. They give deals to licensed architects hoping we promote their brand."

"How much, Rex?"

"I put *nine* thousand dollars down."

"How much?"

"*Nineteen* thousand. It's leverage, Asa. It's tax deductible."

"What's the mortgage?"

"Less than peanuts. Two weeks per year for a luxury hotel suite."

"What hotel?"

"Flamingo. Near Treasure Island Hotel and Casino. Permanent Vegas home of Cirque du Soleil."

"Cirque du Soleil?"

"You know, the highbrow Canadian circus. Guy Laliberté said his troupe wanted to grow a flower in the desert with *Mystère*."

"Guy Laliberté?"

"One of the two circus founders."

"I hate the circus."

"I know. I didn't buy the circus, Asa."

"We could have used that cash for a real vacation."

"Like what, Asa?"

"Like a week in Paris. Or on a Greek island. I'll even take Hawaii."

"Yeah, Hilton gives points so that shareholders can trade their anchor location for other Hilton Grand Vacation properties."

"I read a lot of crap about timeshares, Rex."

"This is the Hilton Corporation, Asa. Come on. It might open business opportunities on the other side of the country."

What he withheld from Asa was the historic knowledge that mobster Bugsy Siegel launched The Flamingo Hotel & Casino a year after arriving in Las Vegas, 1945, and establishing a powerful, organized crime beachhead. Siegel reeled in fellow racketeer Meyer Lansky.

"Rex, look at the crappy furniture in our living room. We need a new sofa, lamps, and a better television. Club chairs."

"Fine. We'll shop for couches over the weekend, Asa."

"Leather couches, Rex."

"Sure. Fine leather. Whatever."

That weekend the architect and his wife went to several discount furniture warehouses and selected a black leather sectional sofa and love seat. Asa impulsively pushed her husband to buy a large oak coffee table for the living room. Rex agreed without any resistance. He withheld the news that he would be flying to Las Vegas the following weekend to inspect his timeshare.

That night after furniture shopping and dining at the Olive Garden in Westbury, Long Island, Rex and Asa made love passionately. It had been a while before they had been this physically intimate. It was something which evaded their daily conversation. That evening, Rex explained to Asa that the erotic hiatus was probably due to his having severe lower back problems. She replied that her migraines were debilitating, and she was avoiding physical closeness. Before they fell asleep, Asa whispered that it would be good to try sex weekly, or at the very least twice a month.

A week flew by. Rex left a note on the kitchen table early Saturday morning saying he needed to see a client in Nevada and that he would be staying two or three nights at the timeshare. He also left three hundred dollars in cash on the table for Asa. He forgot to buy roses at Walbaum's to finish out the table display. The architect forgot to lock the front door upon exiting. It wasn't even seven o'clock and he really needed a cup of coffee. Images of sexual movement flooded his thoughts.

The architect boarded United Airlines non-stop to Las Vegas. The stewardess looked Hollywood perfect. Blonde, young, long legs, and a shapely ass. So, the architect had to flirt.

"What's the inflight movie?" asked Rex.

"The James Bond film." replied the stewardess locking the overhead luggage doors.

"So glad James Bond isn't Jewish. He would be telling jokes to Goldfinger."

Rex Heuermann winked broadly. The airline attendant allowed herself to laugh. She was laughing at Rex Heuermann's diction and his self-caricature. He was as enormous as a Macy's Thanksgiving Day balloon. He was hunched over as if the jet had a drop ceiling. His hands always looked larger in confined spaces. He had predator eyes.

The architect was a few inches from the airline attendant. She expected him to take his seat. His belly was like the hood of an older Buick.

"I'm an architect. Need a house?"

Again, the stewardess laughed politely.

"You look so much like Charlize Theron."

"Really."

"*Mighty Joe Young.*"

"Charlize Theron?"

"*Monster.*"

The airline attendant walked down the aisle. She was done with the architect.

When Rex Heuermann deplaned, he felt the day's travel weighed heavily. Luggage in hand, he got into a taxi. The cabbie was playing loud music. Maybe Bonnie Raitt was singing from her third album. The architect had some stomach gas. He leaned to one side and opened the passenger window.

The Flamingo Hotel was in sight. The cab pulled up. Rex Heuermann climbed out. The air was cool and crisp. His chest expanded. He felt happy.

The front desk was stylishly gold and wood. Reception was polished. Rex Heuermann checked in. He was an owner of a timeshare. His room was four-thirty-five. Room service was available all day and all night. The pool was heated. The elevators were on the other side of the lobby. Rex Heuermann picked up his luggage and looked for the elevators.

The lobby doors opened, and Rex Heuermann stepped inside, followed by Roseanne L'Anse. She was at the hotel as a professional consultation. They were the only ones inside the hotel elevator. He glanced at her eyes. The doors closed and the elevator began its ascent. When the elevator reached the third floor, it stopped, and the doors tried to open. There was an odd noise coming from the doors. Rex Heuermann and Roseanne L'Anse were stuck inside the hotel lobby.

"Christ." said Roseanne L'Anse.

"What the hell." said Rex Heuermann.

"Push another floor button."

Rex Heuermann pushed two higher floors. Nothing happened. He pounded on the elevator doors. Nothing changed. Roseanne L'Anse felt her anxiety climb. Rex Heuermann inserted his fingertips along the doors' central crease. He grabbed and pulled. The doors opened. Roseanne L'Anse let out an audible sigh. Rex Heuermann smiled at her. He dropped his hands.

"Got to love Las Vegas." he said.

Roseanne L'Anse turned her head and walked away.

Chapter Thirty-Four

Four years after Roseanne L'Anse attended the opening of Atlantic City's Taj Mahal Casino Resort, Herb had rented a two-bedroom townhouse with a functioning fireplace a few miles from his office and about twenty-five minutes from the house he once shared with his wife. Roseanne found it curious that he required or desired a second bedroom. They had discussed trying a mediator to guide them through marriage dissolution, but Herb felt that avenue would favor Roseanne financially. She prepared a few spread sheets on how they would save money by avoiding battling divorce attorneys, but Herb intuitively believed that he would fare better rolling dice in Nevada's family court.

Prior to the conversation about a professional mediator, Herb suggested they try a marriage counselor. He even pleaded with Roseanne that their marriage deserved at least a dozen sessions with a good therapist.

"No. It's pointless, Herb."

"There is nothing more valuable than our marriage, Roseanne."

"You're a congenital liar."

"Not true."

"I love you."

"Maybe you do, but I can't trust you."

"Have you stopped loving me?" he pressed.

"I think that I have."

The flashes of anger between them came and went, over days and weeks. Roseanne's therapist supported the decision to end the marriage.

Roseanne served Herb with legal papers. They both hired excellent lawyers. It was approaching satire that, upon court required discovery, Herb's holdings prior to marriage and his private portfolio were impossible to decipher. He was a professional accountant for over thirty years but trying to trace his muddy assets mirrored ancient archeology.

Their house was in both names. Roseanne's financial history was plain and discernible.

Herb thought that her income over the decades surpassed his dramatically. Their IRS statements were helpful proving his perspective, but Roseanne's lawyer scrutinized many of the tax dodges created by her husband. Herb dissembled without shame. A forensic attorney was hired to unearth the mess and the results damaged Herb considerably. Four days before they were scheduled for the court hearing, Herb's attorney proffered a rational compromise. The divorce was finalized April 1, 1994. Roseanne's attorney joked that sometimes April Fool's Day can be a personal triumph.

Roseanne and Herb had their house appraised by a realtor. She then bought out his half. The house meant a lot to her. After all, she had remodeled it personally and it was turnkey beautiful.

Six months after the divorce, Herb had a massive coronary. He died in the hospital after open heart surgery. He was fifty-nine years old. This shocked Roseanne to her breaking point. She was not responsible for Herb's health and his longevity. He was a smoker until they married. However, his serious drinking was something he could not taper. Herb's older brother had blamed Roseanne for his death and there was nothing she could say to remedy this miserable aspersion.

Roseanne attended the church funeral. It rained heavily that day. Black umbrellas dotted the parking lot. She brought two friends from her book club to console her. It was impossible to communicate with Herb's family members. She cried profusely at the memorial service. She prayed for Herb's soul. Roseanne identified the thunderous rain as an act of purification.

"We need to be cleansed and cleansed again." she said to the elderly priest upon leaving the service.

The wind grabbed her umbrella and flew towards the church roof. Roseanne was escorted by one friend to their Tesla, and they drove into the formidable storm, windshield wipers working furiously.

"The priest was judging me." said Roseanne.

Her friends agreed with Roseanne.

Roseanne was crying. She shut her eyes. There were flashing images of Herb as a young, handsome man driving Roseanne in his old, powder blue Mustang convertible to Lake Powell. Their wedding day in Lake Tahoe. Their vacations to Paris, London, and Rome. Ski trips to Park City. Faraway escapades to Machu Picchu, Chichén Itzá, Taj Mahal, Luxor, and Petra. When they went to Cuzco on route to Machu Picchu, they were one week ahead of actress Shirley MacLaine's "Out on a Limb" film crew. It was to be an Inca inspired movie of the week spiritual journey.

Herb was with eternity now.

He would never return to Roseanne.

Roseanne knew today that she would live past ninety years old. Herb would never discover the hardships of old age. Roseanne expected a different fate. Her bed would feel colder now. Even though she was getting used to living alone, her bed grew very cold. The breakfast table would feel cold too. Life would become cold.

Her love would be directly exclusively towards architecture.

The car took the women to the cemetery. Herb would now be buried. The rain was letting up. The cemetery was darker than twilight because of the black clouds. It was weather built for restless ghosts.

The grave looked forbidding to Roseanne. This is his final resting place. God have mercy on you, Herb.

We once loved each other, Herb.

Goodbye. Rest in peace, my darling.

Roseanne turned and looked away. She drew strength from her two friends who held her arms.

The Tesla drove slowly following the exit signs. Turning onto a main road, they found themselves behind a large warehouse truck. Road spray hit their windshield. Roseanne swallowed herself in total silence.

She still had hundreds of photos of Herb at home. She had a good many of his books and music CDs. Roseanne always thought there was one more important conversation to have with Herb.

Herb wanted children. Maybe for a day like today.

He wanted some legacy. He never said that, but she felt it was true.

Herb craved freedom but he feared being lonely. That was Herb's inner mystery.

Roseanne did not go back to work that week. She stayed at home and clung to her bed.

Chapter Thirty-Five

Mir awoke in damp bed clothing from perspiration. He had a disturbing dream which, upon awaking, he was able to recall most of the deranged details. In his nightmare, he contacted illicit business contacts in explosives from Arya's Shiraz region. Mir had paid them with sacks of precious jewels. His entire savings were directed to this clandestine revenge. Mir trusted an experienced Hindi courier to deliver the sacks and to return with a dozen wooden boxes of high explosives. When the courier returned with the boxes that were labeled spices and rice, Mir was given precise instructions on preparing the fuses, the timing of the fuses, and how to avoid mishandling the dangerous cargo. In this fantasy, he was told that court guard dogs could detect explosives, which would be the primary challenge to overcome.

The courier had suggested that Mir trick the dogs with treated, raw meat which put the canines to sleep. Mir was known by most of the patrolling dogs. The bait worked. Mir's building assistants at the Taj Mahal site accepted the boxes without questioning the courier. It was close to nightfall. The crescent moon appeared larger than normal as low cumulous clouds drifted across the moon's face. The nightmare was unrelenting.

Eerily, Mir spotted Ustad Ahmad Lahori climb onto a horse and trotted away from the building site. Mir opened the boxes with great care. He waited for laborers to leave the north side of the Taj Mahal. He handled the fuses and began to bundle the explosives systematically, placed strategically around the partial perimeter. This was the first time he had worked with explosives.

Mir began a small fire using tinder. The sound of crackling twigs was enormous to his ears, magnified by the perverse dreamscape. Arranging the fuse length, he was ready to ignite the explosives. Magically, Mir left the ground and drifted like a leaf in the wind. He found himself on the outskirts of the Taj Mahal grounds along the riverbed. The emperor's guardsmen hurried to capture Mir just as the sound of terrifying explosion ripped through all of Agra. Mir witnessed an inferno of fireworks, broken stone, fractured marble, scaffolding, and metal hurl above the structures.

The luminous moon appeared to be lower and larger than astronomy would allow. The hurricane of debris annihilated all of the guardsmen and the remaining laborers at the site. Ustad Ahmad Lahori was dead, crushed by his own dying horse.

Mir's feet were still not quite touching the ground. It was as if he were on a gravity free rug hurling magically. He wondered if he were killed from the blast and left his physical body. He was transfixed by the magnitude of the mausoleum's destruction. He heard a choir of robed children intoning sacred words. He caught a glimpse of the emperor dying in the midst of the flying fragments of the Taj Mahal. These details were what he could remember from the dream.

He hated himself for imagining the immense atrocity. Mir acknowledged the evil impulse from inside to undermine his decade-long endeavor in collaboration with the world's finest architects. He recognized the burning desire to destroy the emperor's aspirational monument in a single moment of violence. Nonetheless, he found slight respite knowing a nightmare was nothing more than a work of the recessed imagination. His nightmare was not seen or heard by anyone else. His nightmare was removed from daily reality, and it need not serve as a sinister premonition. In short, he had not murdered one soul and he had not damaged a single block of marble.

The dream presented itself as a cryptic lesson. Mir was facing a stark decision whether to avenge Saanvi's death or to keep living as the surviving parent of his two children. Clearly, the nightmare illustrated the visceral sensations of an absolute counterstrike. There would be untold political and financial chaos in Shah Jahan's empire after an assassination at the site of the Taj Mahal. Inevitably, Mir would be caught, tortured, and killed.

Mir found himself talking to Saanvi. He climbed out of bed. Was she in their bedroom? Was Saanvi watching him now? Was she free of human pain?

"Saanvi," he spoke softly and plaintively, "I ask you to communicate with your mother. I ask you to change your mother's thinking. I ask you to mollify your mother's anger. I ask you to communicate with our children. I ask you to comfort them. I will not abandon them. That priority surpasses all priorities, my love."

Along the flooring by the bedroom's doorway, Mir saw a straggly stray cat. It was dark brown with white paws. The cat was focused on something in the corner of the room. Mir remained still, letting the quiet prevail. The cat pounced on some prey.

"What did you catch?"

The cat turned and looked directly at Mir.

"What did you kill?"

The cat sat and cleaned his hindquarters.

"You don't live here."

The cat began to bite his tail.

"Go!"

"Are you deaf!"

The cat continued to ignore Mir. Mir left his bed feeling weakness in his ankles. Mir took a step in the direction of the cat. The cat suddenly recoiled, scrambling out of the bed chamber. Mir pursued the animal in a clumsy footfall, unable to find strength in his legs. Cats normally did not sneak into his abode.

Mir entered the kitchen. Divya was preparing pastries and she had opened the outside door for ventilation.

"We have a cat, Divya."

"What?"

"There is a stray in the house."

"We have no rats." she replied.

"A cat, Divya. A brown cat."

"Where?"

"I don't know. It was in the bedroom."

"Your bedroom?"

"Yes."

"I left the door open, Mir."

"I see."

"The cat will leave before long."

"Maybe not."

"The cat will not hurt the children."

"Maybe it will."

"You were talking in your sleep again. Screaming in your sleep, Mir."

"I had a bad dream."

"Do you want a pastry for breakfast?"

She handed him two small pastries with a rapid gesture. He hesitated and accepted one pastry.

"Eat. You are losing weight. You will get sick."

There was a noise outside Mir's home and footsteps approaching Mir's front door.

"Do you hear someone, Mir?" said Saanvi's mother.

Mir went to look. Outside was Ustad Ahmad Lahori wearing white clothing which was uncharacteristic of his daily outwear. His hat was in his hand.

"Might we be able to talk, Mir Abdul Karim? Forgive me for coming to your home."

Divya could not help but look to see who was outside. She had never laid eyes on Ustad Ahmad Lahori, but she did sense that the visitor was making a professional call. She observed that Mir was unsettled by his presence.

"I will leave." she told Mir, as she disappeared,

"Come in." pronounced Mir formally, punctuated by his open hand.

Ustad Ahmad Lahori propelled himself up the front steps, summoning reserve energy.

"Are you well?" Ustad Ahmad Lahori asked.

"I am in mourning, Ustad Ahmad Lahori."

"Yes, that is why I came here. To talk with you away from the Taj Mahal."

"My wife did not have an accidental death."

"I know about the horsemen in the market."

"My wife was murdered."

"I mourn with you, Mir Abdul Karim."

"What does that mean?"

"I feel the immensity of your tragedy."

"Go away, please."

"The emperor commanded the horsemen. It was meant to intimidate you and me."

"Your wife is alive, Ustad Ahmad Lahori."

"Yes."

"You don't know my tragedy."

"I told the emperor the truth yesterday."

"What is the truth?"

"That I am the court architect and that you report to me. That I am the chief visionary of the Taj Mahal."

"The eternal damage is done, Ustad Ahmad Lahori."

"I do not expect you to forgive me, Mir Abdul Karim. I would feel all that you feel if I were in your shoes. We have a year or two more of design and building. I need you. You need me. We are brothers of architecture."

"Please leave."

"I will fund your family. I will make good my commitment."

"I do not want your insincere generosity."

"I assigned men who will make payments for your children. No matter what happens to me. No matter what happens to you."

"We will both be slaughtered in due time, Ustad Ahmad Lahori. Your manipulation helped no one."

"I honor you, Mir Abdul Karim."

Mir closed the door and contained himself from screaming.

Chapter Thirty-Six

In early August 2016, according to scores of newspaper headlines around the nation and overseas, the "too big to fail" Trump Taj Mahal Resort Casino was about to close after a quarter-century of tenacious endurance, colorful boxing fights, and absurd, business setbacks. The casino hotel was billed by Donald Trump as the "eighth wonder of the world" positioned perfectly on the pricier leg of New Jersey's shore. However, after cascading bankruptcies and a near endless union casino strike in Atlantic City, the Trump Taj Mahal was destined to go belly up.

Roseanne L'Anse had followed the travesty of the Taj's fall from grace. The hotel casino was a part of her architectural portfolio. It was her child. It was her ugly child. She couldn't disown the structure. She was one of the parents. She intended to visit the casino when next visiting her mother in New Jersey. It didn't matter if the casino was shuttered up.

Trump had broken most ties with Atlantic City in 2009 aside from a ten percent ownership in the Taj Mahal's parent company in exchange for the value of his branding name. That stake was erased in March 2009 when Carl Icahn bought the hotel directly from bankruptcy court. Gaming was an industry Donald Trump failed to conquer.

The Taj Mahal Casino Resort, once the crown jewel of the now defunct Trump Entertainment Resorts company, had no choice but to fold after Labor Day weekend 2015, according to a public acknowledgement from Tropicana Entertainment's Chief Executive Officer Tony Rodio.

Roseanne L'Anse never met Tony Rodio.

Rodio blamed the hotel casino collapse solely on the striking union rank and file along with the previous equity owner, Donald Trump's company, who placed its naked bankruptcy.

"Icahn Enterprises which controls Tropicana Entertainment, saved the Tropicana, and to date has lost almost one hundred million trying to secure the Taj when no other party including the prior equity owners who put it into its recent bankruptcy were willing to invest even one dollar to save it," Rodio said, alluding to Carl Icahn who purchased the final shares of the Taj Mahal Resort Casino from Donald Trump in February.

"Currently the Taj is losing multi-millions a month, and now with this strike, we see no path to profitability," Rodio volunteered. "Unfortunately, we've reached the point where we will have to close the Taj after Labor Day weekend."

Over one thousand Local 54 union members were on strike since July 1st, pressing for full restoration of the health insurance and pension benefits that were ripped away from the casino's employees by bankruptcy court in 2014.

In a press release by the president of Local 54, Bob McDevitt, the union assigned gross mismanagement under Icahn's watch, and insinuated blame to the Trump Organization.

Roseanne L'Anse never met Carl Icahn.

"These workers stood up for what every other casino worker doing their job in this town has, and what every other casino worker here has had since gaming was introduced to Atlantic City over three decades ago,"

McDevitt said. "If this is the guy Donald Trump wants to be treasury secretary of the United States, then this country is doomed."

Atlantic City, once seen as a credible upstart competitor to Las Vegas, stumbled hard after the Great Recession of 2007-2009, combined with Las Vegas' successful family-friendly makeover and the placement of Philadelphia casinos. Unflattering reports of the city's wipeout after 2012's Hurricane Sandy damaged tourism, and any plans for subsequent casinos crashed.

On May 21, 2010, North Bergen's Martin Caballero met his only daughter, Jessica, at the Trump Taj Mahal casino in Atlantic City as part of her 22nd birthday celebration. His daughter was planning to club it with friends. Martin Caballero and his girlfriend, Libia Martinez, would stay inside the Taj. Late that evening, Martin Caballero dropped Libia Martinez off at the Taj's entrance and then parked his white Lincoln MKS in the casino's garage. Longtime criminal, Craig Arno, and Jessica Kisby, both from Egg Harbor Township, tailed Martin into the multilevel facility with the intention to carjack him. They were brazening and not too bright.

Caballero, a supermarket manager, parked his car on the garage's third floor. Arno and Kisby in Toyota trailed behind. Jessica Kisby began a conversation with Martin Caballero to distract him from the ambush.

Arno approached with a pistol and ordered Martin Caballero to climb into the Lincoln trunk. Caballero was stunned beyond words fearing that he might die. Armo then commandeered the stolen car while Kisby followed behind in the Toyota. Garage security videos taped the theft, but surprisingly not one security official saw the incident in real time. The lone watchman who was hired to secure the parking facility was thoroughly overworked and overwhelmed.

The Trump Taj Mahal had rolled back its surveillance team budget as the decade was coming to an end. In 2006, according to public documents reviewed by the press, the casino spent just under ten million dollars on security. However, by 2010 the budget was cut over thirty percent.

From police records, between 2008 and 2011, there were four murders involving events within the Taj Mahal Casino Resort. Approximately, twelve percent of the killings in Atlantic City were aligned to the Taj during a period when the other city casinos reported not one associated homicide.

Roseanne L'Anse had read a few stories about the four prostitutes' deaths in USA Today.

Journalists queried the New Jersey's Gaming Control Commission on the scandal as the speculation over Taj Mahal hotel budget cuts played a key role in these four murders. Surprisingly, the Commission wholeheartedly defended the Trump Organization. The series of murders were only part of the larger, dangerous mural at Donald Trump's flagship casino. From 2006 to 2010, there were nearly five hundred violent crimes committed inside or on the grounds of the Taj Mahal, according to court documents reviewed by news journals. In 2009, Atlantic City cops were summoned to the Taj Mahal Casino Resort an average of five times per night which was an extraordinary statistic for a Trump property.

Specific to the Taj's towering garage, records disclosed at least eight thefts over thirty-six months. Despite Taj Mahal workers testifying during court depositions that they couldn't recall detailed criminal acts; the garage was deemed sufficiently perilous to require a security staffer who wouldn't be burdened with cashier duties simultaneously.

Craig Arno drove Martin Caballero's white Lincoln into a filling station about fifteen minutes west of the Taj later that night, while Jessica kept texting his phone. The gas station attendant testified that he saw blood on the rear bumper. Kisby explained to law enforcement that the blood stains on their car came after hitting a deer.

The suspects were arrested May 28, 2010, at the Golden Key Motel in Egg Harbor Township, just outside Atlantic City. Moreover, the bodies of four murdered prostitutes were discovered behind the motel in a ditch over four years ago. The cadavers were apparently unrelated to the Arno and Kisby crime at the Taj and the women's slayings remained unsolved.

In court, it was established that Arno told Kisby to get the knife in their Toyota.

"In your mind, what was going to happen next?" the prosecutor inquired.

"Figured we were going to kill him," she replied blankly.

Martin Caballero's corpse was discovered nine days after the carjacking. The cold-blooded execution dominated the news for months in Atlantic City and Philadelphia, where Arno and Kisby were the media had christened the couple — a lowlife Bonnie and Clyde.

In April of 2008, Vincente Perez killed Arthur Prince on the boardwalk outside of the Taj Mahal after an explosive argument in the casino's poker room. In May 2009, Mark Magee murdered a Taj shift manager Raymond Kot in a game lounge off of the casino floor. It was as though the very air which circulated within the Taj casino drove people to terrifying thresholds.

Caballero's family sued for wrongful death the Taj Mahal and its parent company, Trump Entertainment Resorts Inc., and the case took years to wend through the courts before both sides decided to settle for an undisclosed sum.

Days before the 2008 stabbing death of Arthur Prince outside the casino, Donald Trump made a cameo appearance for the Chairman's Tower—a quarter billion-dollar building named after Trump. The following February, Trump resigned from the casino board of the casino. But by August, he made a bid with his daughter Ivanka to capture Trump Entertainment Resorts and pledging "to make this company great again."

Ivanka truly loved the cameras and the media attention. Some cognoscenti pinned her as the next media whore. Her father swore to the world that she was his princess.

That father/daughter bid was accepted April 2010, a month before Martin Caballero's slaying.

Trump was the powerful face of the company, making his casinos no different from the scores of other enterprises he has aligned to his name. Leasing his name equals the core business and is Trump's *raison d être*. Trump knew how to play lady luck.

Yet in the case of the Taj, that business seemed to be exercising an almost gravitational pull over the criminal set. There was the 11-hour standoff at the Taj with a gun-toting felony suspect in 2009. The arrest of a man for sexually assaulting a 13-year-old runaway there in 2010. The conviction of another man for beating a senior citizen in the garage.

After Martin Caballero's death, the Taj Mahal made security improvements, but the shoddy management remained unchanged. Sixteen months after Martin Caballero entered the Taj garage—Sunil Rattu and his girlfriend, Radia Ghetta, drove a Range Rover to the Trump casino. They went to celebrate a school graduation. When Sunil Rattu and Radia Ghetta drove into the parking structure, their Range Rover was ringed by a small gang. The couple was killed instantly by gunfire., Trump repeatedly assumed no responsibility for these harsh events and Roseanne L'Anse prayed that she would never run into Donald Trump again.

In 2013, the Taj Mahal Resort Casino opened the nation's first casino strip club, featuring exotic dancers wearing less than colorful pink ribbons.

On March 24, 2016, three teenagers dropping in at a large party in the Taj Mahal Resort Casino room on the forty-seventh floor were shot. Seven suspects were arrested in connection with the incident, which was later denoted by the police as gang related.

Almost six months after the Trump Taj Mahal Resort Casino had closed in October 2016, the Seminole Tribe of Florida through its Hard Rock International consortium put out a press release trumpeting its purchase of the casino and its planned transformation to the Hard Rock Hotel and Casino brand. The facility reopened on June 27, 2018, and Roseanne L'Anse flew to New Jersey to experience the celebration firsthand. She found the visit cathartic and yet profoundly upsetting. The Las Vegas architect was given a courtesy overnight by Hard Rock management and, in the morning, she rented a car to see her mother in Morristown.

Chapter Thirty-Seven

In late October 2018, Roseanne L'Anse flew to Pittsburgh to visit her cousin Jesenia on Jesenia's sixtieth birthday. Paradoxically, the two women were closer in middle age than during their twenties and thirties when Jesenia was living in Nevada. Jesenia married a few years later than Roseanne's marriage and often complimented Roseanne as better than a good sister. Jesenia worked as a nurse practitioner for a pediatric office in Pittsburgh's Squirrel Hill suburb. She loved helping children, no matter how fierce the health challenge.

Jesenia's two daughters left Pittsburgh permanently after finishing college. Callie, her elder daughter, became an estate and trust attorney in Hartford, Connecticut. Elaine, who recently turned thirty and completed her MBA at Wharton, was working for Goldman Sachs in Manhattan. There were no grandchildren to report but Jesenia was more than patient. Their optometrist father, Richard, retired in 2017 having growing difficulties with arthritis and Crohn's disease. Richard came from a Jewish East Coast family. Jesenia's husband needed a reliable restroom whenever they were out of the house for a few hours.

Jesenia converted to Judaism when she became engaged to Richard. Her family with Richard was members of New Light Congregation – a vibrant Jewish Conservative community in their Pittsburgh neighborhood. Roseanne tried to visit Jesenia every few years, usually in autumn or spring when the weather was conducive and pleasant.

On the fun itinerary penciled by Roseanne's cousin was the Andy Warhol Museum and the Phipps Conservatory and Botanical Gardens. Jesenia could be counted on being an energetic host. Roseanne was happy to do most anything in comfortable walking shoes. Clearly, Salsa dancing and ten-mile hikes would be low on the architect's list. Her flight back to Las Vegas was on Halloween so there would be no trick-or-treating.

Roseanne agreed graciously to accompany Jesenia and Richard to Saturday morning services at New Light Congregation. Jesenia wanted to show off the synagogue which had notable architectural attributes and was large enough to house three separate congregations on different floors. The building's early life under the Tree of Life "parent congregation" began in 1953 and aesthetically linked its clean, austere façade to Jerusalem with distinctive cream white cornerstones hewn from limestone quarried in Israel. Five years later, the congregation launched a 1,400-seat space featuring multiple, cascading stained-glass windows symbolizing Genesis and life cycle moments. Two generations afterwards, with declining membership as Jews moved to the enticing Pittsburgh suburbs, Tree of Life began renting space in its building to other emerging, affinity congregations.

In 2008, Congregation Or L'Simcha began their residency in the Tree of Life building. After two years, the two congregations coalesced to become the L'Simcha Congregation. The merger added over a hundred to Tree of Life's congregation, pushing membership to over five hundred families. Around that time, Reconstructionist Dor Hadash leased space in the Tree of Life building. Likewise in 2017, New Light, a Conservative sect, left their Pittsburgh location of sixty years to be part of Tree of Life's architectural presence.

Jesenia and Richard took Roseanne to a Chinese dinner Friday evening. The plans for the following day were to arrive at services around 9:45am and leave the synagogue for lunch at a nice French bistro before hopping over to the Warhol Museum. As fate would have it, Richard woke up later than usual and was delayed in his bathroom. They didn't leave their house until half past ten o'clock. When they drove by the synagogue, the area was cordoned off with a legion of police cars, strobe lights flashing, everywhere. The scene was pure bedlam. Single shooter Robert Bowers using an AR-15-style assault rifle had mowed down eleven Jews and injured six. The world just discovered Robert Bowers – a rabid antisemite and psychopath with a repulsive social media manifesto.

Dozens of congregants had assembled in the Tree of Life synagogue for religious services when the massacre started. At 9:50 a.m., Bowers, stocky and bearded, initiated the mass murder off the building's entrance. One floor below, the New Light Congregation congregants feared their deaths would follow immediately the slayings upstairs. Rabbi Jonathan Perlman steered them into a storage closet as a fusillade of bullets exploded upstairs. The killer entered a storage closet where several congregants hid quietly, but it was so pitch black he believed it was vacant. Bowers then abandoned the basement avoiding human contact until ascending upstairs. The police, outside, coordinated rescue strategies, and eventually exchanged horrific gunfire. SWAT teams rushed into the synagogue just after ten thirty. At 10:43 a.m., SWAT searched the basement, where they freed the traumatized holdouts of the New Light Congregation.

Bowers had retreated to the synagogue's top floor, barricading himself behind an office door. Ear-shattering firepower continued for several minutes before the gunman surrendered at 11:08 am. Several law enforcement officers were injured by Bowers' artillery.

"Suspect is crawling, he's injured, SWAT's telling him to continue to crawl at this time," a police officer radioed headquarters. "Suspect is talking about all these Jews need to die."

The Tree of Life Synagogue had been occupied by the three congregations' services when the attack commenced just before 10:00 am. News outlets soon learned that a bris – circumcision rite — was just begun when Bowers wheeled his rifle. Exclaimed the Pennsylvania Governor, "The shooter claimed innocent lives — and injured first responders — at a baby naming!"

Jesenia and Richard were shocked within such proximity of unchecked violence. Their sacred house of worship had been stormed by a psychotic lone gunman, poisoned by America's undisguised antisemites and white supremacists. How could their city fall under the spell of such unrelenting evil, they intoned the question. This was the worst attack on the Jewish community in America's history.

Had God protected Jesenia, Richard, and Roseanne? Why had God allowed Robert Bowers this day in Pittsburgh?

Had Jesenia, Richard, and Roseanne arrived at the start of Shabbat services, it would have been highly probable that Bowers would have crossed paths with them. Jesenia was undone by her tears. This was utter madness. Nightmares weren't this violent. Roseanne too was crying heavily and soon became numb, breathless, tongue-tied. This tragedy was impossible to process. Jesenia intuited that she would probably know the names and the faces of some of the victims.

Richard drove the car nervously away from the synagogue. He was speeding. His hands were shaking from the horror. They turned on the car radio for news updates.

"Oh God . . ." sputtered Richard.

"Where do we go?" said Jesenia.

"Home."

Roseanne, sitting in the car's back seat, shook her head and spotted herself in the driver's rear mirror. Her face was without color. She couldn't find words anywhere. Her heart was petrified by the hour. She began to experience the ice-cold fingers of death.

Chapter Thirty-Eight

Rex Heuermann memorized sections of the Robert Musil novel, sometimes embellishing a phrase or two:

> "His appearance gives no clue to what his work might be, and yet he doesn't look like a gentleman without a profession either. Consider what he's like: He always knows what to do. He knows how to gaze into a ladies' eyes. He can put his mind to any question at any time. He can box and he can shadow box."

On long car drives, the architect would recall such passages and think about the movie version of *The Man Without Qualities*. The idea was a joke since more than half of the book presented little or no physical action. The book was the tyranny of limitless thought. The intellectual's playpen of madness.

Rex Heuermann had a scheduled meeting late afternoon with a quirky, obnoxious developer in Rahway, New Jersey. His name was Salvador Caputo. A previous RH Consultants client from Jersey, Tony Ambrogio, had made the referral. Rex was unclear if the Caputo project would be based in New Jersey or in New York.

Ambrogio told the architect that Salvador Caputo owned extensive commercial property in Rahway near East Jersey State Prison. Ambrogio joked about Caputo's nickname, "The Corkscrew", in Italian circles.

"Hell, some hooker went down on him and saw his prick was like a pig's tail."

Caputo was on "the up and up" according to Ambrogio. The architect knew several details about the Rahway penitentiary. The medium-security complex with 1,225 inmates had been featured in many films and television shows. Its large dramatic dome was a punctuated landmark from US Route 1–9 and New Jersey Transit's North Jersey Coast Rail Line. Architect John Rochester Thomas created the original prison in 1895 on state-owned property, known as Edgar Farm. Former middleweight Rubin "Hurricane" Carter, wrongly convicted and sentenced to two life terms for murder, was incarcerated for nearly two decades at Rahway. Bob Dylan wrote a hit song about Hurricane and Denzel Washington played the boxer in the popular 1999 Hollywood film.

Rex stopped his Chevrolet Avalanche truck along US Route 1-9. He pulled up his drooping socks. He took out his Canon EOS camera and snapped photos of the prison's hubcap themed dome from several angles. He liked the design. Rex was particularly keen observing the institution's faded yellow walls, roof cones, and security towers, projecting the spirit of a European chateau on twenty-one acres. Rex had visited several prisons over the last twenty years, from Alcatraz in California to New York's Ulster Correctional Facility. He pondered the aesthetics, economics, and the practical requirements of penitentiaries, particularly as society was moving rapidly to privatization of jails from coast to coast. Private prisons were big money makers.

Sal Caputo was waiting for the architect at a corner table inside Luciano's Ristorante & Lounge on Main Street. The hour was approaching five o'clock. The restaurant was nearly empty. Caputo looked like the love child of comedienne Phyllis Diller and actor Al Lewis best known as Grandpa in 1960s TV show, *The Munsters*. Caputo was too large to be considered bird-faced, yet his avian nose defined everything about his character. His eyes were set close together, making him appear cross-eyed. Caputo wore a three-piece suit in late spring. His moustache was trimmed and crafted above his lip. He also wore a crooked smile.

Rex could guess the gentleman in waiting was his client. He approached Caputo's table. Caputo stood up. The two men shook hands with Rex squeezing a little longer than necessary.

"I just heard that the cook died. I think we got to go somewhere else."

"What?" Rex asked, tilting his head.

"I'm just joking. Sit down, Rex."

Caputo's hand slapped the architect's shoulder. Rex sat down. The architect's frame covered the table.

"Mr. Caputo . . ."

"Call me Sal."

"Hello, Sal."

"You hungry?" asked Caputo.

"Yeah, I can eat."

"I hear that your name is *The Fixer* or *The Expeditor*."

"Who said that?"

"You know, a lot of people in the Italian community."

"Well, I like the Italian community." confessed Rex.

"Paisanos are good folk."

"Yeah."

"Yeah." smiled Caputo, oozing warmth. "Do you like my necktie?"

The architect's eyes focused intently on Sal Caputo's red polka dot silk tie.

"Nice tie." said Rex Heuermann.

"My mother-in-law gave me two neckties for my birthday. When I saw her last Christmas, she made a scene at the dinner table, shouting, 'So you didn't like the other tie?'"

"I don't have a Jersey license." said Rex.

"I don't care. In Jersey it won't matter. Honest. And if things work out for us in Rahway, I got more work for you in Staten Island."

"Okay."

"You know, Rex, polka dots were symbols of supernatural potency and moral uncleanliness."

"I didn't know that, Sal."

"Interesting semiotics." declared Caputo in raw Jersey inflection displaying his elevated vocabulary. "So, I got a few Rahway buildings with twenty-six apartments. Half the apartments are vacant. Half the buildings house goddamn deadbeats. There's weird plumbing fifty years ago, and – maybe more to the point – things aren't anywhere near code. Hell, the buildings' footprint might be in violation."

"Who told you that, Sal?"

"A Jersey surveyor with a fucking eye patch."

"That's serious."

"Maybe. Maybe not. I knew the former mayor. The current mayor is a prick."

"I can't do much with a surveyor on your back." said Rex.

"I know. I just wanted you to get the full story."

"And what's in Staten Island?"

"More apartment buildings, a garage, a retail building. All need some remodeling and a little magic."

"Who recommended me, Sal?"

"Some Italian guy with a Jewish last name in Newark. Maybe Teaneck?"

"Did you go to my website?" asked the architect.

"Cohen? Goldberg? Lebovitz?"

"Who?"

"Yeah, I looked at your website, Rex. Very nice website. Nice colors."

The waiter came to the table and took their order. Both men went with the fish. Caputo ordered a fine bottle of wine. They talked in wide circles. It was getting close to seven o'clock. Rex pinned Caputo to the transaction.

"I'll send you a contract, Sal."

"Sure. Let's do that. Obviously, we have chemistry."

Rex, still hungry, reached for the bread and olive oil.

"Were you bullied as a boy?" asked Caputo.

"All kids get bullied. Big kids. Small kids."

"How old were you?"

"I don't know. Maybe when I was twelve. The year my father died. 1975."

"Did the crap stop in high school?"

"Not really. There were a few bad days. Teachers intervened in middle school, but they don't give a shit in high school."

"Any of your family or friends land in jail?"

"Why are you asking that?"

"It's no big deal. Just curious."

"My brother, Craig, served time for a DUI and for fatally running down a police captain."

"Well, that's kind of painful to hear. Thank you."

"Don't thank me."

Sal Caputo appreciated the architect's honesty and his discernible discomfort.

"If you're not busy tonight, I have two tickets to Union County Performing Arts Center's show. Tonight. Taj Mahal is singing."

"Taj Mahal?" asked Rex.

"You know that Black old timer, folk jazz guy, blues music, banjo shit."

"Yeah. Oh yeah. Taj Mahal. He's got to be over eighty."

"I can't go. So, you get the pair. Free. You don't want to drive back in rush hour."

Caputo pulled out the tickets and slid them to the architect. Rex appeared confused.

"The Center is a few miles from here. Easy. Concert's at eight."

Rex checked his phone.

"I don't know, Sal. I go to bed early."

"Drop in for forty-five minutes. Parking costs a few bucks. Make me happy."

Caputo picked up the check. The men shook hands and followed each other to the restaurant's parking lot. Again, Rex picked up his drooping socks.

Inside the decorous Union County Performing Arts Center, the lights were still bright. The crowd was at capacity. Rex found his seat midway to the stage. He was chewing gum. His feet began to hurt in these tight leather loafers. The seat to his right was empty.

In the next moment, the lights went dim with the announcement, "Ladies and gentlemen, The Taj Mahal Quartet."

He was about to see an American blues legend play guitar, piano, banjo, harmonica, and weave world music into one evening. Taj Mahal had reshaped the tone and dimension of blues over an enduring 50-year career.

Taj Mahal, Bill Rich on bass, Kester Smith on drums, and Bobby Ingano on guitar entered dancing to broad ovation. Taj Mahal cut a smooth figure in hat and blue denim jacket. He moved like an aged rock star. He acknowledged the fans with a bow and lowered his hands like an ancient priest. The Performing Arts Center had a detectable echo as the crowd settled down. Mahal welcomed everyone, saying, "This is a tune you might not know. It's a story song about a judge, a judge's wife, corn liquor, the 'perpetrator,' and a girl named Nel."

Rex removed his loafers. A young woman snaked through his row and sat next to him. She was dressed in loud colored fabrics, New Orleans beads, and tight, torn jeans. Her hair was dyed strawberry with deep purple streaks. Her perfume was unmistakably pronounced, somewhere sweet and smoky. What Rex noticed most about her were her large hoop earrings, gold nose stud, and vintage round buckle jeans belt. She pretended not to notice the architect and fell into her seat with coquettish abandon.

Rex knew that she was not sitting in her assigned seat. When she crossed her legs, she kicked Rex gently. He glanced at her, but her eyes were on Taj Mahal's band. She lit a marijuana joint after Taj Mahal's third song. Again and again, she crossed and uncrossed her legs, occasionally kicking the architect.

The concert rolled over Rex. He thought the music was very cool. People were dancing by their seats and atop their seats. The woman next to him was dancing wildly too. In the second half of the evening, Taj Mahal played high spirits with the pulsating blues number, "Queen Bee," as the audience sang the refrain, "Rock me to my soul."

"Rock me to my soul." shouted the stoned woman next to Rex.

Rex stayed late and lasted for the two-song encore. He was surprised how much he came to love Henry St. Claire Fredericks, Jr., the singer's legal name before becoming Taj Mahal.

The woman sitting next to Rex, asked him if Sal comped him that evening.

"Yes." responded the architect.

"Me too. Sal buys concert tix but never goes."

This didn't quite add up in the architect's mind. How did she know about Rex's assigned seats?

"This wasn't your ticketed seat. Did Sal tell you I was going?"

"No, Sal tells me shit."

"Do you work for him?" Rex asked as they were leaving the aisles.

"No. We met online."

"I see."

"My name's Tina. You want to get a drink?"

"No, I have to drive back to Long Island."

"Oh, come on. Buy me dinner. Don't disappoint a young girl on a lonely night."

"I'm on a diet."

"No way. You? I guessed you're a marathon runner."

She laughed at the joke. He resented the joke. A scowl swept the architect's face.

"Don't get pissed. Come on. Smile for mama. Just buy me a drink, Rex."

The architect's body became tense, brittle, electric.

"How do you know my name?"

She leaned over and gave Rex a convincing hug.

"Everyone knows your name."

"Don't toy with me."

"I'll tell Sal."

"You'll tell Sal what?"

"Bye bye, big guy."

Suddenly, she vanished from sight. Rex picked up his pace to leave the building quickly.

"The last time I saw Taj was in the 1970s." someone said walking up the stairs with a cane ahead of Rex Heuermann.

Chapter Thirty-Nine

Rex Heuermann took the day off and drove to New Jersey in an upscale rental, an Audi A5. His truck was under repair for a few days. He was listening to the Dave Brubeck Quartet and was enjoying a very elevated mood. The architect had made an appointment with the events planner at Trump National Golf Club Bedminster two weeks ago. For several years he had a hankering to tour the estate. His pretense for the visit was to secure a wedding setting for his daughter Victoria. He had rehearsed in his head how the session should proceed. He viewed himself as an actor on location. The architect wanted to explore the five-thousand-foot ballroom adorned with floor to ceiling windows, the expansive exterior grounds, the clubhouse, the overnight suites, cottages, and the final resting grounds for Ivana Trump.

He felt compelled to see the isolated grave behind the first golf hole, allegedly the only burial on the Bedminster estate. This was certainly a fascination for the architect although he wasn't a golfer and, to the best of his knowledge, the architect wasn't a closet necrophiliac. More to the point, Rex Heuermann was always fixated on how infamous property owners maneuvered around zoning ordinances. Because this was late summer, a month after Trump's first wife was buried at Bedminster, there was a remote chance that he might even cross paths with the former president. It was widely known that Trump preferred Bedminster to Mar-a-Largo from June to September.

The estate, located just off Interstate 78, was about forty-five miles west of New York City. Traffic was not bad once Rex Heuermann passed Newark. He called ahead to say that he might arrive on the early side. He heard back that would be fine. The architect was in business suit attire and wore his most expensive tie, his lucky tie. A few days earlier he had his hair cut neatly which always improved his look.

After identifying himself at the security checkpoint and his appointment confirmed, he was signaled by the attendant to drive into the compound. The architect felt a noticeable tingle in his hands and along his thick neck. He was perspiring despite the car's air conditioner set at maximum cold. Before he left his car, Rex Heuermann straightened his tie using his rear-view mirror.

He walked past a few Bedminster guests leaving their cars. One younger man with gingerbread complexion and sporting a designer golf shirt had his tennis racket and can of balls under one arm. He glanced at Rex Heuermann from a safe distance and registered clear disapproval of Rex Heuermann's near obesity despite the architect's commanding height. The architect gave the stranger a thumbs up salute, dagger eyes, and a gargantuan insincere smile.

The architect was met at the lobby and was escorted through lavish corridors to a discreet sales office. The event planner would be with him shortly, so he was told. He was handed a cold-water bottle that had the Trump logo. Ten minutes later, a stunning redhead in a simple black dress approached his chair. She studied Rex as though he were a luxury cruise line stowaway and offered him her hand.

"Good afternoon, Mr. Heuermann. I'm Cheryl Downing. One of the event planners at Bedminster."

He accepted her hand and rose to his feet. He towered over her.

"Nice to meet you, Ms. Downing. It's exciting to be here."

"Yes." she repeated the thought. "Bedminster is unlike any other estate in the tristate region."

She pointed in the direction of her private office. He walked a few steps ahead of her. The events planner trailed behind until they arrived at her open door. She then passed Rex and entered her room. There was an impressive cherry wood desk and lined bookshelves, but the events planner led Rex Heuerman to a small conference table with four chairs.

"Please have a seat, Mr. Heuermann."

"Thank you."

Rex Heuermann sat in close syncopation with Cheryl Downing.

"Would you like coffee or a cold bottle of water?" she asked.

"No, thank you."

"Congratulations on your daughter's engagement."

"Thank you."

The architect chided himself for sounding repetitive like a trained parrot.

"Victoria?"

"Yes, Victoria. She'll be twenty-six, but I still see her as a teenager."

"You live on Long Island, Mr. Heuermann?"

"That's correct. Massapequa Park. My office's in Manhattan."

"Do you have family in New Jersey?"

"Why do you ask?"

"We always ask our patrons."

She smiled wanly.

"Just a second cousin."

"Is your daughter's fiancé from New Jersey?"

"Yes. Short Hills."

"And his name?"

"I knew that you would ask that."

"Yes?"

"Robert Woodhouse Jr."

She texted quickly to a colleague as Rex took out his wallet. The architect handed the events planner his business card which she accepted without studying it.

"In reviewing your online inquiry, it seems the wedding is eighteen months away."

"At the very least, that is correct. The kids are in no hurry."

"Well, that does give us some flexibility, Mr. Heuermann. Avoiding summer months will help both you and Bedminster. Fees fall considerably during the winter and early spring. February is wide open."

"That's great, Ms. Downing. Black history month."

She smiled rapidly.

"Please call me Cheryl."

"Cheryl."

"Not to be terribly direct but let me give you an approximate scale of costs and particulars."

"Please do."

"Off season, we are looking at eight hundred dollars per person, one hundred thousand dollars for one hundred and twenty-five guests which is our minimum figure even if you are holding an intimate occasion for one hundred guests."

"Sounds quite fine, Cheryl."

"The Trump deluxe package includes eight passed hors d'oeuvres; a choice of three stations with options such as sushi, antipasto, chilled seafood, and a splendid dish called Woks of Fire; and a five-course dinner with three entrée option. For an additional forty dollars per person, guests can have sliders and buffalo wings. Also not included in the cost: *Trump's old-fashioned*, an eighteen-dollar cocktail made with the drinker's choice of whiskey, brown sugar, orange bitters and Angostura."

"And for the vegetarians?"

"One of the entrées will cover that subset."

"And for those who are kosher?"

Her eyes narrowed.

"I'm joking, Cheryl."

"Oh."

"How much do I need to put down to hold the date?"

"Twenty percent of the contract. It's non-refundable."

"Of course."

"If you pay in full today, we can include gratis *Trump's old-fashioned*."

"Honestly, I never pay in full when I enter into a contract. I hope that's okay."

"Yes, naturally."

"Thank you, Cheryl."

"Bedminster customizes your entire day to create the most unique experience that you've dreamed of! Our ballroom is second to none, French door access the countryside, crystal chandeliers, gold chivari chairs, towering ceilings. Lush acreage and beautiful historic architecture as your daughter's wedding backdrop, luxurious on-site overnight accommodations, and our complete attention with only one wedding at a time."

"I've seen in the news that President Trump occasionally crashes wedding events."

"Yes, that does happen once in a blue moon. The guests love when he pops in."

"With secret service men at his heels, no doubt."

"No doubt, Mr. Heuermann."

"And the president likes to make toasts to the bride and groom."

"Yes, that's his charm."

After a disquieting silence, the events planner said, "Bedminster Township is known for large estates, tasteful affluence, and exclusive clubs. In addition to our Trump National Golf Club, Bedminster boasts two other prestigious venues: Fiddler's Elbow Country Club and Hamilton Farm Golf Club. You might wish to compare prices and value."

"Thank you, Cheryl."

"Do you have other questions for us?"

"I wanted to say, and this probably sounds odd, but I once was hired by the Trump Organization to renovate The Trump Building on 40 Wall Street."

"Really?"

"Yes, but not the entire structure. Just the 17th floor."

"When was that?"

"About four years ago. I mostly dealt with Eric Trump, but I also met his brother."

"How lucky for you, Mr. Heuermann."

"In the final stages of the renovation, the Trump Organization began to withhold fees to my company, and I ended up eating some losses. But I love MAGA, and I don't feel that bad about getting stiffed. That happens in my profession all too much."

Cheryl Downing projected a quizzical expression and then directed her eyes to her iPhone which pinged with an incoming text. She read the text.

"I wonder if you could adjust the one hundred thousand minimum in light of my association with the Trump Organization?"

"I don't think we can do that, Mr. Heuermann."

"I would guess that you gave allowances to other patrons."

"No, that's not what we do at Bedminster."

"Is it because you don't like me?"

"Liking you has little to do with our standards of consistency."

"Can you ask your supervisor please?"

"Mr. Heuermann . . ."

"Please, just ask your supervisor and show him my business card."

He handed her the card gently. She accepted it without looking and pretended to smile.

"Certainly."

"Thank you." he replied looking at his wristwatch.

"You're very welcome, Mr. Heuermann." She paused awkwardly and turned her phone over delicately. She then pressed a hidden button under the conference table.

"I wonder, you know, how your wedding guests feel about Ivana's burial a stone's throw from the wedding rotunda. Well, I would love a tour of the grounds."

"We usually do that once a deposit is received."

"You have my business card, Cheryl."

"Mr. Heuermann, there is no Robert Woodhouse Jr. in Short Hills or anywhere in New Jersey . . . unless he lives with his parents?"

"That's exactly right. He lives with his parents, having returned from a short career in London."

"I have to attend to another client, Mr. Heuermann. Thank you for coming in today and do call me when you're ready to place a deposit on that date in February."

She rose slowly and signaled to two tall men in black suits at her door.

"I can also give myself a self-guided tour of the clubhouse, gardens, and ballroom, Cheryl."

"Mr. Heuermann, these men will show you the ballroom on your way to the parking lot."

She extended her hand to Rex. He shook her hand with a firm grip and waited an extra moment before letting go. The events planner felt frightened at the menacing sensation of the architect's throttlehold.

Chapter Forty

Upon exiting the club's parking lot, Rex Heuermann drove in a slow, circuitous route to get views of Trump's Bedminster compound from various points, first within the estate's egress road. The architect took delight in slowing his pace as though he were on vacation. He was quite impressed with the estate's serene layout and serenity. When he was far beyond the sightlines from the security checkpoints and the main building along the county road, he was comfortable stopping to take photos with his phone. The architect felt very important. There was no hurry to drive back to Manhattan or home to Long Island. He had no appointments and no urgent work assignments. The Audi sedan was due back at Massapequa Park's Enterprise Rental the next morning.

The photos were souvenirs and yet they energized him as a faux architectural landscape researcher. He had other interesting points of contact with Trump's world, primarily in Manhattan where he toured several Trump properties. He was an overnight guest at Trump Hotel and Tower in Chicago during the American Institute of Architects National Convention and Design Expo in 2015. He almost had a contract to do a small job at the sixty-eight stories Trump Tower on Fifth Avenue but lost out on the final round of bids.

He even watched a year of *The Apprentice.* Nonetheless, the Bedminster grounds fascinating Rex. An elite championship thirty-six-hole golf course and luxury events manor were now even more multipurpose and mysterious — a personal cemetery for an ex-wife from the Czech Republic. He wanted a photo of the ex-president's ex-wife's grave. He teased himself thinking Ivana Trump was a marauding ghost, with the chic European accent, who haunted northern New Jersey.

In the distance, Rex noticed a red Lexus sedan awkwardly parked on the road's shoulder. He slowed upon approaching and saw a woman talking on her phone. She seemed distressed. Rex pulled behind her car and got out of his Audi. She eyed him suddenly. She too was an architect. Roseanne L'Anse was on her way to pick up one of her colleagues, the chief legal officer at Steelman Partners, who was at Bedminster for a golf event.

"Everything okay? Need some help?" he said as friendly as possible.

"It's a flat. Someone's coming." she said.

"Because I can fix a flat in three minutes."

Rex smiled and removed his suit jacket in a casual motion.

"Did you call AAA? They take an hour to arrive, no matter what the dispatcher says."

"I called Avis. It's a rental."

Roseanne L'Anse studied Rex Heuermann's build. He was a massive linebacker. He held his smile. She was in a pink summer dress which covered her shoulders. Roseanne's hair was much shorter than her years on the Trump Taj casino project. At an age that suggested retirement, she was content showing grey hair in a pixie cut and less eye makeup. She was still trim and athletic. Divorced over a dozen years, Roseanne adjusted her professional appearance to accentuate her attractive features and yet maintain a measure of understatement.

"I just came from Trump's club." said Rex, sensing her discomfort.

"Oh, really." she responded, her attention back on her phone. Her thumbs moving rapidly over the phone's keyboard.

"My daughter's getting married at Bedminster next year." He waited for a reply but there was just a cold stare from her. Rex Heuermann coughed to clear his throat.

"She's so young for a wedding but all fathers have trouble letting go."

"Congratulations." she blurted out avoiding eye contact.

"Well, Avis might be faster than AAA. I can drive you to Bedminster's clubhouse."

"No, really. I'm fine. You can go. Thank you."

Rex threw his jacket over his shoulder like the famous Frank Sinatra album cover and pivoted nonchalantly. He stumbled on the loose gravel and laughed to himself. The architect turned back; his head larger than a pumpkin.

"You see, I'm an architect with two left feet."

"An architect?" she replied without thinking.

"Yeah, I'm a licensed New York architect. I troubleshoot, because who knows what the person before you did?"

Rex opened the Audi door and climbed inside. He started the engine, rolling down his window and the passenger's side window. Using his phone through Bluetooth, he played Stan Getz's *Take Five*. The Audi did not move. Roseanne returned to the driver's seat of her Lexus and locked her doors. She turned on the air conditioning and kept her eyes on the rear-view mirror. She wrote down the Audi's license plate number. He waited a few more minutes until he saw the Avis service truck arrive.

Roseanne was relieved to see Rex Heuermann drive away. She spotted subtle twitching of Rex Heuermann's fingers. She didn't like the movement of his eyes. She assessed a mountain of cruelty behind those eyes.

The Avis serviceman changed her tire and then she drove another mile to Trump National Golf Course. The chief legal counsel was waiting for her at the cocktail lounge. She had a personal nickname for him, Skip. Sometimes she stamped people with secret nicknames. The Steelman Partners attorney was extraordinarily deft with cutting corners and jumping steps. Even his golf game was aided and abetted by a deliberate driver slice on long dogleg fairways. Or she called him Skipper as he sailed Lake Mead throughout the year. Skip tried to talk Roseanne out of moving to New Jersey a year before her retirement. He enjoyed her company whenever they travelled to the East Coast.

Roseanne told Skip and all the senior partners at Steelman that moving her mother into assisted living was a non-starter and her mother refused to live in Las Vegas. Roseanne preferred moving into her mother's three-bedroom house in Morristown. Nevada was the architect's personal history to discard. Relocating east made clean breaks easy.

"Retirement is just death with unbearable consciousness," joked Skip, "while death is retirement without any benefits."

Skip ordered a martini for Roseanne. He was nursing his scotch neat chased by a glass of Perrier on ice. There were also plates of stuffed grape leaves and garlic hummus on the table.

"How was golf today?" she asked.

"Great. Can't complain. Had a birdie on the front nine without cheating." said Skip.

"Was Trump playing?"

"Yes."

"Was he in a good mood?"

"I can't tell anymore, Roseanne. His humor has turned nasty."

"Did you check out yet?"

"Yes. My luggage and golf clubs are ready to go."

"The meeting at the Marriott was pushed to four o'clock."

"Oh, really." said Skip.

"We have ample time to grab a quick dinner and see *Wicked*."

"Oh fuck, not another Broadway musical."

"You said you would go."

"I was drunk."

"Yes, you were."

"Eight o'clock curtain?"

"Yeah." said Roseanne.

"Sorry you had car trouble."

"Avis came right away. But there was a creep who tried playing Good Samaritan."

Skip laughed with characteristic charm, saying, "there aren't any Good Samaritans in this time zone."

Roseanne enjoyed her martini. Skip signed the check. They left the lounge and decided to stroll outside to see the gardens. There were several clusters of guests and golfers milling about the grounds. Birds were singing. Not too distant from Roseanne and Skip was a small entourage around Donald Trump. Roseanne took notice.

"You've met him before?" asked Skip.

"Yes, once or twice at Christmas parties."

"Years ago?"

"Decades ago." she replied.

"I could never vote for him, but I do admire his unyielding will power."

Roseanne gave Skip a scrutinizing scowl, which he thought was endearing.

"I never voted for him, Roseanne."

"But you golf at his clubs?"

"Strictly for business networking, for our company's diplomacy. Try the stuffed grape leaves. Delicious."

While Roseanne and Skip were finishing their drinks, the group following Trump gravitated to Skip's corner of the lounge in pursuit of

Trump while he meandered. It was like an errant queen bee detouring from the hive. Skip rose and greeted the ex-president. Reluctantly, Roseanne stood and lit up with a manufactured smile. There was a photographer taking group shots, paces behind Trump and a secret service detail.

After Donald Trump shook Skip's hand, Skip introduced himself and then introduced Roseanne as one of the principal architects to the Taj Mahal Casino Hotel.

"You look familiar." said the ex-president to Roseanne.

"Yes, we met several times." she replied.

"Oh, really? When?"

"I was a consulting architect for Foxwoods Resort Casino in Connecticut, which you had opposed in 1993 because of the tribal questions you had raised to Congress. But we met more regularly in Atlantic City when the Taj Casino was in mid-completion. And you came to our Las Vegas office Christmas parties in the late 1980s."

Donald Trump was torn between following up with another question or simply turning away to find a friendlier Bedminster visitor.

"I never opposed Foxwoods." he declared.

"Maybe my memory is slipping, Mr. President." she offered softly.

"Yes, I think your memory is slipping."

One of the secret service agents stepped closer, checking his wristwatch.

"You also handed me a cocktail at the Christmas party."

"You must have been a beautiful younger woman back then." Trump confessed thinking this was a solid compliment. He pulled his hands apart as though playing an invisible accordion.

"Yes, I probably looked like E. Jean Carroll's younger sister."

Donald Trump turned abruptly, gave a crude laugh, and reeled in another Bedminster guest.

Chapter Forty-One

Roseanne and Skip checked into Marriott Courtyard just off Fifth Avenue and steps away from the central branch of New York Public Library, nestled in Bryant Park. They had adjoining rooms on the seventh floor. Their business meeting was a few blocks away. Skip was in a buoyant mood and regaled her with quick, political jokes. Some were quite humorous, particularly about the Squad – the four young progressive Congresswomen led by New York's charismatic, self-assured Alexandria Ocasio-Cortez.

The lawyer had enough dexterity to mock social justice warriors while maintaining a convincing humanitarian posture. His barbed jokes were aimed mostly at the so-called naïve solipsism of Generation Y and Generation Z. He ridiculed the sweeping tide of Cancel Culture on the left and on the right. Roseanne L'Anse was diplomatic laughing when the punch lines arrived. Her manner of returning conversational entertainment was discreetly pointing out strangers and predicting aloud what unimaginable bed clothing was worn away from prying eyes. Half the time she turned everyone into a dominatrix or a sex slave.

Roseanne and Skip went to a small Thai restaurant that was a few blocks to the Gershwin Theatre, home to thrice Tony Awarded musical *Wicked*.

They loved the show. They adored the witches. They found renewed sympathy for Elphaba, a misunderstood, savvy girl with emerald-green skin, who eventually became the hated Wicked Witch of the West.

There was a mandatory nightcap at Joe Allen Tavern, loved by the acting community before and after a Broadway performance. They spotted a few thespian celebrities nearby – Christine Baranski, Martin Short, and someone who resembled Harvey Fierstein after a starvation diet.

The next morning, Skip left quite early for a return flight.

Roseanne had another day in Manhattan planned and would join her mother in Morristown that evening. She assured her mother that Morristown was a high priority for Roseanne and that there would be no last-minute postponement. Still, she was taking personal time. Roseanne L'Anse was an architect at a turning point. She suffered a sharp loneliness. She stopped loving her art and loving herself. This wasn't a mid-life crisis. She was well into the often-touted golden years and yet the "sensible rebel" inside her was forcefully resisting acknowledging the fact of age.

She had the hotel store her luggage upon checking out of her room. After her hotel breakfast, she planned to meet an interior designer friend, Vimi Patel, at the Morgan Library and Museum at Madison Avenue. Vimi Patel, a strikingly beautiful woman, was about twenty years younger than Roseanne. They had worked together on several projects.

When Roseanne arrived, Vimi Patel was in the Morgan Library lobby holding a pair of admission tickets. The two women briefly hugged. The lobby was uncrowded and quiet.

The current exhibits celebrated "One Hundred Years of James Joyce's *Ulysses*", the photography of Ray Johnson — "New York's most famous unknown artist", and "Dawn till Dusk: Studies of Light in Marine Sketches" — nineteenth century Europe plein air painting.

Roseanne felt very relaxed with Vimi, who was an attentive listener with an unassuming, receptive personality. They were compatible in giving sufficient time to the exhibitions on each floor. Vimi was curious about Roseanne's short visit to Bedminster.

"You don't know our chief legal counsel." stated Roseanne.

"No."

"Very low handicap golfer and a major GOP contributor."

"A friend of Trump's?" asked Vimi.

"At best, an acquaintance dating back to the 1990s."

"Was he there?

"Trump?" said Roseanne flatly.

Vimi shook her head comically with her dark brown eyes enlarged.

"Yeah, Donald Trump was there."

"Did you meet him?"

"No." she lied.

"I've a theory that he made a pact with the devil. A Faustian contract. That's how he flies his kite so fucking high, Roseanne. That's how he seems untouchable from prosecution."

"Yeah, maybe so."

They had one last gallery floor to visit.

"Have you dinner plans?" Vimi asked.

"No."

"Do you like exotic foods?"

"Sure."

"Ethiopian?"

"Do you have to eat with your hands, Vimi?"

Vimi laughed and nodded in the affirmative. She reached out and touched Roseanne's arm affectionately. They hailed a cab and headed to

Queen of Sheba, Tenth Avenue near 46th Street. The restaurant was tiny, with an exposed brick wall and an open bar. The establishment was on the ground floor of a residential four-story apartment house. There was one open table for Vimi and Roseanne. After ordering food, Vimi asked Roseanne, "Did you ever read Doctorow's *Ragtime*?"

"No. But I did see the movie."

"There's a climactic scene when a Black musician Coalhouse Walker and his buddies storm the Morgan Library, holding the treasured collection hostage and threatening to blow up the building."

"James Cagney played the fire commissioner."

Roseanne's attention was rivetted by Vimi's delicate fingers dancing on the tablecloth. Vimi's hands and her wrists were so slender. Vimi talked with animation and Roseanne found her beautiful. Roseanne realized that she was craving intimacy with Vimi.

When the entrees were served, Roseanne barely touched her plate. She was focused on Vimi's fingers lifting the food to her mouth. Vimi began with injera homemade bread, swabbing from her plate tibs wot, menchet abesh wot, bozena shiro, yebeg alecha, doro wot, gomen wot and ater kik alecha. Roseanne had ordered a skewered beef plate with vegetables and asked for a knife and fork.

Vimi's warm radiance was intoxicating to Roseanne. Her complexion changed indoors to a rich dusky tan and had notable nuances with the lighting from lamps or windows. Vimi's expressive eyes were dark and deep, accentuated by long, thick lashes. She gave Roseanne a delectable calm.

Vimi had a remarkable resemblance to Saanvi Aashi Karim.

The centuries of time ribboned together in a sweeping knot, measured history which closes and returns to the starting point despite time moving forward. This resemblance was not proof of reincarnation, but evidence of immutable identity.

Vimi touched Roseanne's hand after the meal was finished. "Come to my hotel room."

Chapter Forty-Two

Vimi had booked several nights at a highly recommended boutique hotel in Gramercy Park on East 31st Street. The Arlo NoMad was within walking distance to the Empire State Building. Vimi and Roseanne had beverages in the hotel bar. It seemed that the drinking lounge was populated by a young, boisterous crowd, perhaps half were gay. The pulsating dance music was a few decibels higher than a civilized setting in Roseanne L'Anse's professional judgment. The first thing she said to Vimi after they ordered drinks was that the lounge might be a tad too rowdy.

Clearly, the reserve mood had transformed significantly from the cultured afternoon at the Morgan Library and Museum. The alcohol was softening Roseanne to a zone of laxed permission and unchartered adventure. She seemed hypnotized by Vimi's black onyx eyes. They grazed one another's hands while talking quietly. Their interest was mutual and had a wild frisson spark. Vimi asked Roseanne about her week's work schedule.

"I've no more work appointments." she relayed to Vimi.

"Where is your luggage?"

"Checked at the Marriott. I have to see my mother in New Jersey."

"That's nice of you."

"I owe her a visit. It's been some time since."

"How old is she?"

"She'll be eighty-six in two months."

"You're driving there?"

"Yeah."

Vimi smiled serenely. Roseanne forgot her age. They finished their martinis. Vimi signed the check to her room and left a five-dollar gratuity. The neck tattooed bartender bid the ladies a good night and winked at Vimi.

Outside Vimi's hotel room, Roseanne suddenly became very frightened and self-conscious. Nervously, she searched for her phone and then held it awkwardly in her gaze.

"Someone texting you?" Vimi asked.

"No."

"Put the phone away, angel."

No one ever called her angel. Roseanne's face was inches away from Vimi's.

"Sometimes my mother sends me email."

Vimi leaned in and kissed Roseanne. Their lips were moist. The two women became aroused.

"Sometimes I send her email as a response." whispered Roseanne.

Vimi slipped her tongue into Roseanne's mouth, and Vimi's hand reached for Roseanne's. In Vimi's other hand was the hotel room's key card. Vimi managed to open the door without looking. Vimi ended the kiss but kept her eyes on Roseanne's open mouth.

"You taste like a dry martini." she told Roseanne.

"Do I?"

"Vermouth and London dry-style gin."

Vimi pushed the door open halfway, and then kicked the door a bit wider. They entered the room as though performing a rehearsed dance step. A heavyset businessman carrying an attaché walked by and saw the women kissing once more as the suite's door slowly shut.

"How often do you see your mother?"

"I try several times a year." said Roseanne. "But work always had a way of derailing a planned visit."

Vimi ran her fingers through Roseanne's short hair.

"Are you nervous?" asked Vimi.

"About seeing my mom?"

"No, about being in my room."

"Yeah, maybe a little."

"Don't be."

Vimi kissed Roseanne lightly on the neck. The sensation of her heavy, full lips on Roseanne's skin transported the architect from reality to an unknown region. She left the earth. Roseanne felt weightless. This is what astronauts must feel outside earth's gravity. A world apart embraced her. She imagined her spatial position centering within a commanding marble white forecourt, a short distance from a monumental gate of inlaid, decorated red sandstone. She felt symmetry and antiquity. There was cool moonlight and dramatic shadow. She sensed that she stood steps away from a sublime channel of incandescent water which led through the gates of time. She felt a warm breeze on her exposed legs and her abdomen tingled with quiet excitement.

"Where are you?" Vimi whispered into Roseanne's ear.

"I'm with you. I'm in your hotel room."

"Open your eyes, Roseanne."

Roseanne's eyes widened and met Vimi's eyes. Roseanne was crying.

"I saw architecture." she explained to Vimi.

They kissed delicately, maybe awkwardly.

"Stay in the room with me." Vimi instructed patiently.

"There was thick smoke from incense. I saw an imaginary palace."

"That's so sweet. But come back to New York."

"Okay. Okay. I'm back in New York."

Vimi led Roseanne to the edge of the hotel bed. They both sat down.

"Take off your shoes."

Roseanne did what Vimi suggested. She kicked off her left shoe, then the right. Vimi unbuttoned Roseanne's blouse. She fingered Roseanne's slender gold necklace. Vimi pursed her lips and hummed a simple melody. This pleased Roseanne. Vimi leaned in and kissed Roseanne's lips. Roseanne's phone rang but the call was ignored. The women clasped each other's hands. The electric sensation in Roseanne's hands was palpable. Roseanne's pleasure mixed with a traceable thread of guilt. Naming the guilt was not possible. Vimi paid no attention to Roseanne's guilt. The thread of guilt soon vanished.

The heavy linen bed covers were removed. Vimi drew the curtains to lessen the window glare and engineer a degree of privacy. She then removed her V-neck cashmere sweater. Vimi had no bra. Vimi then unfastened Roseanne's bra. The two women embraced tenderly. Their bodies spilled onto the queen size mattress. Roseanne uttered a soft sigh. Vimi asserted her movements like a graceful dance. What followed was the longest kiss Roseanne had ever experienced.

More clothes were removed. They were naked.

"Roseanne."

"Yes?"

"Roseanne."

Vimi brought her hand between Roseanne's thighs.

There was a knock at the door.

"Housekeeping." said the unseen hotel staffer.

"Not now. Thank you." exclaimed Vimi.

The door opened part way, slowly. Vimi jumped out of bed and slammed the door shut.

"Come back in a couple of hours." shouted Vimi.

She returned to Roseanne.

"Sometimes I think no one can hear my voice." she told Roseanne.

Roseanne quivered as Vimi's hand went higher than before. With her eyes shut, Roseanne again found herself transported to a marble white forecourt. There was a scent of night-blooming jasmine. There were faint sounds of finger cymbals or ornamental bells. She saw the glitter of gold and the vibrations of brass instruments. It was as though Roseanne had been stimulated by a hallucinogen. She resisted the temptation to tell Vimi about these sensations, lest Vimi judge Roseanne's sanity.

Vimi brought her open mouth to Roseanne's waistline and tongued her summer tan line. Roseanne dropped her arms, moaned, while her wrists went limp. In a few moments they were making love despite Roseanne's sudden languor. The elephant-headed Hindu God of beginnings and embarkments appeared to the Las Vegas architect. Ganesh, often worshipped before grand enterprise, was the proctor of intellectuals, artists, and authors. Why was an elephant's trunk in this hotel bed?

Roseanne gazed below her breasts and abdomen. She no longer recognized her own body. She studied Vimi's head from this unusual angle, which was equally erotic and awkward. She imagined Vimi's long flowing hair move like ocean kelp, undulating rhythmically. Vimi's perspiration was intoxicating like exotic perfume. The silhouette of Ganesh vanished in synch with the percussive sounds like rain on a tin roof. When Vimi crept up to Roseanne's face, they kissed again and suddenly Roseanne felt a tender bite on her neck.

Chapter Forty-Three

In late September 2022, Rex Heuermann was contacted by Antoine Amira. Amira ran a popular YouTube channel devoted to quirky urban profiles from New York's five boroughs. Amira, who seemed to be a jovial, half-intoxicated Frenchman in love with Manhattan's jovial side, made several phone calls to RH Consultants and emailed the architect a few links to Antoine Amira's previous video interviews.

Amira fawned over many of his guests, flirted with others employing effeminate ironies and soft ball questions. Rex watched the YouTube interviews. He researched Antoine Amira online. There was nothing negative to glean. Amira was a legitimate professional with a traceable video channel and several thousand YouTube subscribers. On first viewing, Antoine Amira looked like a gay, cooking show co-host. Amira seemed to get through life by expansive Madison Avenue facials weekly and Norman Vincent Peale positivism daily.

In short, the architect was flattered by the invitation and agreed to participate.

They set a convenient date. The first Thursday in October. No questions were sent in advance to the owner of RH Consultants in order to keep an air of improvisational fun. It rained heavily that afternoon.

Bespeckled Antoine Amira wore a thick, colorful scarf around his neck. Amira was slightly smaller than most men, but next to Rex Heuermann he looked like a growing adolescent in knickers. Worse, he personified an elf on a large expensive account. Amira had a crew member handle the camera, the microphone, and tripod. She looked like a college intern and kept silent.

"Bonjour Realty," declared Amira to the camera, "is a celebration of New York City and its people. We're going to show the most amazing city on Earth thanks to who we are and what this city is about. Every Tuesday, we will go further than any other real estate agent in our lunchtime *L'Interview*. We aren't just showing apartments, but the closest, charming bodega, the best twenty-four-hour laundromat, the cheapest cup of coffee. I am Antoine Amira and I promise you that we will find all the wonderful perks that make New York City heaven on earth.

Every Thursday, Bonjour Realty interviews extraordinary guests - from real estate agents to subway performers. These interviews will be like no other, NYC is the world's most perfect stage."

Amira's assistant signaled that his sound levels were good. Amira and the young woman were inside RH Consultant's Manhattan office. It felt as though the architect was looming over them.

"Hello, Rex. How are you doing? I brought my assistant with me. I hope you don't mind."

"No, I don't mind. I see it's raining."

"Yeah."

"Yeah." said the architect.

"Yeah."

"You said you like to do this outside but Mother Nature's not cooperating today."

"Ha, ha. Let's dive in." laughed Amira, adjusting his scarf.

"I wasn't looking forward to doing this under a wood scaffold and pigeon shit."

The two men sat at the architect's desk.

"So, please tell us, who you are."

"I'm an architect." pronounced Rex Heuermann with pride.

"But you're not a typical architect. Could you explain to our audience what you do? Not the design part of your business, but your role as a *facilitator*."

"I do architectural troubleshooting and all sorts of negotiations with the city building department. We do standard stuff, handling filings, petitions for exceptions. I have other clients who are architects, and my firm handles their interactions with the city. We do a big business with out-of-city architects because they're afraid of the city officials."

Rex Heuermann employed his bulky hands with genuine animation.

"When a job that should have been routine suddenly becomes not routine. Yeah, so I get a phone call. Whether it's an old building or they need somebody to maneuver the 1938 building code. You look surprised when I say the 1938 code."

"I am surprised." gushed Amira, as the added office lamps bounced light from his glasses.

"People don't always understand when it comes to building codes. It's like Latin or Greek. They never read the administrative sections. I accidentally landed into this niche. Really. It was mostly due to my first job in 1987, working for architect Harvey Rothenberg, on Spring Street. In that year, a new law came out regarding handicap access and Rothenberg worked for several non-profit agencies.

"Go on, please."

"The architectural firm told me to go meet with the city and I did. I was effective with city bureaucrats. So, Harvey Rothenberg said, go do it again. And that's how the whole thing started with the developmentally disabled. That's where I cultivated my building code skills along with my design work and drawings. And the one thing I learned quickly was the building department could not understand their own codes. They were fucking idiots, excuse my French."

Amira laughed and whispered to Rex to tone down the expletives. Rex nodded.

"They're overwhelmed by the size and the complexity of the building department. And whether it's a restaurant, a place of assembly, a 40,000 square foot retail space or a someone's co-op with twenty-year-old application pre-dating personal computers, I'm the guy to solve your headache."

"You're brilliant, Rex Heuermann. Bonjour Realty hasn't yet met a man of your talents."

The architect flashed a neon smile revealing most of his amber teeth.

"Often the problems that arose didn't fit the code book situations and the planning examiners working for the building department were just flat dumb about this. So, part of my job became educating the city. That takes a lot of diplomacy and patience."

"I bet." smiled Amira.

"I'd tell the examiners that there were limitations to their own archaic codes and, therefore, workarounds were absolutely essential. I was the one-eye guy in the land of the blind."

"Yes, brilliant. Great metaphor."

"And it was soon time to start my own firm. This was the early 1990s. Sometimes computers solved regulation problems and sometimes they created them. I could pivot between antiquated paperwork and computer software. I had everything committed to memory."

Amira motioned to his assistant to come in with a new angle on the architect's face.

"Most architects will go to an outside consultant, *an expediter*, and beg for a minor miracle. And I'm that guy. I go to the city desks and prove that I get all the administrative procedures, all the crazy codicils, and I always remind the city that I have a license to practice architecture. I tell the city how I feel and what I think they should do. And the city gets on board because the department grunts trust me completely.

"I think this is so interesting about your dual roles," Amira insisted, "because you can build things and you can make formal petitions work like fairy godmother gold dust."

"Let me also say that I still dream of being the architect of total innovation."

"Yes, of course."

"You don't understand."

"I don't?"

"You don't. An architect competes with God. We build large. We don't build small."

"Yes, of course."

"I always wanted to visit South Korean. The nation has been underappreciated regarding its architectural advances. I've seen ample design power and innovation in their culture's design ambitions with their historical identity. Their contemporary architecture is efficient, confident, and brash."

Amira intuited that the architect was on a lost tangent, but Amira was wrong.

"South Korea, in my view, has made jumps in two key aspects: middle class residential and commercial high rises with or without retail. Both modalities are closely aligned to Korea's key attributes. Individuality, social bearing, and a deep respect for tradition. A popular Korean design element pays homage to the traditional Korean home, Hanok, while gracing the building with a very modern attitude. There's a new, cascading Korean market—young professionals desiring to acquire the best of western culture without trashing their Asian heritage. South Korean residential structures ranges from intimate infill homes to dwellings with gargantuan spaces. These new homes blend traditional features — interior patios, reflecting the spirit of inner plazas found in Madang, which is traditional Korean aesthetics, with flawless contemporary lines beyond simplicity. Sometimes the reverse is true, traditional aesthetics counterpoising intricate, conceptual statements."

"Your sophistication comes naturally to you, my friend." slathered Amira.

"I believe that as we go through life, we are permitted to see unusual patterns which on first glance appear incongruent and lack meaning. Sometimes these are coincidences of events. But despite the leap of time, the span of geography, these odd patterns link and define a powerful concept. My architectural journal has benefitted greatly by the patterns of personal destiny."

Amira, suddenly bored, looked at his wristwatch and coughed softly.

"Alright, my last question Mr. Heuermann. If you were a tool or an object to help your craft become even more spectacular, what tool would you be?"

"That's an interesting question. I know because I do have many tools in my toolbox. One of the things I learned from my father was furniture building. He was an aerospace engineer who built satellites and had time to build furniture at home. In fact, I still build stuff in the same family workshop. I inherited my father's house on Long Island. So, I have one tool that's pretty much used on every job and it's actually a cabinet maker's hammer. It's a tool that is persuasive enough when I need to persuade someone."

"Something or *someone*?"

Rex Heuermann guffawed.

"Persuade *someone* and it always yields excellent results. At the end of the project, whatever the furniture, it always helps. Comes out beautifully.

Sometimes I have to be the heavy framing hammer. Other times I have to be the lightweight hammer, just to nudge things along."

"Great, we got it. That's it, folks. That was Rex, owner of RH Consultants. So, if you have any building regulator issues, go see him. He's the ace."

Amira stopped the camera. The interview was a wrap. Both men rose to their feet and had their sunglasses in hand. The Frenchman ignited his charisma one last time.

"Okay guys, you know the drill. *Share, subscribe*, and *like* my YouTube channel. Very important. *Like my channel!*"

He looked at the architect and Rex Heuermann was ready.

Amira stopped the camera. Both men rose to their feet and had their sunglasses.

"It's selfie time!" said the architect.

They both donned their sunglasses.

"You're fast, Rex. One, two, three. Can you smile?

"I am smiling." said the architect.

Chapter Forty-Four

Roseanne L'Anse drove with deliberate caution on the route to Morristown, New Jersey. All arteries were congested well past the Hudson River. She eventually got on the I-80 Express going westbound, passing Parsippany-Troy Hills when the traffic lessened. Roseanne had phoned her mother with a rough estimated time of arrival. She told her mother not to make dinner plans since Roseanne had a deli sandwich and sour pickle in the rental car.

Roseanne parked carefully in her mother's driveway. She slid a piece of cardboard under the car engine in case the rental had an oil leak. These were precise instructions from her mother. Roseanne L'Anse's mother was the paragon of neatness reinventing a more perfect Martha Stewart lifestyle. Certainly, one reason for Roseanne's drive and stamina to shaping a successful architectural career came from her mother's inordinate immaculateness and an enduring, untreatable obsessive-compulsive disorder.

Her mother met Roseanne at the front door. They embraced first. They kissed on the cheek. Her mother squeezed Roseanne's arms. It was a loving form of inspection. Roseanne noticed her mother was wearing a strange, new perfume and her eyebrows were tweezed aggressively.

"Roseanne, my neighbors are making me crazy."

"New neighbors?"

"Yes. Six months or so."

"Noisy?"

"No. No. They are looking into my windows."

"You've curtains, Mom."

"Yes, I know I've curtains."

"Did you have dinner?"

"Soup and salad. Not quite dinner, but filling. What happened to your neck?"

Roseanne's mother pointed to a hickey under Roseanne's left earring. Vimi was very frisky in the hotel room, and she was adventurous with her teeth.

"It's nothing. Probably a cat scratch."

"Whose cat?"

"There was a cat in the conference room."

"Roseanne, don't shovel shit in my house."

"You want me to tell you the truth?"

"Of course."

"I slept with a woman last night and we had very unchartered sex."

"A woman?"

"An interior designer."

"Why the hell would you sleep with a woman?"

"Well, she was very attractive and about twenty years my junior."

'Oh, well, that explains everything."

"That's so accepting of you."

"Weren't you dating a college professor from UNLV?"

"Briefly."

"Six months at least?"

"Maybe that long. I don't remember anymore."

"What do you mean – *'you don't remember?'*"

"My memory is spotty."

"Really?"

"Your memory is worse."

"So?

 "I want to help you."

"Help me?"

"Help you, yes."

"Do you think I need your help?"

"Your diabetes. Your balance problems. Your doctor visits."

"I have no balance problems, Roseanne. I'm a Libra."

"You fall out of bed more times than a tabby with vertigo." said Roseanne.

"Are you going to lecture me about bone density?"

"I could lecture you on bone density or mental density. Which do you prefer?"

"No lectures tonight, Mom."

"You told me I've the skeletal structure of a parakeet."

"That's half true. But very funny."

"How the hell can you spend a night with a woman?"

"I need the bathroom."

"Answer me, baby."

"Oh, Christ. How can I live with you?"

"Did you go down on this woman? Or did she go down on you?"

Roseanne walked to the bathroom just beyond the home's living room. Her mother followed close behind. Roseanne forgot to lock the bathroom door. In the next moment, her mother opened the door and kept the discussion rolling.

"Are you going to see this woman again, Roseanne?"

"I hope so. Yes. Are we out of toilet paper?"

"Use the tissue box." said her mother as if in rehearsal of a Broadway play.

Roseanne concentrated on urinating. There were sound effects.

"Do you really expect to live with me in Morristown?"

"It's an idea. Nothing more than an idea. I have good ideas and I have awful ideas."

"Why do you want to be back in the East Coast?"

Roseanne grabbed a few tissues and wiped herself.

"I left Steelman Associates. I'm thinking of consulting work in the tristate area. I'm not ready for full retirement."

"This is all about your lifetime mourning over Herb." she threw a sharp look at her daughter.

Roseanne stood and straightened her clothes. She washed her hands and studied herself in the mirror. She fidgeted with her hair. She tried to imagine how Vimi assessed her fleeting beauty.

"I'm almost sixty-five. This can't be happening. I remember when you were sixty-five."

"I scared you when I was sixty-five."

"Yes."

"Herb was so good to you. He spoiled you."

"Let's not talk about Herb, Mom."

"You'll be lucky if you found someone as gentle as Herb."

"Stop."

"Do I see liver spots?"

"No! No liver spots!"

Roseanne's mother leaned in to look at the neck bite gifted by Vimi. Was this pleasure for her daughter? Is it forbidden pleasure? Would it cost a lifetime?

"What was her name?"

"Vimi." said Roseanne, feeling like a virgin.

"Vimi?" echoed her mother.

"Vimi."

"Is she Black?"

"No. She's brown."

"How brown?"

"She has ancestry from India."

"This excites you?"

"I don't know. I don't think so."

"How did it feel when you saw her in the morning?"

"As sexy as the night before."

The two women left the bathroom.

"She's not from the U.S. and it shows."

"Where is she from?"

"India."

"India is so unclean."

Roseanne began to giggle and laugh.

"India carries the past. The deep past. India."

"I'm going to bed, Roseanne."

"Tired?"

"All day."

"I make you tired, mother."

"You used to call me, mom."

"I feel like a man when I'm with her."

"You should have had children, Roseanne."

"Goodnight, mother."

"I left fresh linen on your bed. A towel too."

"Thank you."

"I'm very proud that you an American architect."

"I know."

"It was a men's profession."

"Not anymore."

"You didn't bear children. You became a man."

"That's either a stupid thing to say, or you are succumbing to dementia, mother."

"I'm incontinent, Roseanne, but I have my fucking wits."

"Do you prefer to inhabit assisting living in the land of Formica?"

"Or you will laminate my memory?"

"Assisted living is expensive."

"I don't care."

"I do."

"And I can't stand my psychiatrist. He wants me to give him five stars on Yelp."

"Dr. Milton's on Yelp?"

"You know something, Roseanne?"

"What?"

"Architects want to live forever."

"You're right, mother."

"I don't want to exist for eternity. That would be hell."

"I would like a long life."

"You have an old soul."

"Do I?"

"Older than mine, that's for sure."

"Sometimes I think I'm your parent."

For some reason, Roseanne's mother didn't hear that remark. She looked vacant for several long moments. It was the shortest coma in history.

"We never leave the earth. We just come back."

"That makes sense." Rosemary replied.

"Does it?"

"We come back if we love someone."

"And who do you love, Rosemary?"

"Vimi. Moves. Me."

"What does that mean?" Her mother flung back, "I love her. And maybe. My death will precede yours.

241

Chapter Forty-Five

The formal celebration of Agra's Taj Mahal began in 1648, after a day and night of heavy spring rain which seemed to cleanse the region magically of dust, dirt, and grime. There were over a thousand attending in the early morning, separated by class status and wealth. Hundreds were turned away due to security measures. The emperor ordered two-hundred-armed palace guards to secure the entrance and the grounds proper. Decorations were kept at a minimum, mostly cut flowers, in order to avoid visual clutter.

The larger ceremony was an accommodation to the overflowing crowd which spread throughout the estate's gardens. As the day unfolded, the private ceremony was staged in the Taj Mahal's inner courtyard. There were expansive fireworks and festive music. Shah Jahan and his guests were dressed in their finest clothes. The emperor gave a speech in which he praised Mumtaz Mahal and expressed his gratitude to the architects and builders of the Taj Mahal. He pointed to the select men seated in chairs behind him on the elevated platform, built temporarily for the emperor's public remarks, and anchored the entire public proceedings. Ustad Ahmad Lahori and Mir Abdul Karim were prominently visible in the regal chairs. The emperor's family were also seated behind him.

The exquisite white marble dome, dominating the structure's sculptural statement, overpowered the viewer standing close by, but achieved an organic balance with the surrounding grounds seen from a far distance. The Taj Mahal's tomb was set majestically against the plain across the river and it is this natural background that rendered the apparent prestidigitation of hue, shadow, and radiant light. It seemed pointed that, through their reflection from the garden pools and the River Yamuna, men and women witnessed a mercurial and ever evolving view of the Taj Mahal. The colors, as if by design, changed incrementally from dawn to sunset, and from winter to summer. The Taj Mahal sparkled like a rare diamond under shining evening stars helped by an infinite inlay of gems along white marble. The Taj Mahal appeared salmon pink in morning, elephant tusk white before evening, and purely golden under a majestic, full moon.

Ustad Ahmad Lahori, dressed in a white formal robe, declared at the ceremonies, that these color changes represented the sublime moods of phenomenology and the leaves of eternal beauty. Mir Abdul Karim, also in formal white, stood by his side. The other team of designers were lined in a row behind these two lead architects.

The rectangular base of the Taj Mahal was explained by Ustad Ahmad Lahori as an expression of symbolic viewpoints of a magnificent woman, and the four precepts of wisdom for a lost humanity. The rectangular base employed proportions that were considered divinely mystical.

"The main gate is not unlike a veil to a woman's face," spoke Ustad Ahmad Lahori, "which must be held gingerly, lifted delicately, without fear or accident on a nuptial night."

Mir Abdul Karim then spoke, as he was signaled by the emperor.

"The rectangular base of Taj is in itself symbolic of the different sides from which to view a beautiful woman. The main gate is like a veil to a woman's face which should be lifted delicately, gently, and without haste on the wedding night. When standing inside the mausoleum's main gate, our eyes will be led to the glorious arch which framed the Taj Mahal."

The placing of the tomb at one end of the quadripartite garden was always a strong and aesthetic decision by the designers. Rather than situating the tomb logically in a central axis, dramatic depth and perspective were accentuating. Furthermore, the raised tomb struck many as an innovation to raise the direction of gazing eyes rather than an act of blasphemy. The tomb, elevated on a square platform with the four sides of the octagonal base of the minarets magnify the architectural conceit. The top of the platform could be accessed via lateral stairs found in the southern side's center. The complex, ground plan of the Taj Mahal demonstrated the harmony of balanced composition. The octagonal tomb chamber in the monument's solar plexus, defined by the portal halls and the four corner chambers. The exact concept was repeated on the upper floor. The exterior of the tomb was square in its final realization, with austere chamfered corners.

The imposing double storied domed chamber, which housed the cenotaph of Mumtaz, served as an idealized octagon in execution. The exquisite octagonal marble lattice screen encompassing the cenotaphs redefined workmanship to the highest standards.

The fabulous inlay artisanship appeared both understated and punctuated. The borders of the frames were inlaid with precious gems. The cenotaph of Mumtaz Mahal had been centered in a sacred geometric chamber. The upper cenotaph was essentially illusory as the real tomb was secured in the lower crypt, keeping with a traditional practice found in the great, imperial Mughal tombs.

The four wonderfully tapered minarets at the corners of the platform contributed a profound undiscovered realm to historic Mughal architecture. Besides projecting a spatial reference to the mausoleum, the free-standing minarets gave a three-dimensional grace to the building.

The most impressive detail in the Taj Mahal compound, next to the tomb, was the main gate which stood proudly in the middle of the forecourt's southern wall. The gate was flanked on the north by twin arcade galleries. The garden in front of the galleries was segmented by four quarters and two walking paths. Each quarter was separated by the tight cross-axial walkways, on the Timurid-Persian persuasion of walled off gardens. The eastern and western enclosure walls sported a well-defined central pavilion.

The Taj Mahal's debut presented the immaculate idea of symmetry and grandeur, with an emphasis of bilateral equilibrium straddling a central axis on which the key elements flourish. The brick-in-lime mortar veneered with red sandstone, marble, and inlay work of precious stones. The mosque and the guest house in the Taj Mahal complex exhibited red sandstone in contrast to the marble tomb at the heart of the structure. Both structures had a huge platform over the terrace. Both the mosque and the guest house appeared to be identical buildings. They had a massive oblong chamber featuring three vaulted bays. The frame of the portal arches and the spandrels were fronted by white marble. The spandrels were defined by flowery arabesques of stone intarsia and the strong arches silhouetted by rope motif.

Unseen by the multitude and by the emperor, Mumtaz Mahal's ghost was present, walking the grounds and looking at the swirling crowds. She was barefoot and cold. Her hands and extended fingers were sinewy. She wanted to touch a human being but was not allowed to do any such thing.

Mumtaz Mahal's ghost vanished and reappeared behind Ustad Ahmad Lahori and

Mir Abdul Karim. The two men were still seated on the stage platform. She spoke to both architects, but they could not hear her. However, Mir Abdul Karim did sense her spirit. The emperor was close by, yet Mumtaz Mahal's ghost was invisible to her husband's eyes. The emperor was too obsessed by the Taj Mahal to notice her ghost. She began to sing a childhood's song before she changed into a wisp of smoke.

"I am asleep in my mother's bed.

I am knee deep in my father's head.

I am a little girl lost in the woods and trees.

I am a sweet child swept up by the seven seas.

Chapter Forty-Six

Rex Heuerman stepped out of his office building at 385 Fifth Avenue and saw the Manhattan summer streetscape appear serene, friendly, and pastoral. He calmly strolled down Fifth Avenue and East 36th Street, after a long workday as the sun set balletically over midtown. It was well past eight o'clock, Thursday, July 13, 2023, and he was coatless wearing creased khaki trousers with a brown leather bag over his shoulder, unaware he was being tailed by three plain clothes police detectives who were about to arrest him.

The architect turned to walk south on Fifth Avenue. There was happy energy to his jaunty step.

The police team believed it was much safer to apprehend the architect near his place of employment rather than at his home, knowing he had a large collection of weapons in Massapequa.

The detectives, showing their badges, surrounded him after he was about a block from his office building.

"Mr. Heuermann, you are under arrest." said the lead detective.

"For what?"

"For murder."

"Three counts of first-degree murder." said the largest detective in the stark black necktie.

The lead detective informed Rex Heuermann of his Miranda rights.

"I want a lawyer." said Rex Heuermann.

One of the detectives, nodding like a thug that he heard Rex Heuermann, muttered an audible, "Yeah, of course, pal."

The same officer positioned himself behind the suspect. He instructed Rex Heuermann to place his right hand behind his back. The officer then pressed the single strand of the oversized handcuff against the architect's wide wrist. The same action followed for Rex Heuermann's left hand. The architect was now cuffed in plain view of Manhattan pedestrians. He puffed out his chest like a gorilla under attack.

The four men walked down Fifth Avenue and bystanders were watching the police action. The shortest and happiest detective began to whistle a Rolling Stones song, *Dancing with Mr. D*, from their 1973 *Goats Head Soup* album. The cop captured Keith Richards' opening guitar lick and kept adding volume while staying in tune. He suddenly remembered the opening lyrics and sang, *"Down in the graveyard where we have our tryst."*

Mr. D was either death personified, or the devil incarnate.

Mr. D was not the architect.

Mr. D was not Rex Heuermann.

This was the acrid stench of a public Manhattan arrest.

There was no way that Rex Heuermann could see that the detectives looked remarkably like the palace guards who brought Mir Abdul Karim to the emperor nearly four centuries ago. Their skin complexion was much lighter than the palace guards, but their stride and their hand gestures were completely identical. The detectives led the suspect to their car two blocks from the arrest.

A kaleidoscope of chaotic thoughts and images twirled within the architect's agitated mind in the first minutes of being in police custody. He saw staccato video news clips of the Gilgo Beach murders from a dozen years ago. He heard Long Island broadcast voices from *Talkradio 77*. He thought about the Adolf Hitler books, *Mein Kampf* and his sequel *My New Order*, which Ivana Trump told her lawyer Michael Kennedy, were visible in their bedroom by her husband's night table during her Trump marriage. He recalled the day his mother punished him for eating too much Halloween candy. He imagined a miniscule New York State prison yard with rabid rats and the wretched prison food. Musil's fictional, imprisoned character Moosbrugger from *The Man Without Qualities* blinded his pained mind's eye. The hard-working, eccentric architect became the madman Moosbrugger. He heard Miles Davis' cinematic score for the Louis Malle 1958 film *Ascenseur pour l'échafaud* (*Elevator to the Gallows*). He remembered the recent Liz Gargus film *The Lost Girls*, seen on Netflix, delving into the unsolved, scandalous Long Island murders of young sex workers. He remembered the older, well-regarded prison movie, *The Shawshank Redemption* based on the Stephen King book. He had a fleeting image of himself alongside a dilapidated boat on a Zihuatanejo beach in Mexico during a brilliant sunrise, a modified ending of the King story. On the remote sandbank was Antoine Amira, wearing a flamboyant scarf, sunglasses, and Bermuda shorts, from Bonjour Realty. He held two Piña Coladas.

Rex Heuermann was arraigned on three first-degree murder charges and three second-degree murder charges in the deaths of Melissa Barthelemy, Megan Waterman, and Amber Costello, according to the court documents. The Long Island architect was also a suspect in a fourth killing of Maureen Brainard-Barnes.

Court papers stated that Rex Heuermann was allegedly linked to the deaths using cell tower data, a witness's detailed description of his Chevrolet Avalanche truck, and most damning, the DNA samples from hairs found on three of the victims. Law enforcement also stated that they discovered that the architect used an online account to access images of his alleged victims and their families.

Rex Heuermann was whipped into the future.

He thought he was invincible. He thought he was the sharpest tool around.

He was startled to realize he had multiple personalities.

He knew his anchor personality. That was his truest personality. The "no bullshit" architect. The police had to believe that along with the district attorney and the judge. Rex Heuermann was the problem solver for all public buildings. He was the very best problem solver in all of New York. New York still needed him. He saved people a ton of money.

The arraignment was sped through. There would be no bail. Suffolk County Police seized more than 280 firearms from Rex Heuermann's Massapequa Park house in the days following his July 13th apprehension. Along with the weapons, a child-sized, blonde doll encased in a large glass and wood box, with carvings of flowers, was removed by police officers. The doll's long hair was braided. A red bow adorned the doll's head, and the figurine sported a crimson outfit.

Rex Heuermann felt estranged from his wife and adult children.

He felt estranged from himself.

He swore to God that he was not Moosbrugger. Rex Heuermann was a regular guy with a good soul. His temper was just an act. It was a dance step. Entertaining.

The cops were getting under his skin. His jail clothes gave him an instant rash. He lost his appetite. He became constipated. He wanted to sleep in his own bed. The prison staff taunted him. He didn't deserve this treatment. Was death an option?

Rex Heuermann was given an hour of exercise outside. No one else was allowed to be in the fenced yard with him. The guards were strict about the time. One prison guard was demonstrably friendly to him. The guard was nearing retirement age, overweight, and had an asthmatic wheeze at the end of his workday. The guard told the architect that he kicked smoking cigarettes a few years ago under doctor's orders. The guard showed interest in the architect's building and design career. Rex Heuermann began to trust him and answered most questions about the architect's initial aspirations.

The guard surprised Rex Heuerman one morning by bringing him a plastic, cream colored Taj Mahal replica, no bigger than a few inches. He told the architect that he found the India souvenir on Etsy for three dollars plus shipping. The architect accepted the model, and he thanked the jail guard.

Rex Heuermann knew that the salacious TV coverage would be a tsunami. His life and career were ruined overnight. Would a good attorney make a difference? Who would be his best character witness? How big would the legal bills be? Would Rex Heuermann die inside prison?

Why did the detectives avoid arresting Oak Beach residents Joseph Brewer and Dr. Peter Hackett, he wondered with immense indignation.

The architect wanted his freedom. He wanted to build buildings. Life had few genuine pleasures.

He thought about the four lost women — Melissa Barthelemy, Megan Waterman, Amber Costello, and Maureen Brainard-Barnes. He thought about Shannan Gilbert too. Were there other slaughtered women to be unearthed? Were they all around the same age, same lurid career, and physical description? Were they all leading double lives as prostitutes and strippers? Were there tortured, murdered men? Were these men business partners who drove the girls to their job sites?

He thought often about Jesus. Jesus was watching him and that was okay. He thought about the eternal suffering of the human race. He felt the large suffering of Christ. He heard the sermons inside his head, echoing as if he were in a towering European cathedral. He received the notion that an open-heart approximated confession. The architect was cognizant of original sin governing and inflicting every man and woman on earth. Death purged that sin, cleansing the atmosphere overhead.

There was the sermon Jesus made on the Mount: "For if you forgive other people when they sin against you, your heavenly Father will also forgive you. But if you do not forgive others their sins, your Father will not forgive your sins."

Whom would the architect bestow such forgiveness?

There were people in Rex Heuermann's world over the years that he could reimagine into three vivid dimensions and elevate above his eyes, holding in his memory faces and profiles of the special people. He knew their names. He understood their identities. He suspected their secrets. Everything was redolent. It didn't matter to Heuermann that the distinction of comprehensive recognition would be mutual. The irony of the situation stung the architect. The paradox of a successful New York architect trapped inside a foul-smelling jail cell seven feet wide by ten feet long was monstrous. He was emotionally paralyzed, silent like a medieval monk, unable to escape the Suffolk County Correctional Facility, victimized and slandered relentlessly by the New York media, and now shunned by his family. He would soon discover by November that his wife, Asa, entered into a lucrative, seven figure deal with Peacock on a television documentary series that will track the Heuermann family as they struggle with the architect's criminal trial and their ruined lives.

The architect fell into a massive, petrifying clinical depression.

"I have to wake from this nightmare." said Rex Heuermann. "Or I will be damned forever."

Chapter Forty-Seven

Roseanne L'Anse was living with her mother for nine months. It felt like nine years. The dynamic between them was often bumpy and intense, although love was never far from the daily dissonance. Her mother craved power and all the oxygen in the house. In her younger life, her mother was much harder on Roseanne, but in the last few years came a tender profile. Her mother appeared frightened and fragile now. Once a high-octane personality, her mother seemed lethargic, distracted, pained, and confused in every cognitive way. Roseanne stepped into the parent's role. This was a necessity.

What made Roseanne's life strained within her mother's New Jersey home was endless free time. Retirement was forced on her. She had more productive years ahead thanks to her creative muscles. Her design partners were more leveraged than she intuited. She was blind to the office coup. But she rationalized the outcome which painted her mother as the top priority in Roseanne's shrinking universe.

Placing her mother in an assistant living facility was out of the question. Her mother lost the art of keeping and cultivating friends. Companionship was as vital as a roof over one's head. Her mother failed to be a friend to herself and shifted into being a person of deliberate self-abuse. These factors may have contributed to a health crisis. Over Memorial Day weekend, Dorothy L'Anse had a massive stroke and was admitted to Morristown Medical Center. The doctors were treating her for a thrombotic stroke caused by large blood clots forming in an artery. Roseanne's mother was in very serious condition. The lead doctor explained where the next few days might go. Dorothy L'Anse might die. She might come through but there is the risk of losing significant functions including speech. Optimistically, she might display a strong recovery but that could take up to a year or more.

In Roseanne's mind the thoughts were swirling about, and all were negative. Roseanne wanted to sleep in the empty bed by Dorothy L'Anse. The hospital had a strict policy regarding family members staying overnight. Roseanne befriended the night nurse. This led to the retired architect's success in sharing her mother's hospital room for the first night, at least.

This family was down to two survivors. Roseanne came into the world in the same hospital as she occupied now. Roseanne was flooded by a feeling that Dorothy L'Anse would pass away before Memorial Day.

Talking to the night nurse, Roseanne heard anecdotes about stroke victims. Some stories were encouraging. Some were miserable. Her mother looked like a candidate for the latter. Roseanne always imagined her mother would live to be one hundred. Her mother was built of steel. She didn't have bones. She had metal beams.

The night nurse left the room and indicated this was a good time to sleep in the empty bed and quietly left the room. Roseanne thought about actresses who recovered from severe strokes, like Sharon Stone. Roseanne's brain for a brief second began to implode.

It was as though Dorothy L'Anse's daughter was attempting to match her mother's medical condition. It was as though Roseanne L'Anse wanted to experience dying. There would be no pain after obliteration.

Roseanne L'Anse kissed her mother's forehead. She then sat on the empty bed and removed her shoes. There was a second bedsheet which she pulled above her legs and torso. She rested her head on a soft pillow. The hospital room light was dimmed. There were low volume, electronic sounds of medical equipment originating from the nurses' station. Within a minute Roseanne fell asleep.

A fragment of a dream lingered the next morning. Roseanne was with Vimi. It was a sensual fantasy. The two women, hand in hand, were hiking up a hill of a national park. At the summit, Vimi's tongue entered Roseanne's partly opened mouth. The tongue grew in size and length, eventually filling her entire body. She was transfixed by the magic of this aggressive kiss. Nonetheless, the image of the fantasy and the meaning of the fantasy hadn't bothered her. Roseanne's focus was on her mother's body in the hospital bed.

The days and nights blurred together as the week unfolded. Dorothy L'Anse was released to a physical therapy clinic for long term support. Roseanne kept her mother within Morristown. Vimi had phoned and Roseanne invited her to stayover in Morristown.

"There are trains twice an hour, takes about an hour from Penn Station." said Roseanne over the phone.

"I'll come out Friday night." said Vimi.

"Thanks."

Roseanne L'Anse knew her life was transforming rapidly. She did not want to lose her mother, but she feared that her mother would be thoroughly incapacitated. The architect was looking forward to retirement but did not relish the prospects of being servile to a woman in her mid-eighties. The architect loved opposing aspirations. The benefit of free time from work. The opportunity to nurture her mother through old age. If her mother doesn't recover from the stroke, there would be little free time. There would be no privacy for the architect.

"Vimi."

"Yes?"

"Thanks for training to Morristown."

"I'm happy to help in any way, Roseanne."

"The doctors are giving me mixed signals."

"Doctors don't communicate well."

"She can't talk. She can't write. Can hear what I say but little reaction."

"Any face or head movement?"

"A little. But hard to read reactions."

"Eating?" asked Vimi.

"Liquids seem to go down. Soup. The chewing reflex isn't present."

Vimi gave Roseanne a long hug, while caressing Roseanne's hair.

"How are you holding up?" she asked the architect.

"Irrationally, I find myself wishing to be back in La Vegas."

"That's understandable."

"Is it?"

"Do you want to beat yourself up, Roseanne?"

"My career hit its horizon. My mother's physical life is over."

"Are you Catholic?"

"No."

"Maybe you can hire an aid a few days each week?"

"I thought about that."

"Good."

Vimi touched Roseanne's arm gently. Roseanne was confused. She craved a kiss, but she couldn't initiate the kiss. She expected Vimi to kiss her.

"Are you hungry?

"Vimi nodded in the affirmative.

"I could prepare a salad."

Roseanne gave Vimi a tour of her mother's New Jersey house. Roseanne turned on lamps and lights along the way. The home appeared tidy and well maintained.

"I missed you." Vimi told her.

"I missed you too." Roseanne volunteered, but not smiling.

"It will be nice to have breakfast together."

"Oh God, I think we're out of coffee."

"I'm fine with tea."

Vimi saw Roseanne cry.

"It's taking my breath away." said Roseanne swallowing her words. "I see life without her. But I occupy her home. My mother's turned into a living ghost."

"Don't think of her that way."

"How else to think?"

"I'll take you to India."

"Why?"

"Because life stems from India."

"Vimi . . ."

"Life comes back, Roseanne. Incarnate becomes reincarnate."

A quiet curtain fell. Roseanne closed her eyes. The women kissed.

"Vimi . . ."

Vimi led Roseanne to the guest bedroom, although Vimi never set foot in the house. Vimi undressed Roseanne. Then Vimi disrobed. Her hand moved a body. A body moved her hand. Roseanne was moaning to transverse the centuries. She was never going to die.

Chapter Forty-Eight

Rex Heuermann was perspiring heavily in his prison cell. He had no cellmate. The authorities did not feel the situation was safe for two men, given Rex Heuermann's explosive profile. He was being held at the Suffolk County Correctional Facility in a 60-square-foot cell. The prison guards were under instruction not to engage in extraneous conversation with the prisoner. Most observed the order. His first weeks during the incarceration, he was on a suicide watch. He exclaimed several times during the ordeal that he was an innocent man who contributed to society beyond the Good Samaritan.

"When Heuermann was incarcerated, that first week, he was either laying on his back or with his back against the wall and really he slept a lot," announced Sheriff Errol D. Toulon Jr. at a press conference. "Now, the last couple of times I've seen him, he's sitting up on his bunk. He may be reading a book. So, he's really acclimated to jail life."

The Sheriff surmised that Rex Heuermann seemed not to move around the jail much or visit the recreational area that he has access to throughout the day.

"He seems very convicted to stay to himself, not speak to anyone, not communicate more than just the basic needs of interaction between a correctional officer and someone that's incarcerated," stated Sheriff Toulon. "Heuermann does meet with Catholic clergy for private prayer services once a week - with two cameras rolling at all times. He has requested it, and he seems like he's going to continue. It's a neutral, safe party that's supposed to bring some solace and some comfort, spirituality through his spirituality."

The jailed architect missed his wife, his daughter, and his son. He tried to reach out to them but was rebuffed. He missed his architectural office and his clients. His architectural website was taken offline. He missed his collection of guns. He missed the Greek diner near his building and the diner's breakfast special, two eggs, bacon, toast, home fries, coffee, and small orange juice for nine dollars. He missed the morning New York Times. He missed his bathroom and his padded furry slippers. He missed having sex. He thought about sex obsessively within his prison cell. He hungered for his freedom. The architect, as best that he could, kept up with the media on his unfolding case.

He received very few letters from business friends and associates. He was hurt by the discernible indifference among his loyal clientele. There was a long-handwritten letter from Sal Caputo offering the architect a loan for his legal defense fund.

The architect had learned, from breaking news reports on the Gilgo Beach murders and from his attorney, that in 2010 amidst the initial investigation into the Long Island serial killings, a crucial piece of information had surfaced that went unheeded for over a decade. It came from an unsavory source: the pimp who knew and befriended one of the victims, Amber Lynn Costello. This unnamed witness approached Suffolk County authorities not long after Costello's disappearance. He revealed a chilling detail: he had suspected who was responsible.

The hesitant pimp described his dramatic encounter with an unforgettable stranger he characterized as a "bulky ogre" who drove a green

Chevrolet Avalanche. This giant, he claimed, had been seen with Costello shortly before she vanished. The pimp's description of the Avalanche was detailed, and the vehicle was not very common. According to news outlets, the pimp spotted the vehicle leaving an area where another victim, Melissa Barthelemy, was last seen alive. This detail, coupled with the victim's connection to the New York architect made the tip all the more compelling. It was beyond disconcerting to crime pundits on cable shows that Long Island law enforcement dropped the ball at a critical juncture or, far worse, that there was a cover-up for a variety of unethical or self-serving reasons.

To Rex Heuermann, the recent dragnet and arrest proved absurd, and he felt like a cursed creature from a Kafka story. The media hammered the scandalous details of the pimp's 2010 testimony left ignored while the Gilgo Beach murders haunted Long Island. A dozen years later, when a newly formed task force took a renewed look at an extremely cold case, that the New York architect emerged as a prime suspect. To the architect, this proved worse than a destiny laced with poison.

Rex Heuermann had a series of frightening dreams in his prison cell. He had a fear of spiders and bedbugs. He felt things crawling on his body at night but saw no insects. He had sensations of tiny fire ants entering his rectum, stinging him, consuming his membrane. He had dreams about an invisible devil who bit his private parts. He had dreams about Donald J. Trump sharing his prison cell. These Trump dreams began with prison guards escorting the former president into Rex Heuermann's cell. This made no sense to the architect. How can the State of New York force an ex-president to share a jail cell with an accused sex serial killer? In his dream Rex Heuermann stood up to show respect for the new prisoner's arrival. Rex Heuermann was inches taller than Donald Trump. Trump appeared frightened entering the cell as though he were about to meet his torturer, his Long Island rapist.

The Secret Service entered the cell just behind Trump. The agents surrounded Rex Heuermann and frisked him thoroughly. One agent ran his hand up Rex Heuermann's leg and reached around the groin. The architect felt mortified by the grip of the African American agent. In utter horror, Trump was watching this spectacle. The other agent barked at Rex Heuermann that Trump gets the lower bunk. The ex-president could not be expected to climb a ladder. The Secret Service examined the top bunk and lower bunk for weapons and for bedbugs. There were no weapons and only a few spotted insects.

Trump, in this nauseous nightmare of Rex Heuermann, would not look at the architect directly. Trump heaped disdain on his cellmate. Trump was wearing lady's sunglasses with rhinestones along the stem and there was a hint of red lipstick. His nails were painted plum. In Trump's point of view, his cellmate was an odious lump of clay. To Trump, this squalid cell and wretched, larger inmate were more than an offensive inconvenience. The Secret Service agents, before locking the jail bars, had comforted their boss by saying that this incarceration with a white-collar goon was a temporary logistics problem. In a few weeks, Trump would get a private cell with cable television, heated toilet, and a wet bar.

One version of the dream had Donald Trump expand to his cellmate, Rex Heuermann, on the hot microphone scandal of the Hollywood Access videotape.

"Grab them by the pussy, come on!" said Donald J. Trump in this dream, "doesn't mean exactly what it sounds like. You got to stroke the pussy, Rex. And then they come to you like a little kitty waiting for a nice meal. It's so bad when the fake news fucks you up the ass."

In this surrealistic somnambulant skit, Donald Trump and Rex Heuermann were drawn together. They did not look dissimilar. They both projected towering height, stout chests, rotund bellies, broad shoulders, prying eyes, and tree stump necks. Face to face they could be looking into a funhouse mirror. They both were too large for daily life yet they both had a lifelong birthright about demanding sexual pleasure at their naked command.

A variation of the Donald J. Trump prison nightmares including delicate personal matters which Rex Heuermann tried to purge from memory. These were ordeals over hygiene. There was the vignette of the toilet bowl minus a lid. Rex Heuermann, in the dream, waiting for Trump to fall asleep before using the toilet. However, his cellmate's bowl movements spun around the clock. Therefore, Trump forced the architect to wear a blindfold. Because of extreme hemorrhoids, Trump needed an hour on the toilet, and he was plagued by extremely loud flatulence. The lack of ventilation within the prison cell made the former president's bowel movements absurdly torturous.

Trump would talk to himself during the entire toilet ballet, often giving a spoken inventory of his office trophies at Trump Tower while prancing inches closer to the toilet. Perhaps Trump was enacting a personalized version of Samuel Beckett's *Molloy*. The architect observed Trump distributing his invisible trophies among his four imaginary pockets and sucked them like lollipops. Trump was exceedingly oral in his captivity. He pretended to have sixteen trophies, four in each of his four pockets. Two pockets of his trousers and the two pockets of his black cashmere overcoat.

In the defecating ritual, Trump's exaggerated posterior oozed over the toilet seat. The architect was baffled by these recurring dreams and the memory of putrid odors.

Rex Heuermann had asked the correctional facilities authorities within a day or two of his incarceration to see a priest. This was important to the architect.

The request was granted a few days later. The architect could not choose which priest would be chosen. That was acceptable. An hour was scheduled for early afternoon. The architect combed his hair neatly then was escorted by two guards to a secure room with a reinforced glass window.

The priest was quiet, partly bald, mid-sixties, thin, short, and walked with a slight limp. He had a warm, toothy smile despite an austere, stiff facial composition. Rex Heuermann self-identified as a Catholic upon meeting the priest. He added that going to church was part of his childhood experience. The priest nodded in approval. They sat down at the same time and rested their hands on a wood table.

"I am here for you." said the priest.

"Thank you, Father." said the architect. "It's terribly lonely in a small cell."

"Yes. I try to imagine what it might be like. May I call you Rex?"

"Yes."

"Thank you."

"My wife refuses to see me."

"I'm sorry to hear that."

"I have horrible nightmares."

"Are you eating?"

"Yes."

"Exercise?"

"I'm allowed to walk an hour each day."

"You are in solitary confinement."

Rex Heuermann nodded his head. He turned towards the tempered glass window and noted a prison guard monitoring the meeting.

"Do you have a bible?" asked the priest.

"I do."

"Can you read every day?"

"I can try."

"Good."

"My daughter is the age of these Long Island victims. I think about this a lot."

"It is a community tragedy."

"It's a sick community."

"Is there else something you wish to say to me?"

The architect's eyes dropped low, and he gently bit his lip. He tasted his own blood.

"Is there something on your mind?"

"What does God want?" asked Rex Heuermann.

"God wants to give eternal life to those who open their hearts to Christ."

"How do you know this?"

"I'm a priest. Every priest knows this."

"Did you know this before you became a priest?"

"I think I did know this as a child. But in time the idea was reinforced in beautiful ways, my son."

The architect felt warmth at this turn in their conversation.

"I'm not guilty."

"I didn't ask if you were."

"You know everything about my case."

"I know enough."

"What do you think I did?"

"That's not my purpose today."

"What is your purpose?"

"Each week I make rounds. Sometimes in hospitals. Sometimes in jails."

"And?"

"Hospitals and jails house souls."

"Do you try to heal the sick, Father?"

"I try to do some good."

"But can you heal the sick?"

"In the hospitals I try. In the jails I try harder."

The priest thought deeply and quietly.

"When did you want to become an architect?"

"I guess when I was a boy. Around eight or nine. We had an encyclopedia set in our living room and I liked to page through the volumes randomly. I came upon pictures of the Taj Mahal and thought it was from another planet. I thought it was amazing. I wanted to build the Taj Mahal."

"Thank you for telling me that." responded the priest.

Rex Heuermann leaned in and was inches from the priest's face. He could smell the priest's sour breath.

"Seeing Christ in any prisoner is the key to my ministry. We turn to St. Dismas, the accused who was crucified next to Jesus, the 'good thief' and the patron saint of inmates, to assist on behalf of those who serve long jail time. I also rely on St. Barbara, another patron saint of convicts, and St. John Cafasso, the patron saint of jails, who fed prisoners, heard their confessions, granted prisoners absolution."

"Can you give me absolution, Father?"

"I understand."

"Can you answer my question please?"

"I don't know. Not today. We need to continue our dialogue."

"I didn't expect absolution today."

"It will be nice to see you again."

"Yes."

"Let the guards know you want another visit."

"Yes."

"Say ten Hail Mary's."

"You will come back to visit?"

"Yes. Be truthful, my son."

"I will, Father. God bless you."

Chapter Forty-Nine

On the perfect midsummer day when Mir Abdul Karim met Saanvi Lal Chiranji, there was a total solar eclipse, July 1, 1628. They were in Delhi attending a large wedding event over a series of days. The gathering, perhaps three hundred guests present, was within a courtyard of a three-story structure of orange and red stone. Saanvi Lal Chiranji was a distant cousin to the bride. Mir Abdul Karim was a friend of the groom's father. The air was fortified by late blooming flowers, fragrant open pot cooking, and smoky incense. The families of the bride and groom viewed the eclipse's timing auspiciously. It was traditional to perform one major segment of the nuptials during a solar eclipse to be followed by a segment during a lunar eclipse. People were calling the sky, "the great Ring of Fire."

The celebration included spontaneous dancing and singing. Some inebriated party revelers were scantily clad, using strategically placed scarfs. Musicians were strolling about while drummers were atop a crimson platform of polished cherry heartwood. Saanvi Lal Chiranji loved to dance. She was a gifted dancer and, with her thick long hair, one of the most alluring women at the wedding. Mir Abdul Karim spotted her immediately from one of the upper balconies. He asked a few guests if they knew the dancer's name. Some called her Lakshmi in error. No one seemed to know

Saanvi Lal Chiranji, but that did not deter Mir Abdul Karim. His instinct was dominating his legs and this very personal hunt. It was not the power of unbridled lust inside Mir Abdul Karim, but of his latent spiritual curiosity. Saanvi Lal Chiranji's flowing robe of silk was multicolored, visually poetic, and carried the elegance of her choreography underscored by the twitching, animated fabric.

He finally approached her. She noticed him from the corner of her eye. He blew her a kiss and kept an open palm suspended in midair. It was a stupid gesture. At least, that is what Saanvi Lal Chiranji was thinking.

"It is a beautiful wedding." said Mir Abdul Karim.

"Yes." said Saanvi Lal Chiranji while dancing slowly.

"You look like the bride."

"She is my cousin."

"So young to marry."

"Yes. She is young."

"So perfectly pretty."

"You have an accent."

"I am from a far land."

"Where?"

"Arya. Shiraz."

"Why come to Delhi?"

"I build. I am an architect. I have work here."

"An architect?"

"Tall towers. Exotic domes. Kiosks that trick the eye. Temples which will last centuries. Palaces that defy time. I will be a great architect. History will record my name."

"Are you drunk?"

"No."

Mir Abdul Karim took her hand and tapped it with his forefinger.

"When I touch a girl's hand and tap three times, she will feel the Ganges River."

She laughed. She laughed again.

"And how do you do that?"

"I am water."

"You are water?"

"Yes."

"I thought you were flesh and blood."

"If I were flesh and blood, I would eventually die. Because I am water, I will never die."

"You make me laugh."

"That is good to know."

"We will see the eclipse of the sun." she said with energy.

"Yes. This is fortuitous."

"Will you be going back to Shiraz soon?"

"No. I will stay in Delhi."

"Do you like Delhi?"

"I do." he said, picking his teeth with a fingernail.

"I think Delhi is too big. Maybe Agra is better."

"Can I kiss you?" asked Mir Abdul Karim.

There was silence between them, and the partygoers were the ocean of sound.

"Can I? Please?" asked Mir Abdul Karim.

"I do not know you."

"My name is Mir Abdul Karim. Now you know me."

He leaned in without hesitation. She parted her lips. They kissed.

"That was nice." spoke Saanvi Lal Chiranji.

Her eyelashes were long. Her dark eyes burned him. His hands trembled when she reached for him.

"What is your name?"

"Saanvi Lal Chiranji."

"Do you fear the night?"

"If I am alone, yes."

"What else do you fear?"

"My father." she said.

"Why is that?"

"If you ever meet my father, you will know."

"I wish to meet your father."

"He is dead."

"When did he die?"

"A year ago. Or yesterday."

He gleaned that the pain felt like yesterday.

"I am sorry for you."

"Thank you." she said demurely.

"Will you dance with me?"

"Why do you wish to dance?"

"The gods are telling me that I must dance with you."

"You hear that now?"

"Yes. Very loud. That is what I hear and what I see."

"What do you see?"

"The Ring of Fire. A solar eclipse."

"Yes."

"Marry me, Saanvi Lal Chiranji."

"What?"

"I do not want anyone else to have you."

"You sound like my father."

"I am not him."

"I hope not."

Mir Abdul Karim lowered his young face and reached for her luscious locks of jasmine hair. He was overcome by her perfume. They kissed again as the vast sky turned red. Their hearts fused as one. He loved Saanvi Lal Chiranji and Saanvi Lal Chiranji loved his infinite spark of light.

Allan Havis is a Professor of Theatre at University of California, San Diego. His dramas have been produced at major theaters nationally and abroad. He is the author of nineteen full-length published plays and edited three American Political Plays series — the newest "American Political Plays in the Age of Terrorism" with Bloomsbury. His previous novel, "Maddie Q" by Willow River Press came out last year having followed his 2022 novel, "Clear Blue Silence" by Ktav Publishing. He also published two novels for young adults — "Albert the Astronomer" by Harper/Collins and "Albert Down a Wormhole" by Goodreads Press.